Spy Tails

001

BarbarianSpy

www.**BarbarianSpy**.com

This book is copyright © habu 2014
habu asserts his right to be known as the author of this work..
Published by BarbarianSpy in 2014
Cover design © S Bush 2014
Cover image: All Manipulated: man with gun
Copyright:gosphotodesign, cityscape Copyright:sepavone, coin
Copyright:eldadcarin
E-Book ISBN: 978-1-922187-76-5
Print ISBN: 978-1-922187-79-6
All rights reserved

BarbarianSpy
Jindalee St
Toronto, NSW 2283
AUSTRALIA

Spy Tails

001

by

habu

Table of Contents

Introduction

This anthology is pure fiction.

Nothing like this would happen in the real intelligence world. Wipe from your mind even the slightest thought that anything like this has already happened in the collection of intelligence down through the ages. There would never be a special unit in U.S. intelligence, for instance, that collected intelligence the time-honored way—by providing sexual favors and subornation. There would never be an Agency special unit informally known as the Candy Store. This unit would not have five informally separated sections: male on female, female on male, male on male, female on female, and anything goes. There would certainly be no use of male homosexuality, and society's censure of that, to recruit and control foreign intelligence assets as is fantasized in the sixteen stories of this anthology, which is the first of two volumes of spy tales

The dirty little truth is that the easiest, most assured way of collecting intelligence is not torture. It, rather, is the "giving" to someone who knows what you want to know what they want most, in exchange for the information they know. And it is in being especially prepared to do so if what they want the most is illicit—that is, for instance, connected to male homosexuality. And you can be assured they will give you the most useful information and continue to give it to you if you continue to give them what they want to have—but cannot acknowledge they have gotten, or want to have—and holding over their heads the threat of collapsing their whole world if they don't continue to cooperate.

But even if this is the easiest and most assured way of collecting intelligence—and has been used as such down through the ages, it, of course, could not happen in the Western world. The United States and its allies simply do not condone the existence and use of gay males in their intelligence services. This simply is not a way in which intelligence is collected in the Western World.

It's just as farfetched a thought as the notion that countries would listen in on the private conversations of their closest foreign allies (put smiley face here).

So, do enjoy this collection of short stories presenting a fantasy depiction of the techniques and methods of collecting intelligence through the dispensing of gay male spy candy. But don't for a moment think that it does happen, or that it ever could. It's pure fiction, yes it is. And if you enjoy this collection, be sure to check out the second half of it as well, habu's *Spy Tails 002*.

* * * *

These sixteen stories show an aspect of intelligence work very much in the vein of Graham Greene and John LeCarré but delving into spy craft operations that go well beyond where either of these authors dared to go. The reality of spying is that it isn't all Agent 007 glamour. There is a nasty, cynical, and even arousingly sexual underbelly to it, and these stories don't shy away from showing that, or from ignoring the difficult questions of the morality of taking advantage of the vulnerability and weakness of men who have a weakness for men in the pursuit of chits in the power games of nations. These stories not only show the substance of spy craft, but they also show how men are suborned to be Candy Store agents and then how they use other men to extract what their handlers want. Four of the stories ("Breaking the Banker," "Double-Cross Express," "El Presidente," and "Murmansk

Delights") feature an agent handler, who appears regularly in habu's spy writings, Sam Winterberry.

Geography is also a hallmark of habu's writing, and the settings of these stories cover the globe: Europe ("Around and Around," "Breaking the Banker," "Brussels Seduction," "Double-Cross Express," and "Hidden Flute,"), northern Russia ("Murmansk Delights"), Southeast Asia ("Bangkok Defection"), South Asia ("Black Box"), the Middle East ("Breaking the Banker," "Brussels Seduction," "Ethiopian Cabin Boy," and "Hostage to Need"), the Mediterranean ("Ethiopian Cabin Boy," "Hostage to Need," and "Labyrinth"), Africa ("Hidden Flute," "Hostage to Need."), and the Caribbean ("Dominican Showdown," "Hurricane," and "Interviewing a Dictator"), and South America ("El Presidente").

Such spying activity is everywhere; put your finger down anywhere on the globe and you will find men trying to coax secrets out of other men—and using whatever it takes to get them.

Most of these stories are set in the present, but "Colonel's Treasure" is set in the American Revolutionary War and "Labyrinth" is set on a mystical Mediterranean island. Both serve the purpose of illustrating that spying is the second-oldest vice of man.

"Hostage to Need," focusing on a European oil company's machinations to maintain its presence in a North African potentate, exhibits that espionage transcends national politics and is rampant in the world of international business as well.

But, of course, this anthology is pure fiction.

Around and Around

Colonel Dieter Kielman, assistant to the assistant German attaché to NATO Headquarters, Brussels, Belgium, leaned his long, rangy body against the frame of the open French door leading out onto the wrought iron balcony that he dare not step out onto. The Hotel Amigo, no matter how friendly and accommodating to the type of midday tryst he had come so willingly to enjoy, was not as sturdy as it appeared. Kielman was naked, flaccid in post fuck, and was smoking a cigarette, as he always did after taking the young Belgian, Guido.

"Come back to me, Dieter," the small, effeminate female impersonator from the Au Fou Chantant cabaret whispered in the husky voice he affected to turn his clients on. "I want you inside me again."

"It's late, Guido. I have appointments." Kielman did, however, lift his gaze from the Gröte Markt street activity below and look back at the mussed-up bed. Guido rolled onto his stomach and lifted his buns in a provocative stance and fluttered his long eyelashes at the German military officer.

"You never have enough time for me," he said, with a pout. "You never make slow love to me."

"That's because you like to be taken swiftly and hard," the German answered. "You like to be driven. I can tell in your response."

"I like to be driven by you, at least," Guido cooed. "You have a master cock. I'd let you drive me all day. Come back to bed."

"I don't think so."

"Well, then," Guido said, coming up on his knees and gathering the tangled sheeting around him, "who bathes first? Or do we do it together?"

"I'll go first," Dieter answered, and he flicked his cigarette out over the balcony and stood up straight, nearly six and a half feet of sinew and power. "You need to cover yourself before I return from the shower, though, or I'll surely be late."

Guido waited until he heard the shower start and then he darted out of the bed and over to his jacket and extracted a small digital camera. The colonel had left his briefcase by the door, beside a small desk, the surface of which Guido found very convenient as he slipped documents out of the briefcase and photographed them as quickly as he could. He was only half finished with the papers he had found in the briefcase, though, before he heard the water being shut off in the shower.

He barely had everything back in order and was on the bed once again, when Kielman came out of the bathroom, naked, and rubbing his wet hair with a towel.

"God, I told you to cover yourself," he muttered in a throaty voice.

Guido was on his back, the small of his back arched up on a pillow, his legs spread, and one leg held up by one of his hands. His pert little balls and hole were pointed at the bathroom door.

"Sorry," he whispered and then fluttered his eyelashes at the German. "Just doing some exercises while I waited. You've seen my cabaret act. You know a boy has to be limber." And then he added, in his huskiest voice, "But are you sure you have appointments you have to go to? I see a luscious German flagpole standing at attention."

Kielman was on Guido like a lion on a gazelle. He was at the foot of the bed in two long strides, grabbed the little Belgian by his hips, and lifted him up and slammed Guido's slack hole back on his reengorged cock, achieving a bull's eye in one swift slide. Guido's weight had gone back on his shoulder blades, as his pelvis was now suspended up in the air, being slammed hard back and forth on Kielman's impaling cock. Guido's fists scrabbled at the tangled sheeting and his legs flopped back and forth akimbo as the powerful German pumped him hard. He was crying out and groaning and grunting and writhing under the onslaught of the ravishing German colonel's powerful cock.

Guido's small balls were slammed up into his body with each of Kielman's savage thrusts, and his thin, boylike penis hardened up and dribbled into a great spill, as he cried out at Kielman's taking being exactly what he wanted—just as Kielman had told him. Kielman arched his back and roared at the ceiling and ejaculated deep inside Guido's ass.

"Now see what you've done," Kielman said in a stern tone, but with a wide smile on his face, when he had let Guido's spent body fall off of his cock and onto the bed. "Now I will definitely be late for my afternoon appointment. Now I will have to take another shower."

Guido lay there, panting, collecting his strength, genuinely close to exhaustion as he listened for the shower again. As soon as the water started, he dragged himself off the bed and over to, first, his jacket, where the digital camera was, and then to the briefcase by the door, and once more started taking sheets of paper out of the briefcase and laying them on the desk top and snapping away with the camera.

He did enjoy fucking, but the German colonel was almost too brutal for him. The things he did for the Americans, he was thinking, as he once more heard the water stop in the shower and he reached for his trousers. He'd need to be at least half dressed this time. He'd photographed enough, and he didn't think he could survive another cocking just now from the dominating Colonel Kielman, assistant to the assistant German attaché at NATO headquarters.

* * * *

Guido was walking rather gingerly as he left the Gröte Markt and moved into the Kolenmarkt area. But now he was back on turf he was comfortable with. The Fontainas café on Rue Marché was home base for him, where he picked up the tricks that paid for his apartment. On his entertainer's salary at the Au Fou Chantant he could never have lived alone; he would have had to find a daddy to care for him. That would have been OK before he connected with the Americans, but now he needed to be freer with his time, ever ready to go where they needed him to go and do their bidding. He'd never felt as alive as this before he'd connected with the Americans.

They were there, each sitting at a table, their tables adjacent to each other, in the shadows under the awning. Frank and Felix, Guido's controls. Always together, Guido had never met separately with only one of them. This made Guido feel special. He must be a valuable asset, he was thinking. And they met him at a gay-friendly café. He thought that meant they considered him special too. They were meeting him in his own element.

As Guido approached the café, Frank got up and moved to Felix's table, leaving the other one free for Guido. Guido sat, being very careful not to try to make eye contact with either Frank or Felix, just as they had taught him. He ordered a coffee and a brandy. He drank them slowly, just as he had been taught. And tense as he was inside, Guido mustered all of what he'd already been taught in the cabaret and looked casual and totally uncaring. This was just another performance for him, just one of the many talents he brought to the art of espionage.

Guido called for the bill, and as the waiter left to ring up his accounting, Guido reached into his jacket pocket and took out money to pay the bill with. He also surreptitiously— just as Frank and Felix had taught him—extracted the small digital camera he had used on Colonel Kielman's papers in the Hotel Amigo room and put that on the chair facing the table where Frank and Felix sat.

When the waiter returned with the bill, Guido engaged him in small talk while handing him the money and Frank took up the camera on the empty seat between their closely positioned tables.

When the waiter was gone, Guido swept up the camera that was now on the chair, slipped it into his jacket pocket, and, without looking at either Frank or Felix, rose from his chair and sauntered out of the café, seemingly without a care in the world—but, in fact, needing to get a move on to be in place for his next scheduled assignation.

* * * *

Guido walked into the lobby of the Bedford hotel. He saw Lao Jen sitting primly over on a tufted sofa shielded from most of those strolling through the lobby by a leafy palm tree. Between the sofa and the palm tree was a standing ashtray filled with sand. When Guido entered the lobby, Lao Jen stood and moved to the elevators and Guido walked down the line of storefronts running along the side of the lobby before slowly moving over to the sofa behind the palm tree and sitting and resting for a few minutes. When he'd dug into the sand, however, and come up with the slip of paper with the room number on it, he too moved over to the elevators. Lao Jen was no longer there, but now Guido knew all he needed to know.

Guido was very proud of Lao Jen. Lao Jen had been his own acquisition, and what had given him his entrée with the Americans. Lao Jen was merely a driver for the Chinese embassy in Brussels, just a lackey who was always there in the background but never seen. Lao Jen also had a secret yearning. He went to the Au Fou Chantant cabaret to live his dreams vicariously.

The Chinese embassy chauffeur, the invisible man no one even knew was around as they were driven around the city, doing their business, talking their Chinese state secrets, was talkative and melancholy when he had too much to drink. He also had developed a liking for the little female impersonator, Guido, who glided across the cabaret floor and fluttered his eyelids at him.

Guido had offered his services to the American embassy frequently. He'd gone in and out of the American embassy so often that even the manager of the cabaret had started referring to him as "our little American spy."

Guido rather enjoyed being called that, even around the club while he was working. Guido admired spies; he'd always wanted to be one. And he wasn't dumb; he knew that the best way to get information was not by torture but by giving the one with the information what they wanted—and then making them want more and more of it, until they were willing to do anything to get it. And if you could find what they wanted that was also a deep secret and you could fulfill their secret, dangerous dreams, you were home free. Guido knew what candy was in the world of espionage. He'd read about that. And he knew that to some men he definitely was candy.

The Americans had shown no interest in him at all, however, until he had met Lao Jen and found out what Lao Jen could tell him, without the Chinese even knowing Lao Jen was listening. Suddenly, at the mere mention of Lao Jen's name when he brought up this name in one of his walk-ins to the American embassy, his new friends and controllers, Frank and Felix appeared, all interested and happy to make him an in-country asset with the hope that one day it would get him to America with a comfortable annuity. They had let him develop Lao Jen himself, and they had trusted him enough to help him hook up with and exploit the German colonel as well.

Guido hadn't noticed Lao Jen for some time in the cabaret, and this is what had made the importance of Lao Jen dawn on him. Lao Jen, the menial chauffeur, was the perfect mark—an invisible man, just part of the furniture, something with no ears or brain. In other words, the perfect person to overhear unguarded conversations. Guido had read about that; he knew such things. But before Guido realized the importance of Lao Jen, Lao Jen had already conversed with the club manager and shown that he had enough money to invite Guido to his table, where Guido learned not only that Lao Jen fancied him but that Lao Jen also liked to impress him with what he knew.

Lao Jen was already on the bed, ready for Guido when the young Belgian entered the darkened Bedford Hotel room.

Guido came over and stood beside the bed as Lao Jen sat on the side of the bed and slowly and sensuously undressed him, stopping now and then to glide his big, calloused hands over the smooth body of the dancer and to kiss his nipples and belly and to take Guido's precious little cock and balls wholly into his mouth, sucking Guido's balls up into his cheeks, and then causing Guido to sigh and moan by humming and moving his hands around to cup Guido's buttocks and insert index fingers into the young Belgian's channel to open him up.

Guido hovered there, held up by Lao Jen's strong hands and his sucking lips, and moaned quietly at the slow, methodical attention he was receiving. Lao Jen continued sucking him until he gave up his ejaculate, and then Lao Jen gently raised Guido up with hands gripping his waist and slowly, ever so slowly lowered Guido into his lap, facing him, and onto his thick, erect phallus.

Guido sighed and moaned as he was slowly pumped up and down on Lao Jen's cock. He ran his hands into the Chinese embassy driver's hair and guided Lao Jen's lips to his nipples. Guido lowered his lips to his Chinese lover's ear and whispered to him.

"Tell me of your day. Tell me of how stupid they were in what they would say with you there."

And Lao Jen did.

Later, as they were stretched out on the bed, Guido's buttocks plastered to Lao Jen's crotch and Lao Jen slowly, relentlessly, forever moving his cock deep inside Guido, Guido turned his face to Lao Jen and whispered, "Yes, yes. I love you so much. But I am sad for you. You were so tense. You need to get rid of the tension. They must be treating you so badly at work. Tell me all about it. Tell your little one what cares of the world are hanging on your head. Don't keep it locked inside. Tell me."

And Lao Jen did.

Later, when Lao Jen heard Guido turn on the shower in the bathroom, he rose from the bed and fished around in Guido's jacket pocket. Finding the camera and extracting the cartridge, he opened the drawer where he earlier had stashed a laptop computer and had everything on the cartridge transferred and was standing by the bathroom door, ready to take his turn in the shower, before Guido came out of the bathroom door.

They kissed at the door and told each other how much they loved each other and how good the other one was in his lovemaking before Lao Jen entered the bathroom and Guido dressed, using every trick he'd learned in the theater to remember, almost verbatim, everything Lao Jen had shared with him.

* * * *

They met in a large, leafy-green park in the middle of the city, Guido and Frank and Felix did, one of many in the center of the hustle and bustle of international life and intrigue, where one could lose himself in a forest of trees and bushes and feel they were alone in the countryside.

Still, the three drew very close to each other, as Frank and Felix looked excited and listened intently while Guido repeated to them all that Lao Jen had told him. They didn't take notes, and Guido was duly impressed that they could remember it all.

Guido was beaming when they left, each walking out of the woods in the center of the park in a different direction. They had praised his work highly and had said they would set up yet another assignment within a week or two. Guido felt he definitely was in with the Americans now, on his way to a career in espionage and to a cushy retirement in the United States. Los Angeles. That's where he thought he'd go. But maybe San Francisco. Maybe they'd let him work in a cabaret there. No reason for him not to be able to use all of his talents. But then maybe they would want him to go out of the country on assignment. Maybe they realized just how broad and useful his talents were.

Frank and Felix rendezvoused at the Fontainas Café again, knowing that Guido was expected at the Au Fou Chantant cabaret for the first show of the evening and wouldn't come there to see them at the café when they weren't expecting to meet him. It, in fact, was one of their favorite places in Brussels. This was where each one of them also came to be comfortable and to find male companionship on nights when the tension of their work threatened to overwhelm them.

"Did you get it?" Frank asked.

"Yes, piece of cake," Felix answered as he raised the small digital camera for Frank to see. "He had it right there in his jacket pocket. He never felt the exchange."

Frank laughed. "And he never knew that we didn't switch cameras in the first place and that the bogus papers we had Kielman make available to him are now in the hands of The Chinese embassy spy, Lao Jen—where they undoubtedly will be trusted as genuine and will fuck up Chinese analysis of NATO plans for months, if not years."

Felix joined in the quiet laughter. "And do we use the Belgian again?"

"Naw, I don't think so," Frank answered. "He's a dumb little bunny. Nice ass, though. Maybe we can string him out long enough for each of us to get a ride. He sure looks at you with puppy dog eyes."

Bangkok Defection

I froze in the middle of talking about the next season of the Bangkok Chopin Society at the ambassador's residence, as the ambassador walked into and around the side of the room to get into another room. I don't know if I audibly gulped or not, but none of the women—and the few men— sitting in a circle of upholstered chairs and couches in the commodious room obviously meant for entertaining seemed to notice. The ambassador himself, though, as if he'd heard me react to his presence, turned at the door of the room he was entering and looked directly at me. If he had a reaction of surprise or concern, he was too much the trained diplomat to give one. He just inclined his head a bit, gave me a controlled smile—I had every impression it was directed at me—and then turned and left the room.

I returned my attention to the meeting, having been invited there by Lidka Basher, the ambassador's wife, because the East European country sponsoring the annual Chopin competitions in Warsaw this year was mustering all of the international Chopin societies that had formed to invite their chief executives to sit on the presidium of the next competition. I had, in a convoluted way known only to such social organizations and to the embassy policy to "engage with the country's public," been roped into the presidency of the Bangkok Chopin Society for the coming year, and thus was being invited to Warsaw. I had had no intention of attending and had told my seniors at the American embassy as much, fearing that I'd done something wrong in even being approached by a communist-country embassy, this still being during the Cold War. But my seniors showed no concern at this nondiplomatic contact with communist diplomats and made clear that they had other ideas altogether.

"We would like to get close to the ambassador of that country, very close," the chief of station in the embassy, the most-senior U.S. intelligence agent in country, had told me. "You are to foster, not avoid this contact."

That was a surprise. But this was my first posting. I knew I had a lot to learn about this spying game. So, I'd come to this meeting, intending to follow my chief's directive but not really to make the contact he wanted me to make. I'd tell him that I hadn't even seen the ambassador, that he wasn't part of the committee. But now that I had seen him, I planned on saying it was just fleeting—that I hadn't had the opportunity to talk with him. Fate had other plans, though.

I perhaps would have known about the ambassador if the chief of station had shown me a photograph of him, even though the contexts were so different that maybe I couldn't have recognized the photo. But he had neglected thus far to do so. He, however, seemed already to have known that I would make contact with Ambassador Bacher and even how that would transpire.

Luckily, I wasn't expected to make more of a contribution to the embassy residence meeting on Chopin Society activities, because my mind kept wandering back to where and when I'd previously encountered the ambassador.

It had been in the sauna of the men's gymnasium club I went to in Bangkok—a very special sort of club that flourished in hedonist, "whatever" international cities such as Bangkok.

I was sitting in the lap of the Indian doctor who had originally seduced me in that sauna some months earlier, facing away from him, toward the door of the sauna, and riding his cock, when the man I now knew as Ambassador Jacek Bacher came into the sauna. He stood there, tall, thin, graying hair at the temples and on his chest, and distinguished looking—

perhaps in his fifties, but handsome and well muscled—with just a towel wrapped around his waist, and watched me rise and fall on the Indian's cock with interest and curiosity rather than surprise. Other than a twitch in his cheek muscles, the man initially didn't move while the doctor held my waist in his hands and helped guide me—up and down, a couple of revolves, with me leaning forward then, putting my weight on my feet, and the Indian doctor slamming his long, long, thin cock deep up into me a few times, me huffing at the depth he managed, before pulling me back to rise and fall on the staff myself.

After a few moments of observing, Bacher's towel dropped and he fisted his cock, which looked to be thick and long in contrast to the thin, wiry, tallness of him. The trimmed bush at his groin revealed that he'd had darker hair as a younger man, and his ball sac hung low and heavy. I looked on, mesmerized, the heavy gold signet ring on the middle finger of the slender-fingered hand he was stroking himself with catching my attention, as his cock lengthened and thickened impressively before my eyes.

The two—the Indian doctor and the stranger I didn't then know from Adam—must have known each other well, because the Indian doctor spoke up in his singsong voice that had helped seduce me and then to do whatever he wanted me to do. "Come, Jacek, join me inside him. He's a delicious piece. He knows the double."

And, indeed, I did know the doubling, thanks to the Indian doctor, who had spent months developing me to be able and willing to take anything he suggested.

The man hesitated, but only for a moment, as the Indian doctor's hands went to the underside of my thighs just below the knees and he lifted and spread them, rolling my pelvis up to where the man would be able to see the root of the Indian's cock inside me as well as the rim of my hole clutching the cock.

"Are you sure?" the man asked in a husky, heavily accented voice in a mix of guttural tone but perfect British diction. Despite the question, which, in any event, was directed at the Indian doctor, not to me, I knew he would have me because already that long slender finger with the signet ring was inside me and along the upper side of the doctor's buried cock, and he was rubbing the rim of my opening with the gold metal. I gasped and reached down and, cupping his balls with one hand and his dick with the other, pulled the cock toward my hole.

"Fuck me, oh, god, fuck me too," I murmured, letting him know that he was more than welcome to join the Indian inside me.

"He will open right up for you," the doctor assured him. "I have trained him to double."

And, indeed, the Indian doctor had trained me to take two men at once. At first men with thin cocks like his, but eventually rough thugs with thick cocks. And, if truth be known, I had come to thoroughly enjoy the feel of two cocks inside me at once, especially liking the feel of two active dicks, moving in and out in a countermovement, rubbing against each other, the men breathing heavily and groaning at the effort, as I speculated which of them would come first. This was barely a year before the scourge of AIDS reared its ugly head—a time when every man in Bangkok was still barebacking. Every man pursuing an even more ultimate fuck.

Of course I had reported this sauna encounter to my seniors at the embassy—I had done so the first time the Indian doctor had seduced me here in the sauna and then taken me to his home and fucked me three ways from Sunday, only letting me go when I was crawling across the floor toward him, begging for the cock. I knew that there was no keeping secrets from the secrets specialists in the embassy. And I had expected to be sent home in disgrace. But, to my surprise, my seniors had been pleased and had said that they had known I would succumb to the wiles of other men—even if I hadn't known it or, even if suspecting it, had had no intention of falling to it. The psychological tests I had taken to enter the service had pointed to that, they said, adding that those tests supported the decision to hire me. My seniors said that now I would be even more useful to them and that I was to continue seeing the Indian doctor and letting him train me to male sex.

The COS told me that having the Indian doctor indoctrinate me just saved him the trouble of seeing that it was done.

It was then that they explained to me that the oldest techniques of spying were based on sex, on fulfilling someone's sexual desires to the point that they belonged to you, whether willingly or not. My tradecraft training hadn't been accelerated, the station chief told me, because of my great intellect and natural abilities, but because I was blond, cute, cut, and fit the profile of a man who could be fucked by another man—and still fuck women, as needed.

They left little doubt that after I was fully trained for it, I would be using it to further my government's interests, whether the target was male or female.

I have thought on more than one occasion since then that the Indian doctor was actually in the employ of my seniors in the Agency, and that the most important part of my Agency training occurred here, in Bangkok.

Having been assured by both the Indian doctor and me that I would take his cock along with the Indian's, the tall stranger hadn't waited for a second invitation. He was crouched between my raised and spread thighs and, with grunts and groans, was allowing me to guide his cock to my entrance and force it inside me, above that of the Indians. I let loose of the cock when the bulb cleared my sphincter muscle, not being sure I could take him further and grabbed his ribs as if to push him away. But he was forcing his way deeper into me and I just gripped his sides hard and began to pant.

He faltered, but I whimpered, "Yes, yes," to egg him on, wanting this fuck, wanting to please my Indian teacher. Being willing to endure how it started for where I knew it would lead. I moaned and whimpered as I always do at the first entrance of even one cock, until my opening and channel had got the measure of what I had to take. But the Indian doctor was whispering encouragement in my ear between moments of sucking on my earlobe and even biting it to at least partially reposition the pain I was enduring while the tall stranger was saddling his outsized cock.

I realized that the Indian and this man had done this before, though, because, once saddled, the Indian's cock remained dormant, although still hard, inside me as the stranger bottomed and began to stroke. The stranger wrapped one fist around my cock and stroked me and grabbed my waist with the other, while the Indian continued to hold my thighs raised and spread.

Harder, deeper, faster, the stranger fucked, his balls making a slapping sound on my butt cheeks that reverberated around the wooden walls of the sauna, while I writhed around between them, giving little cries—almost ashamedly cries of pleasure and wantonness—while the stranger pulled hard on my cock and fucked me hard like he was the only one inside me. Slap, slap, slap, the sound of his balls thumping against my butt cheeks, was synchronized with the thrusting of his cock. I moaned and arched my shoulders back deeper into the Indian's chest, rolling my pelvis up to the stranger, wanting him deeper inside me.

"Harder, deeper," I cried out in a moan-tormented voice, wantonly wanting there to be no question what I wanted from the man. My reaction inflamed him to renewed vigor.

But he wasn't the only one inside me. The Indian's cock came to life too, and he was counterstroking me and sucking and biting me on the earlobe and singsonging to me how good I was doing and how sweet my ass was.

I came first and then the stranger and only later, as the stranger pulled out of me and wiped himself with the towel while standing there and watching the Indian lapping me again, did the Indian doctor come. Then he just gently moved me aside, off his cock, with me exhausted and filled with the cream of two men, turning over on my side on the sauna bench. The two of them left the sauna arm and arm then, speaking in low tones. I wanted them to be remarking what a good double lay I was, but I had no inkling what they were discussing.

I hadn't seen the tall stranger in the men's gym since that evening, although it wasn't the last time the Indian used me to double or turned me over to one or a group of men, as he fancied.

That night, the evening of the meeting on Chopin societies in the ambassador's residence, I was approached by a young Thai man dressed in a chauffeur's uniform, after the meeting dispersed and while I was walking across the compound to the gate, where I'd parked my car out on the street.

Whereas many Thai men were small and thin, although being well muscled, this man was tall and bulky and heavily muscled. "Compliments of the ambassador," he said to me in a low voice, as he drew near to me and other people who had been in the meeting drifted by toward the compound gate. "If you have a moment, he would like to have a word with you in the garden."

It was more than a word Ambassador Bacher had. He—and the chauffeur—fucked me, together, in a garden pavilion beyond a swimming pool in a back corner of the compound.

Both were thick, and I gasped and huffed at taking them both, with the ambassador lying on his back on a lounge bed, his thick, long cock pointing straight up at the ceiling of the pavilion, while the hulking chauffeur lifted me as if I weighed nothing and settled me down on the cock. Immediately afterward, he was straddling the ambassador's thighs, grabbing and spreading my butt cheeks, and rolling my buttocks up to his own thick, deep thrust inside me.

They pumped me hard and deep—both pistoning me—there in the dark, the ambassador worrying my nipples and cock, while the chauffeur held my waist with one hand and pulled my head back to his shoulder with the other, his hand covering my mouth and nose to muffle the cries I was making at the much rougher and more brutal double fucking I was getting than I had received from the ambassador and the Indian doctor in the men's gym sauna.

I would complain about the brutality of it, except that I thoroughly enjoyed it. Yes, there was more pain—at least until the emotional pleasure swept over me that there were two men working me, wanting me, enjoying me together. The roughness of it was arousing as any other aspect of the fuck. I couldn't get past the thrill of this sensation of desirability. I'd always want more of it; it would block out any pain involved. And I had been trained well to take it. The only thrill that approached it was being on a chain—we called in being on a string in Bangkok in those days—with men standing in line to fuck me, all of them watching me being fucked, all of them wanting to be inside me too, all of them getting their turn. But in those circumstances, the men weren't having intimate sex with each other at the same time. Nothing served this fetish as doubling did. My only guilty thought was what my employers would think about it. I would have to tell them. They couldn't learn that I was keeping anything back from them.

I protested that my car was there outside the compound when the chauffeur was pulling me toward the embassy limousine, saying he would drive me home. But he paid no attention to me and could—and did—manhandle me at will.

The ambassador was sitting, naked, in the center of the backseat when I entered the limousine, and I sat in his lap, facing him, and fucked myself on his tool during the ride back to my own compound. The chauffeur stopped short of my compound, on a dark cul-de-sac where the buildings were still under construction, and joined us in the backseat, crouching over my buttocks and thrusting up inside me for a second double fuck.

In the morning my car was parked in my spot in the embassy apartment compound parking garage. I remarked on this mystery to the chief of station when I got into the embassy and had told him about my nocturnal encounter with the ambassador—and his Thai chauffeur.

"We drove your car back for you," was all he said.

"What now?" I asked, trying not to think of just how much my own people knew about the encounter and, perhaps, how much of it they were responsible for. "How do I get out of this Chopin Society business and avoid this situation?"

"You don't," was the reply. "We want you to cultivate the ambassador. We think he's ready to defect, and we want him to defect to us. You just have to fuck him. We will pitch him. You are the candy for the deal. Blackmail, if necessary."

Oh. That was my first operation for the station to this effect. I was to become less naïve about these matters later—much less naïve.

* * * *

My "affair" with Ambassador Jacek Bacher, if it could be called an affair, went on for two more months before he disappeared from my life altogether. I attended two more meetings, hosted by his wife, Lidka, during this time, but the ambassador didn't appear to me there again. Instead, I would periodically receive notes in my mailbox at my apartment compound from the chauffeur that just listed an event happening somewhere in the city. He would say no more in the notes or sign them, but if he thought he was fooling anyone, he was the fool. I certainly wasn't fooled. I knew that someone from the station was reading them before I received them—and I turned every one that I received over to the station chief, as well. I was holding no secrets while still being amazed that the Agency could have a stringent policy on sexual activity and still use me in this way.

Without exception, the station chief directed me to make every assignation.

Most of the notes were about sporting venues. I played tennis on the embassy circuit. So did Ambassador Bacher. And I went to the horse races at the Bangkok Sports Club near the corner of Wireless and Ploenchit roads as did many of the rest of the diplomatic community. So did Ambassador Bacher. The ambassador's car would pick me up at a bar near my apartment compound on Soi 51 an hour before the event. Sometimes the ambassador and the chauffeur would fuck me somewhere private at the event. He always seemed to have an isolated, well-appointed room he could use at any venue. Bangkok was famous for accommodating such needs.

More often than not, though, it would be the ambassador lapping me himself on the way to the event and the limousine being parked somewhere hidden on the way back and rocking on its springs as both Bacher and the chauffeur took me together in the backseat. At the actual event, my seat wasn't anywhere close to the ambassador's. Apparently he thought we were being discreet. It didn't take me long to notice that we were being watched by agents from the station.

Bacher said he couldn't get enough of me, and he started to talk of me coming back to Warsaw with him. And I believe he had become that infatuated with me; it came across in his lovemaking, which was becoming less frenetically rough and more attentive and sensual. When I told the station chief this, his eyebrows raised, and, with that simple gesture, I "got" that we would move on to a new phase.

Less than a week later, the Indian doctor summoned me to his apartment. Ambassador Bacher was there. But so was another man, a man I knew in passing but who I had no idea was interested in other men. He was of German ancestry but was an expatriate American, Gerhard Kemp by name. And he owned and operated a well-regarded architectural firm in Bangkok. He was on Lidka Bacher's Chopin Society committee as well as I was and was a big financial backer of the expatriate arts community in the city. He was married to a Thai princess and moved in circles of Bangkok society even above that of the diplomatic community.

He also had a thick, if not long cock. He was on the beefy side, but not quite what I'd call fat yet. And he was quite athletic and vigorous. It wasn't until he was plowing me from between my thighs, as Bacher leaned back on the edge of the Indian doctor's examining table and held me in front him with his cock deep inside me and his hands on my waist, that I realized that I had seen him around the men's gym I went to. He had always been absorbed in a vigorous workout so I hadn't connected him to the underbelly side of the gym.

Until now.

He was stubby enough that it was Bacher who had to hold deep inside me and let the architect, buried only shallowly in my channel, make hard jabs into me and, periodically, revolve his thick cock near my entrance to make the most of his size. The cock could reach my prostate, though, so I could pant and moan—and spout—for him as well as the next man.

The Indian doctor brought the three of us together a few times after that. After the sex, I'd be sent on my way. The doctor would see me to the door, sometimes even coming out of the apartment with me and only separating when we were down on the street, leaving the other two men in his examination room. I could see, in passing, that two glasses and a vodka bottle had been set out on the dining room table each time. I didn't know at the time who they were for—and only later did the significance of them hit me.

But that was only for one more month, until the evening of the Chopin piano concert I went to at the Bangkok Opera hall. As president of the local society, I had been invited to sit in Ambassador Bacher's box. His wife, Lidka, was the honorary sponsor of the concert, so we were in the king's box. Kemp and his wife were there too. And, to my consternation, a political officer from the American embassy was in the box as well.

Nothing untoward happened until the interval, although I could feel the heat coming off the ambassador as he took occasional glances in my direction. There was no pretense, I knew, in how much he wanted me, how hooked he was on me. The Indian doctor was still lending me out to his friends during this period, and I was finding that I melted more to a rough thug than to someone as elegant and refined as the ambassador. So, although I liked him well enough and enjoyed being doubled by him, in particular, he did not hold me in thrall. Certainly not as much as the Indian doctor did, with his variety and his mesmerizing voice—and with perhaps the longest cock I'd had in Bangkok, a cock that was like a snake and could kiss my channel walls from any direction with its rubbing bulb and almost seemed to be able to suck on my prostrate until I came in prodigious flow.

At the interval, the men in the box were separated from the women. The women were sent down to the lobby to mingle with the other high rollers in the audience. The men withdrew to a nearby parlor for, the ambassador said, a smoke and a stronger drink than they were serving in the lobby. As we were ushered toward that room, I realized that the ushers were all station assets from the embassy. I knew then that something was coming down, something important.

31

We had all been wearing tuxedos, and all looked very good in them—as good, I had to say, as we looked out of them. The ambassador and Kemp started taking theirs off as soon as we entered the small parlor. The political officer from the American embassy stood at the closed door to the corridor and motioned for me to disrobe too. I knew then that he was from the station as well.

Bacher and Kemp fucked me, standing, with me suspended between them, my knees hooked on Bacher's hips and Kemp's dick pressed shallowly inside me from the rear. This time, Bacher was urged to take the lead in the fucking, and he did so, with gusto, coming first and then withdrawing as Kemp bent me over the arm of an upholstered chair and finished with his ejaculation. Bacher was invited to take me again, and did so in the same position.

Only afterward, while we were toweling off with wet cloths and dry towels provided, did Bacher begin to "get" what had transpired and why. He'd never asked about the political officer at the door, watching the double fuck intensely. But when he was putting his tux back on and murmuring that it probably was well past the time we returned to the opera hall, Kemp gently placed a hand on his chest and said that Bacher's evening at the concert was over, that they had something to discuss.

Kemp motioned me to dress and leave, saying I would be driven home from there. He was taking charge, and now the assignations at the Indian doctor's apartment and the two glasses and bottle of vodka on the doctor's dining room table each time, and my leaving and the two men staying all came together. Kemp wasn't just a highly placed German-origin American businessman in Bangkok. He was one of us—and probably the senior agent here. This was his defection operation.

As I headed for the door, I looked back at Bacher, who looked sheepish and somewhat confused and lost even as Kemp was pointing out the cameras attached high on the walls of the room, their lenses pointed down to where the two men had stood and shared me.

I was surprised—but in later years wouldn't have been—to find that the chauffeur who drove me home from the opera hall was Bacher's own chauffeur, who obviously had been embedded on Bacher's staff and was part of the operation. He stopped in the familiar quiet cul-de-sac short of my apartment compound and pounded my ass hard in the backseat. He was thug and rough enough for me, and I continued to see him and writhe under him for the rest of my tour in Bangkok.

Weeks later I read in the newspaper that Ambassador Bacher had defected to the British in Singapore—everything well away from Bangkok. His family had been sent to London ahead of him. All neat and tidy.

"Regardless," the station chief said to me, looking down at me over the rim of his glasses, as we "discussed"—with him not sharing all that much—this matter in his office later that morning, "I don't think it would be wise now for you to accept that invitation to the Chopin competitions in Warsaw this year. You should arrange for your vice president to go. She's a classical pianist and you play show tunes, so I think you should manage to rationalize the switch."

"Oh, also," he said, as I was leaving his office. "There's a Russian freighter captain in town whose ship, we think, is carrying Russian arms to Vietnam. He's a rough thug, but we know that he likes your type. Rodney will brief you and arrange the encounter."

"Yes, sir, I understand," I said, as I turned and left the office. Not a preferred double, but the "rough thug" aspect was intriguing.

"And he has a first mate he likes to include in the play," the station chief called after me. "We have an officer in place on board who might be included too."

Even better, I thought, as my smile broadened. I was beginning to get a handle on my job here.

Black Box

One might ask what I, a young American, was doing in a seedy bar and male bordello on a dusty street in Peshawar, Pakistan, walking down the stairs from the rooms overhead after having serviced a Pakistani military officer. And, indeed, that's exactly what the fine-looking fellow in a well-pressed safari suit who was lounging against the bar asked me when I reached the bar and positioned myself at the perfect nonthreatening, but possibly available, distance from him.

He was quite presentable indeed, and an American himself, as revealed by his accent, and he was giving me a friendly smile, so I picked one of my less acerbic responses. "I'm here having a drink, if anyone is paying."

That, of course, was the very shortest version of how I came to be here. The longer version was rather painful and wholly unflattering, so I didn't talk about it much. The truthful version is that I had been working in male porn films in Jersey City, of all places, and the director of one of my movies said he was taken with me and my commanding stage presence, and did I know that the best pay for male porn stars was to be had in Karachi—of all places? I didn't know that, and I didn't take into account that the director was a South Asian himself and one with a particularly shifty-eyed appearance. He offered to pay my way to Karachi, saying he happened to be going there himself, and I bit. Barely there, he promptly sold me to a chieftain in the unmannered tribal areas in the north, along the Afghanistan border, and I spent a good three months in his harem being defiled by all and sundry. When he had grown tired of me, I was dumped on the streets of Peshawar one early morning to look out for myself. Considering what else he could have done with me and no one ever the wiser, I decided to feel gratitude and thank my lucky stars.

I was saving for airfare back to the States, and this bar and bordello was where I was doing the saving, such as it was. It certainly was a step up from being tumbled on a dirty rug in a mud hut by sometimes two burly men at once—although not much more than a baby step up.

You thus could say that I was in pretty desperate straits and open to almost any half-way reasonable suggestion for changing my lot even slightly for the better. And that's why Steve's proposition, when he got around to pitching it, didn't sound half bad.

"I'm standing drinks over here, if you're interested, yes," the handsome, well-muscled man of about thirty said. "My name is Steve, by the way. And you're . . . ?"

"Ken. You can call me Ken," I said, as I moved over beside him, close enough for him to make a move if he wanted to. "And I'd do almost anything for a gin tonic," I added, remembering one of my most frequently used pickup lines.

"Almost anything?" Steve asked right on cue, and the palm of his hand went to the small of my back.

"Well, 2,000 rupees plus that gin and tonic would get you anything," I said. I turned and smiled at him, and he grinned back at me as his hand moved down to cup my buttocks.

He fucked me on the same narrow bed in the small room upstairs where I had sucked off the military officer not more than thirty minutes earlier.

Steve was a fast mover at the bar after our signaling was over; I hardly had time to down my gin tonic before he had me twisted to where he was letting my butt know he had a raging hard on—and quite a good-sized one too—and he had one hand on my basket and the other running up under my shirt and searching for my nipples.

There were only a couple of other men in the bar. A few were enjoying the view, but none were showing any surprise, having seen me more or less in this position a couple of times a day. I'd seen the dicks of everyone I could see from the bar myself on days when they could scrape up the necessary rupees.

When we got to the room, he told me to strip—all of the way—but quickly, if you please. He wanted to see me in the altogether, he said, but time was short. While I undressed, he did so as well, neatly folding his clothes. He had an athlete's body, tanned and perfect except for a few scars on an arm and his side that could be either gunshot or stab wounds. They didn't run long enough to be surgery scars.

Perhaps I should have put a halt to everything then. But I didn't. He already had money out and on the nightstand—somewhat more than the requested 2,000 rupees.

"Do lube and condoms come with the quoted price?" he asked.

I opened the top drawer of the nightstand, and he leaned over me and reached in and took out a professional-size tube of lubricant and two condoms. He held the condoms up for me to see.

"I put 6,000 rupees down," he said. "We square so far?"

I nodded and leaned back against the side wall, my shoulder blades touching the cool, moist mud brick, and rolled my hips up at the edge of the bed and spread my legs.

He fucked me hard and fast and deep and expertly. And I gasped at the thickness and depth and rapid pistoning and came a long time before he did.

"Stretch out on your stomach," he said in a low voice after he'd spent his first condom. I did so and he sat on the bed beside my hips and started massaging my back and thighs and butt.

It felt nice, something I didn't usually get from a client except for the few who fancied they were in love with me and thought they could, eventually, convince me I was in love with them too if they treated me right. This mostly meant they wanted their fucks for free. I could have been in love with an

37

exotic prince if he'd swept in and taken me away to his mountain palace. But none had ever ventured into the bordello in this section of the city to my knowledge.

Steve ran his hand between my thighs. I sighed and opened my legs to him, and he encircled my cock in a fist and started rubbing my piss slit with a lubricated thumb.

And while he was slowly masturbating me, he offered to be my saving prince.

"You married to this place?" he asked.

"Not particularly."

"I'm taking a walk in the mountains and could use a companion. Fancy some fresh air for a couple of days?"

"Last time I checked I wasn't due a vacation," I answered.

"It would only be for a couple of days."

"I don't have hiking . . . ahhhh, yes, yes, like that . . . I don't have hiking boots."

"I'd outfit you," he said. "And it wouldn't be a vacation, really. I'd pay you 20,000 rupees."

"And fuck me how many times for that?"

"Oh, maybe five times—unless you wanted more, of course. That would be double pay."

"I don't know . . . yeah, maybe." Business had been slow; it was the wet season, and the men were out watching their women work the fields during the day and coming home exhausted in the evening from seeing how hard the woman worked.

"In that case, here's another 2,000 rupees," he said as he reached over and took more money out of his wallet and laid it on top of the 6,000 already on the nightstand. "Sit up and blow me. I want to know how well you suck before I'm sure about taking you along."

Steve stood up beside the bed, and I sat up on the edge and palmed the hollows below his hips and beside his hard-muscled buttocks and opened my lips to his erect cock. I sucked on just his glans and flicked his piss slit with my tongue until he groaned, palmed the back of my head, and forced my lips farther up his shaft. I didn't think I'd be able to take him all in, but he proved me wrong to a bit of objecting and gagging on my part.

He was breathing heavily and I could feel him shuddering—always a sign that I was delivering satisfaction—when he pulled away from me, made me roll the second condom on his cock, and told me to lay belly down on the bed again. I opened my legs as I felt him pull my cock up between my thighs. And then he gave my cock some attention with his mouth as he crouched between my legs. His lips and tongue went to my hole, and despite all advisories from me that I was close to coming again, he tongue-fucked my channel and slowly pumped my cock with his fist until I did, indeed, come.

He took up a pillow that had fallen to the floor and inserted it under my belly, raising my pelvis to him, and then he stretched out on top of me, closely fitting his body to mine, and I widened my stance as his cock slid into me. He quickly encased my thighs in his, though, causing me to gasp and groan at the tight filling of my channel by his thick cock, and plastered his lips to the hollow of my neck as he slow fucked me for an eternity.

After that there was no question whether I was going with him or that his fucking me just five times as we climbed that mountain of his would fully satisfy me.

I didn't count on how cold a walk in the mountains along the Pakistan-Afghanistan border north of the Khyber Pass would be.

He was as quick and insistent on getting off on that hike as he'd been about getting me into bed. He didn't even give me a chance to ask him why he was taking that walk.

I really should have thought about asking him that before we set off.

We took a Land Rover as far up into the foothills as we could and then hiked for a while and stopped at a rest station built for mountain climbers at the base of a mountain that looked pretty much like the Rockies to me. But maybe a bit higher. OK, looks can be deceiving. Probably a great deal higher.

After dinner, taken in silence because I was already exhausted just by the short walk from the Land Rover, Steve disappeared outside. I stepped out into the cold to see what he was up to and found him holding some sort of beeping metallic box and turning it in different directions, listening to the change in the beeping. It had a needle on it too, that seemed to insist that it wanted to point up the mountain. I saw Steve smile and then he turned and saw me, and I saw him give a little frown.

I started to ask him questions about the beeping box, but he bustled me inside, threw me down on one of the cots, and fucked all of the questioning out of me, leaving me a heap of satisfied sighs—at least for the moment.

It was still dark when he woke me up again with his cock plowing my depths. And when he'd spent another condom, his own this time, we bundled up and started our slow hike up the mountain.

We made remarkably good distance, entirely, I'll report, because of Steve relentlessly driving us on. Twice on the trail he stopped and told me to go take a piss or something over to the side, and I saw him open his little beeping box and take bearings again.

Before nightfall, we had reached another rest stop cabin on the side of the trail. I heard Steve mutter, "Ah, good, they're still here," which was my first clue that we no longer were alone on the trail.

Three men were in the cabin when we entered it. All of them were hulky and bulky and Slavic looking. They were speaking Russian, which, I'm happy to say, I heard a lot of in Jersey City, so I know how it sounds when I hear it. Can't understand a word of it, of course. Which was too bad, because the three were looking us over real good and muttering to each other.

Surprise, surprise, Steve spoke Russian too, and then I found out that the man who seemed to be their leader, a muscle-bound dude who stood a head taller than the other two and whose name was given as Sergei, also spoke passable English.

I don't know what Steve told them in Russian, but they settled right down and became quite friendly.

They had brought vodka. And, more important, they were happy to share. Steve said no thanks, he didn't drink vodka, but when he produced chocolates from his backpack, the Russians seemed to forget any tendency to take umbrage at his failure to drink with them. I did drink with them, though. I didn't get drunk, but I got tipsy—too tipsy, in fact, to be much use to myself for what came later.

While we all shared dinner rations, Steve took me over to the side and gave me a serious look.

"Listen, you are a loyal American, aren't you?" he whispered.

"Well, yes, of course," I said. "I'm not really in Peshawar because I have anything against America. Just circumstances, you know."

"What I'm going to tell you now can't go any further than you. You must never tell anyone. If I thought you would, I'd have to kill you."

"No, really?" I said, amused. But then I wasn't all that amused anymore. He was smiling—grimly, though. But it was his eyes. They weren't smiling at all.

"These guys are Russian spies," he whispered. "They're after something I've been sent by U.S. intelligence to retrieve, and I . . . we have to make sure I get there before they do. Can you understand that?"

"Spies? Get where?" I muttered back. "Does this have anything to do with that beeping box in your backpack."

"Yes, of course," Steve responded, his voice laced with exasperation. "But we can't talk long; they'll get suspicious. I'll just tell you straight out and you nod your head if you're with me. If you're a loyal American. This is very, very important."

I nodded my head—not really for practice, but he was so intense and had such a strong grip on my arm that I wanted him to know I'd die for America, if I had to. I'd even sing the "Star Spangled Banner," it that would help—although even in these circumstances I couldn't guarantee I'd hit that high note in the song. And when I thought of it, I wasn't actually sure I knew all of the words—which meant, of course, that I was a born American rather than a naturalized citizen who had to memorize a lot of shit like that to get his membership card.

"A plane went down on the mountain," Steve whispered, his voice intense. "A reconnaissance drone. Something so new and different that almost no one knows about it. It was locating Al-Qaeda leaders. And it went down. And somehow the Russians know about it too, although only I have the homing device to be able to walk directly to it. I've got to get to the plane first. There's a black box and some other gear that I must retrieve. Understand?"

I nodded my head. One of the Russians came over and refilled my vodka cup. Both Steve and I smiled sweetly to him, and then he went back to where the other two Russians were huddled. Sergei had his hand high on the thigh of the sitting Russian, and the other one leaned down and planted a kiss on Sergei's lips as he squatted and folded himself into the bundle.

Steve gave a low whistle. "OK, that's it. I was told that was it, but now I know. Here's what we are going to do. Ken, Ken. Focus, look at me. Read my lips. I have to say this fast and very low."

I turned to him and focused on his lips. There seemed to be two sets of them, though. I obviously was drinking too much vodka too fast.

"I have to go on ahead tonight to the wreckage and retrieve what I can," Steve whispered. "You have to stay here and occupy the Russians. Understand? Try to keep them from noticing I haven't come back from taking a leak. I'll be back as soon as I can to pick you up and we can go back down the mountain while the Russians go on up looking for what's no longer there. Understand?"

I started to nod my head and then realized it didn't make complete sense to me.

But before I could say anything, Steve had reached over and pulled my sweater over my head. He then put his arms around me from behind and palmed my nipples and called out to the Russians, "Say, Sergei. You like my friend here?"

Sergei looked up—in fact all three looked up—and I could tell that they did like me, that they liked me a lot.

"Ken here is a male whore," Steve continued in a friendly, casual tone. "I bought his time down in a bar in

Peshawar. Brought him along so I could fuck him in the evenings."

Three sets of Russian eyes widened up to saucers. I could tell that they all understood English well enough.

"You want to fuck him tonight? Only 20,000 rupees and you can all have him. I'll go outside. I'll sleep in the shed outside. You can all fuck him all night long. Only 20,000 rupees. What do you say? Look at this chest. Young American piece. You should see his nice hole. Good fucking, I can assure you."

I never saw 20,000 rupees appear so fast. And with only mild vodka-impaired objection and struggle from me, which the Russians enjoyed immensely, they did, indeed, fuck me in relays most of the night, with one Russian cock barely vacating my channel and my mouth before another plunged in and started pumping away. They were so engrossed with me and with each other that none of them ever showed any curiosity about where Steve was.

Toward dawn, they were all exhausted and in a stupor from having imbibed more vodka than I had and doing more vigorous fucking than they should have done in the thin atmosphere, and at last, saying I had to take a piss, I painfully rose and pulled on whatever of my warm gear I could find in the dark—the Russians never having bothered to make me take off my hiking boots while they fucked me—and hobbled out the door.

My timing was perfect. I was still creating yellow snow not far from the door to the cabin, when a bright light on the side of the mountain, a good bit farther up than where I stood, blossomed up and caught my attention. Seconds later I heard a low, rumbling boom. Not loud enough to wake the Russians, I am happy to say, but loud enough in combination with the slowly waning bright light up there outlining a hump on the mountain to know that Steve wasn't just retrieving a black box and some portable secret gear from that crashed plane up there.

I also wasn't dumb enough to believe that Steve was coming back this way to pick me up.

I felt in the pocket of my parka and found that Steve had stowed the Russians' 20,000 rupee in there. At least he'd done that much. This, with the 20,000 he'd given me back in Peshawar, might be enough to get me as far as Karachi—a good two centuries forward toward civilization. That is if the Russians didn't get suspicious when they woke up and found that Steve wasn't here anymore.

"Ah, well, that's life. My life, certainly," I muttered and, with a sigh, turned my nose downhill and started off at a slow, painful gait, hoping that Steve had left the keys in the Land Rover—knowing, though, that he either had not, or that he had every intention of getting there before anyone else did.

Breaking the Banker

Henri Bragger looked around the seminar room at the World Bank symposium in Washington, D.C., giving a nod here and a little smile there. He was among old friends—or at least long-time colleagues. His own Swiss bank, the Banca Privata Reichstein, was one of the most reputable—and safest—banking institutions throughout the world. And he had been with the bank over thirty years now. He was at the top of his world, with a secure position in playing traffic control for all international transactions coming into and going out of the BPR; a beautiful and rich second wife, Karyn; and two university-student children, who were beautiful in their own right and who worshipped him and didn't blame him for his first divorce. His ex-wife had been decent that way; she had said nothing to the children about the incidents that had led up to the divorce and, anyway, that whole period of his life was more than a decade behind him.

And here he was, in Washington, on a panel of world banking leaders, advising the industrialized nations on how to get out of their shared economic crises. His panel had been very successful, and he had come into this one on secured international bank transfers to rub shoulders with his peers and to rest his brain before he was to appear on his next panel. This seminar wouldn't be taxing; there was absolutely nothing anyone had to teach him about secured international bank transfers.

After glancing around the room, Henri's brain signaled that he had passed on something interesting and a bit disquieting, and he scanned the room again. He almost didn't pick up on it, but his eyes finally focused on a younger man sitting several rows back and to his right. Henri might have let his gaze travel over him again, because in identifying his peers, his brain was gauged to men and women in their fifties, as he was, not men as young as the one who now was giving him a smile.

That smile. Yes, he was a younger version, probably not connected at all, but reminiscent of Sa'eed. Henri hadn't thought about Sa'eed for years—or at least intentionally or very long at one time—or at least that's what he pretended to himself. Sa'eed was part of his closed life. And the Germanic in Henri worked hard at keeping closed internal doors closed—and locked.

Henri looked at the young man again. Dark-complexioned and handsome, a son of the Levant, with a sultry look, velvet brown eyes, and black curly hair. The bittersweet memories crowded into Henri's brain, and perhaps he should have gone to a seminar with a less-familiar topic, because his brain disconnected entirely from the droning of the German banker at the front of the room and roamed back twenty-five years, back to Beirut.

* * * *

It was the silky voice he had and his sultry good looks, even in maturity—especially in maturity—and what he read to me, yes, certainly that too.

Sa'eed Maalouf was a writer and scholar of Arabic literature, destined to be a major writer and, even then, a professor at the American University of Beirut. And I was a young banker, in my late twenties, on an internship in our Beirut branch, and with a pregnant young wife at home in Geneva. I was studying at the American University in the evenings, intent on learning Arabic and the culture of the

46

region, already having decided that specialization in the oil-rich regions of the world was ideal for a banker. I also was lonely, and full of myself, impressionable, and in a place exotic in ways that were way beyond my world in Switzerland.

At my beckon, Ibrahim crossed the stifling hot room, an old ceiling fan ticking overhead, and sat down on the edge of the divan where I was reclining, ready for the night and reading from one of my forbidden books.

Ibrahim looked at the cover of the book and gave a low laugh, "And is this the cause of those sounds I hear in the night, Mahmud? You have no need of such books as these."

He laid his palm on my belly and leaned down and looked intently in my face as his hand descended lower, watching the changes in my expression, listening for the soft moaning from my lips, his face like a mirror, reflecting his own rising passion in response to mine.

Please turn down the lamp, Ibrahim, I murmured.

We were in Sa'eed's study at the university, a large room, opulently furnished with Oriental carpeting, massive overloaded bookcases, a large mahogany desk, and in the far corner, wedged behind bookcases, a low divan, spread with tapestry pillows and one overstuffed club chair. The ceiling was high, and an old fan ticked away overhead. It was late in the evening, with little light filtering through a tall, dusty, uncurtained window behind the desk.

Sa'eed, in his customary white dishdasha tunic, was reclining on the divan, reading to me in Arabic from *The Red Velvet Jacket*, slowly, in silken tones, endeavoring to help me pick up the richness of the language. The text was almost poetry as written in Arabic—and even more so as Sa'eed spoke it—and I was concentrating hard to understand all the nuances of a language that was so much more expressive and visual than mine.

This reading was all too visual, and even though I was blushing and Sa'eed was murmuring that I need not dwell on the deeper meaning of it as much as how the language was being woven on the surface, I found myself responding in ways that embarrassed me.

I was not a novice to homoerotic texts or even to youthful experimentation in the all-boys prep school I had attended in Zurich. But I was a husband now and soon to be a father. I'm sure I could have resisted if I hadn't been alone in an exotic atmosphere, with a handsome, honey-voiced poet exhibiting a special attraction to me.

"Come, come over here, Henri, and sit on the divan beside me and take up the book and read to me. Here, I will find another passage. Ah, yes, this will do. The verbs are not too difficult."

I sat beside Sa'eed's hip, and he brushed his fingers along the hairs on my forearm as I concentrated hard on speaking the words properly.

The night is so quiet out on the sands of the desert, a day's journey between the oases. The warm leather of the camel saddle slides gently across my belly, as I dig my fists and toes into the sand and stare up at the stars, searching for the largest, panting, his hot breath on my neck, his teeth nibbling at my ear, his chest rising and falling on my back and his strong hands holding my wrists. Never before feeling so filled, so deeply pene—

"No, Sa'eed," I said, my voice breaking, my trembling hands lowering the book. "I don't think I can—"

He had drawn his dishdasha off and was nude underneath. He was sitting behind me on the edge of the bed now, his thighs enclosing mine. One hand on my belly under my shirt and the other hand unbuttoning my shirt and fly. He was breathing heavily on my neck and raised his lips to my ear and took my lobe in his teeth for a moment before I heard that soft, arousing voice of his.

"I think you can. I think you must." He had encased my now-freed hard cock in his fist. "I will be gentle."

"Please, can we turn out the light?" I murmured in a shaky voice.

In darkness, I felt my body being lifted up on the divan, and my thighs spread and Sa'eed kneeling between them. He was reciting verse to me in a singsong voice.

The velvet sheath whispers its sadness at the wandering sword
The sword hears the song; its blade shimmers and sings in return
Searching for its velvet sheath, singing to it to open to the sword .
. .

My legs were raised slowly onto Sa'eed shoulders, and I felt the cool, oiled fingers at my entrance, and I moaned and felt my hips begin to roll as my prostate felt the touch. I closed my eyes and went with the passion of the moment. He was still speaking of the sword and velvet sheath as he entered me, and I cried out and he thrust deeper each time the word sword was spoken.

Afterward, after Sa'eed's lips left mine and he had declared me as his—and I had not demurred—he gave a low laugh and whispered, "Next time we leave the lamp on."

My awakening to Sa'eed's world was followed by a blissful summer with pledges and plans for meeting after I returned to Geneva. On my final day in Lebanon, as I was approaching the departure gate at the airport, I was called aside into a small room and shown photographs of more than one of my couplings with Sa'eed. I was told that, of course, the men present in the room could fully understand a love between me and the poet, but that I had to return to Switzerland to a family and Sa'eed had to remain in Lebanon, where such activities were illegal and severely punished. But, of course, if I were to cooperate with the needs of their organization, they were sure that none of these photographs would come to light.

But what could I do, I asked, so besotted at the moment that Sa'eed's safety was uppermost in my mind.

Quite simple, they said. They knew that, with my training, I could manage an assignment to the Arab section of the Banca Privata Reichstein, a bank in which their organization, a patriotic Palestinian organization, wished to open a secret secured account. All I needed to do was to smooth that and, as I rose in the bank, as they knew I would, to work in the organization's interest.

I never saw Sa'eed again. He answered my letters for a while—and sent me the love poetry he was working on, but it never seemed convenient or safe for us to meet again. And then, barely more than a decade later, he was dead, killed in a bombing in Lebanon during a time when there was so much bombing that no one knew for sure who set what bomb off against what target and for what purpose.

But by then I was firmly trapped into handling the secret bank account interests of more than one Arab revolutionary organization. And after I discovered I couldn't be as clever as I thought in pursuing my proclivities in Geneva and my first wife divorced me, I did all I could to close off that aspect of my being. I remarried and started all over again.

* * * *

Henri snapped out of his flashback in time to chat and greet at the close of the dull seminar. He looked around the room, but the young man who had caused his remembrance was not in sight.

However, the young man was in the next seminar where Henri was impaneled, and it took all of Henri's strength to stay in the discussions and not let his eyes drift to where the young man was sitting, smiling at him throughout.

"Hello, Herr Bragger, wonderful comments. I'm sure they will help us set a new path in our economic plans."

"Umm, thank you," Henri said rather perfunctorily, not the least because he suddenly felt unable to breathe. The young man had walked up to the panelists' rostrum as the seminar was breaking up and colleagues were making quick, brief comments to each other before they rushed off to their next session. Henri—reluctantly—moved to turn away and join the departing crowd, but the young man placed a hand on his forearm, and Henri felt the electricity of the touch race up his arm. With resolution mixed with an almost sensual forbidden and forbidding pleasure, he turned back to the young man.

"I'm sorry, if you are in a hurry, Herr Bragger, but I wanted to meet you. My name is Salim. Salim Maalouf, and I work at the U.S Department of the Treasury and saw your name on the list of attendees."

Henri hadn't really heard anything beyond the "Maalouf" part.

"Maalouf. Not—?"

"Yes, that Maalouf. The writer, Sa'eed Maalouf. He was my father. I know about you. That's why I wanted to meet you."

Knew about him? Henri's brain was bursting. What context was there in that? What did this young man know about what transpired between him and his father all those years ago. Was the young man going to denounce him on the basis of family honor? Or was it something else altogether that he knew—Henri's connection with the Palestinian organizations purpose perhaps? Henri was doing everything he was being asked to do; why would they be sending someone to Washington, D.C., to contact him directly? But, hadn't the young man said he worked for the U.S. government? Was Henri's complicity with Mideast terrorist groups—something that had now become quite an international crime—being exposed? Or was it both family honor and criminal activity? Or something else altogether?

"Listen, I don't have a seminar scheduled now," the young man said. "Do you? Perhaps we could go somewhere quiet for lunch?"

Did Henri really have a choice? The sudden shock of it left him almost speechless—and without choices.

They lunched in a dimly lit alcove at a discrete little restaurant in Georgetown, and Henri was both relieved and aroused that Salim seemed to only know of his relationship with Sa'eed as being lovers; nothing was mentioned of Henri's business with secret Palestinian bank accounts and Sa'eed's possible connection with that.

"I never could forget what my father said of his love for you and the consummation of that love," Salim said.

"He told you of that?" Henri asked. "Weren't you rather—?"

"My father was a very special man; and we were a very special family. He spoke of everything. And he lived life deeply, even with his own family. He wrote of you and let me read it."

"He wrote of me?" Henri asked, feeling a bit breathless.

"Yes, my father had much love to give," Salim answered. He reached over and took Henri's hand and traced the lifeline on Henri's palm with his forefinger. Henri began to tremble. The young man was beautiful and sultry. He had his father's voice, rich and with unexpected, exciting rhythms. Henri had cut himself off so completely from the past, that it was like a flood of memories when the dike was breached.

"His favorite story he read to me before . . . well it was of you. Did you read any of the writings about you that have been published?"

"Yes," Henri answered in a small voice. "Or at least I hoped they were about me—that our couplings meant as much to him as they did to me."

"And to me also." Salim reached up and cupped Henri's chin with his hand so that Henri had to stare him in the face. "I want the same things with you as you had with my father."

Both men had rooms at the Willard hotel, and Salim made the practical suggestion that they use his room rather than Henri's, as there were European colleagues of Henri's with rooms on the same floor as his.

* * * *

I was his from the moment we entered the room, he made that perfectly clear. The shades were drawn and one light was on, at the side of the bed.

We stood just inside the door, facing each other, close. He cupped my face in his hands and kept my eyes trapped with his as I—at his demand—unbuttoned my shirt, unbuckled my belt, and unzipped my trousers. Then his face and hands disappeared from view, traveling down my chest and belly, and, trembling, I was being held up by his palms cupping my buttocks and my cock in his mouth. His hands were spreading my buttocks and fingers were entering my channel.

Memories were crowding in, and I felt like my spirit was rising out of my body, being transported to another place, another time, another man. I was being taken by Sa'eed, and it was his name I murmured.

I was on my back on the bed, my knees bent and legs spread, my Arab lover was between my legs, his chest hovering over mine. I cried out in long-dormant passion as a hot cock slid into me, deep, and held there as I felt him throbbing and still filling out, deep inside me. He cupped my head in his hands again and held his beautiful, sultry face just above mine. His milk-chocolate eyes possessed mine.

"Recite your poetry to me, your love poetry," I sighed, seeing Sa'eed's face above mine. "In Arabic." I loved being fucked to Sa'eed's love poetry.

"I don't know any poetry," he answered. "My cock is my poetry. My cock will sing your praises."

"No matter," I answered with a sigh.

And then, just before he started to stroke inside me, once again a memory stole up from the depths of me, and I whispered, "Shall we turn off the light?"

"No," He answered. "I want to see the working of my cock reflected in your eyes. That is poetry to me." And he was smiling, enjoying every flicker and pop of my eyes as his cock explored every nook and cranny of my channel.

"Your moan," he whispered, "Your moan told me you liked that phrase."

"Yes, yes," I whispered, moving into a deep, long groan.

"And you liked that better. My poetry is reaching you, each stanza making you sing."

"Yes, yes, yes," I moaned. "Oh, gawwwd!"

And after that there was no more talk, as I moved my hips in motion with his and he took my lips in his—and I drifted off into a reverie of my nights on the divan in Sa'eed's university study.

* * * *

The next morning Henri fled Washington, leaving the conference early and rushing back to Geneva with the breathless tale that he could not stay away from his Karyn and his children for one more evening.

He was good then, a devoted husband and father, and diligent in his work, only permitting his eyes to glaze over for a moment or two in remembrance of his afternoon in the Willard Hotel, still having trouble keeping straight who it was—the father or the son—who had made love to him.

Life had almost gone back to normal for him; it had been nearly a week since he had locked himself in his bathroom and stood under the shower and masturbated to the memory of his fucking by the ghost of his long-lost lover.

Thus, it was a shock when he looked up from his desk one day and standing there in the door, smiling at him, was Salim Maalouf.

"I had a room available at the Kipling Hotel on the Rue de Navigator. They have a very private elevator and they ask no questions," was all Salim had to say.

* * * *

I was bent over the bed on my belly, my arms spread out wide, held at the wrists by strong hands, my legs spread, and Salim's cock sliding into me. I knew it was Salim now. No illusions. I no longer needed Sa'eed as a buffer. I had had weeks since the encounter and I had worked it all out in my mind, had relived the taking by the son—not the father—over and over again. This was a strong, young, virile cock stretching my channel walls as it moved up inside me.

His chest was hovering over my back and his lips were in the hollow of my neck. He raised them and nipped me on the ear lobe and then put his mouth near mine. "You wanted Sa'eed last time," he growled. "Well I have found some of his love poetry, if that's what you want."

The velvet sheath whispers its sadness at the wandering sword
The sword hears the song; its blade shimmers and sings in return
Searching for its velvet sheath, singing to it to open to the sword .
. .

At each use of the word "sword," he thrust his cock deeper inside me. I struggled again with the confusion of who was covering me and making love to me.

"No, no, Salim," I protested. "It's you I want, not the ghost of your father."

"Then this is how Salim fucks his men," he barked. And he turned me and flung me to the carpet, bringing me up on all fours and mounted my ass like a dog and pistoned me with long, rapid, deep strokes and slapping my butt with the palm of his hand as I cried out and grunted and moaned—and came in three gushes on the carpet. But still he rode me, until my knees and palms were bruised from carpet burns and gave out and I went down flat on the floor while he rode me some more—to his own completion.

I loved every second of it. I'd never felt so taken before.

* * * *

"I suppose you wondered why I came to Geneva," Salim said as we were laying in the bed and enjoying a smoke and talking of his father—with me doing most of the talking. Salim didn't seem all that interested in talking about his father.

"Are you going to tell me?" I asked. I hadn't, in fact, wondered a bit why he was here. I had assumed, foolish old man that I was, that he had come for me, that he couldn't stay away from me—but I couldn't say I'd actually thought about it. I could tell by his asking of the question, however, that there was something he wanted to tell me—no doubt something he wanted me to do for him. And I was right.

"I am more or less, as we say in the States, on the lam," he said.

"What have you done?"

"Nothing, of course. But there seem to be some Treasury Department funds missing."

"How much?"

"Not much. About $120,000. A computer system upgrade was contracted and delivered, but somehow the payment is missing."

"And you want me to help you?" I knew the answer to that question, so I just continued on. "How?"

"Can you launder the money for me?"

I had done many things that were not completely on the up and up in my career—especially in the similar favors I did for Arab groups—and I was in love. So, my answer was not that much of a decision for me.

Our trysts in the Kipling Hotel room continued until I informed Salim that his money was clean. The cocking that afternoon after I told him his money was clear seemed a little desultory, but I reasoned that even young men would have their off days now and again.

When I came out of the shower, Salim was gone, and an expensively suited middle-aged man of military bearing was sitting in the club chair.

"Hello, Herr Bragger," he said. "I am Sam Winterberry of the American embassy, and I believe that you are the principal attendant of several secret Mideast terrorist bank accounts at the Banca Privata Reichstein."

* * * *

All through my "chat" with Mr. Winterberry, I kept waiting for the accusation that I knowingly was working with the Mideast terrorist groups—that they had had me under their thumbs for years—but that wasn't even hinted at. I was treated like I was a completely honest banker who just happened to control the traffic in Arab banking transactions for BPR and could be approached just because I was so smitten with a homosexual lover that I would do illegal things for him.

And thus my quandary. What they were asking me seemed low risk to them—but to me it was a death sentence—and quite possibly for my wife and children too.

"We want all the information you can give us on any Mideast organization with a secret account at the bank that we ask you about, and promptly when we ask, Herr Bragger."

"Is that all?" I asked. I was jumping at shadows; I knew that this was too elaborate of a scheme for that to be all.

"When we are closing down the groups, we want you to transfer their funds into a U.S. government account," Winterberry said. And he had the audacity to smile as he said it.

"The risk," I said.

"Is minimal," Winterberry said.

"Is phenomenal," I countered. And Winterberry didn't know how phenomenal it was. All it would take was a hint of what I'd done on one account to reach the still-viable holders of other accounts, and I and my family would be dead. And after just a few such groups being hunted down, the rest would be able to figure where the information that brought them down would come from.

"My family," I said.

"Will be protected," Winterberry answered.

There was no arguing. Winterberry just didn't know it all, and I couldn't tell him all. And it was dangerous enough even with what Winterberry did know. Already my brain was spinning. I would have to transfer assets—there was a slight chance I could disappear on both of my oppressors. And I would have to force something that would cause Karyn to divorce me quickly and my children to part with me so publicly and irrevocably that the terrorists thought there was no bond at all between us. I was a dead man, but I would do what I could do for my family. Maybe a real mistress to anger my wife. Not reveal my homosexuality, of course. I could not humiliate my family that way—and my first wife had been good enough to keep the secret all these years—but another woman, that might work. At that contemplation, of course, my thoughts went to Salim.

"And Salim?" I asked Winterberry.

"He will be there for you as long as we are pleased with your efforts," Winterberry said, with a smile.

At least I'll die happy, I thought.

Later, after Winterberry had gone, my Arab lover did return. I refrained from recriminations—it was far too late for those to matter anyway—and when he had proved, because of my response, to have regained all of his vigor and virility, he fucked me silly, first missionary style on the bed and then, when I was washing the sex of him off me in the shower, he took me there too, my belly against the wall and his cock lifting my feet off the soapy tiled floor with the force of its thrusts.

"I'm so happy you'll be helping us out and that you and I can be together," he murmured.

I would indeed die happy.

One thing I needed to know, regardless, which I asked him when he had agreed to let me spend the night in his bed and we were in the dark in an embrace.

"Tell me one thing, please—and it doesn't matter either way—but I would like to know. You are not Sa'eed Maalouf's son, are you?"

"No," he answered with an edge of slight regret in his voice, which I noted with appreciation. "My name is Jamil Jallud. I'm third generation American. You can call me Jaime. And, as you may also have guessed already, I don't work for the U.S. Treasury Department."

Brussels Seduction

It had just been a kiss and a grope in the underground garage of the American embassy in Brussels. I'd pulled away from him and told him that he'd misjudged—that I wouldn't report him that time, but that he'd misjudged me and he should stay well away from me from then on or I'd have to report him. I wouldn't report him, though, I didn't want there to be any spotlight on a junior consular affairs officer in his first overseas posting.

And Dieter Jouret hadn't misjudged me. When I opened my apartment door two nights later, after I'd had time for the momentary encounter with the golden hunk of a local embassy driver in the dark of the subterranean garage to play over and over again in my mind—extrapolating to the possibilities of it—I just stood there, dumbfounded and trembling. I put up no resistance when Dieter entered the apartment, shoved the door shut with his foot, picked me up in his arms, and carried me into the bedroom. I lay there on the bed, chest heaving in ragged breathing as he pulled my sweatpants and briefs off—I had been bare-chested—and knelt between them and worked my cock with his mouth and tongued my ass.

I had spread my legs for him myself, my heels digging into the edge of the foot of the bed, and my hands buried in the blond hair of his head—and moaned. God, how I'd moaned as his mouth worked my cock, balls, and asshole. I nearly lifted my butt off the bed and squeezed his skull as he swallowed my balls and sucked them while two fingers worked their way into my ass.

I'd said nothing, made no effort whatsoever to tell him to stop—to repeat that I wasn't like this and would report him.

I obviously *was* like this. I'd been like this all through my first year at college, letting a senior jock spike me after a night at a beer hall—and then his friends as he spread around that I could be had—stopping only when I woke up one morning in a fraternity house and realized that all of the brothers in the house who had wanted to had known me, in succession, throughout the previous night. I was frightened and disgusted not because they had done it—or even that I had allowed myself to get so drunk that I didn't prevent it—but because I had enjoyed it.

I had been shocked when one of the fraternity brothers said that this was what I'd been rushed by the house to do. To be the house punch. To take a train whenever the brothers felt so inclined—that my willingness to be fucked had been spread all over the campus. I'd packed up my stuff and left the house that day. And I transferred colleges my second year. My father had been miffed, as he'd been in that fraternity and in that college, but I couldn't tell him why I'd left other than that I had found I didn't like fraternity life—and that college didn't have the major I wanted to pursue. The latter was true. I decided I wanted to go for foreign affairs—of the diplomatic kind. I wasn't looking for a French guy to spike me.

I swore off on sex with men after that and thanked God that the Foreign Service exam polygraph didn't include any lifestyle questions such as that.

I hyperventilated, with my own hand going to my cock, as Dieter stood up between my legs, stripped down to reveal a glorious, heavily muscled body, and a huge erection, and smiled down at me while he snapped the condom on the cock.

Thinking back on having sworn sex with men off, I thought that at least he wasn't French—but then I realized that I was beginning to hyperventilate and be a little crazy.

"Am I right? You've been fucked before?" Dieter asked, as he smoothed the condom out along his thick cock. "I know you want it now, but it makes a difference whether you've had experience."

"It's been a long time . . . but, yes."

He came down on top of me between my spread legs, took my head between his hands, and possessed my mouth with his to cover my groans as he worked his cock inside me. He was big; bigger than most I had taken. When he was saddled, he released my mouth and looked down into my face, smiling, as I arched my back and started to pant in answer to his beginning a slow pump.

"It's OK? It's good for you?" he asked as he, at first, gently pressed in and pulled out.

"It will be good," I answered with a whimper. He hurt like hell now, but memories were coming back. He was as thick as anyone I remembered at college. And I couldn't deny that I had become addicted to the cock there before determination pulled me away from it.

"It's good, then," he murmured. "I'll fuck you good."

He took me the first time in long, slow strokes, holding me close, whispering to me, as I lost the battle of not acknowledging his right of victory and started moving my pelvis with him and rubbing my heels on the backs of his thighs.

The second time was rougher, demanding more of my cooperation and involvement, as he put me on all fours, crouched over me, and fucked me doggy style.

Later, as we were finishing up a beer and a snack at the breakfast table, I gave up all—answering his demand and gesture by standing and coming to where he sat, lowering myself in his lap, as he encircled my torso with his arms, and fucking myself on his staff.

"Do you have any fantasies?" he asked me in a murmur as I was rising and falling on his cock, and my thoughts went back six years, to my first year in college, and I leaned over and whispered in his ear, not being able to voice it aloud.

The next Saturday Dieter was driving me to Amsterdam. I knew I was being rushed, but he'd opened a door for me that had been closed for six years and that I hadn't realized haunted me as much as it did. And when he'd told me what he was offering, I hadn't hesitated to tell him I was interested.

The club was entered through a half-basement door in an alley off Reguliersdwarsstraat. The cobbled-stoned street we walked down, with glassed cubes projecting out of the second floors of the buildings with scantily clad men in them, hawking themselves, left little question what section of the city we were in. Some of the men were young, some black or Asian, some hairy, some dressed in leather. A sign in the alley saying "Satyr's Gehölz"—"satyr" being self-explanatory and "Gehölz" meaning "grove"—was blinking on and off in red neon lights over the door. We were met at the door by something as close to a satyr as possible with a man—bare-chested, the chest sprinkled with gold dust; hairy, animal-skin pants rising low enough to show a fringe of pubic hair and open at the crotch, although the doorkeeper had a codpiece covering his genitals; black ballet slippers giving the hint of cloven feet; a goatee; and devil's horns on the head.

The wait staff in the main room was dressed the same, but without the codpiece. Four of the entertainers on the stage that was sunk at the far end of the long, narrow room, descending in tiers with banquet tables on them, also were costumed as satyrs. The fifth entertainer, a young blond man, bound to and facing an X cross and being lightly switched by the other four, was simply naked—and beautifully formed.

Besides the cross bar and two lounge beds on the stage, there were the skeletons of two trees in the background with neon-colored cylinders hanging from their branches instead of leaves. I had no idea what they were until, as we stood at the bar, and Dieter encouraged me to drink a head-spinning drink, the young man on stage had been released from the X cross and been laid on one of the lounge beds. His ass was turned toward the audience, his legs spread and bent, his feet on the edge of the lounge bed. Two satyrs, one crouched on either side of him, were spreading his ass cheeks, revealing that his channel was gaping open—capable of accommodating more than one of the satyrs at the same time.

Dieter leaned over toward me and whispered, "Yes, it as you imagine. Does it arouse you?"

"Yes," I answered simply.

The four satyrs had immediately begun to fuck him. They were grabbing the cylinders off the trees. The cylinders were condoms. They took him two by two.

We hadn't been in the main room long before Dieter and I had been escorted to a smaller room off a corridor entered through a beaded curtain, and three satyrs, in succession, fucked me on a lounge bed while Dieter watched.

"You said you fantasized a train, being on a string. Do you want more? Do you want what the young man on stage—?"

"Not yet. Not now," I answered, frightened at the prospect.

The experience and the promise of what it might move to far exceeded the fantasy I had whispered in Dieter's ear, and I felt trapped. But it was my own released desires that entrapped me. I was a wildcat in bed in my apartment with Dieter that night.

He lay flat on his back on the bed, allowing me to spread-eagle him and bind his arms and ankles to the corner posts, and I rode his cock hard. I rocked back and forth on the long, thick, hard cock, taking it deep into my channel. My back was arched, and I was rubbing and pinching my nipples hard with my thumbs and fingers.

"Yes, ride it. Fuck yourself," Dieter murmured, smiling up at me. I slitted my eyes and imagined myself one of the men in the glass cubes on Reguliersdwarsstraat in Amsterdam, offering myself blatantly to any man coming along who wanted me. I had never been so wanton. In the fraternity house I had been drunk and I just lay there, with my legs open. Here I was exercising fantasies I never even knew I could entertain.

"Release my right hand," Dieter growled. "And raise yourself a bit on your knees. I'm going to take over the fuck."

I continued to stare down into his eyes, in a half trance, as I slowly rocked on the cock and fiddled with my nipples.

"Now," he commanded.

Shocked back into the present, I did as he bade. There was enough play in the bindings on his ankles that he could bend his knees and elevate his thighs. When he did, he pitched me forward a bit over his chest. I had to prop myself up on the heels of my hands on either side of his shoulders to keep myself from collapsing on his chest. With his free hand, he cupped my cock, giving me a sheath to slide in and out of as my pelvis responded to the rhythmic thrusts inside my channel of his cock. We came nearly together as we were kissing. And when we did, I collapsed on his chest.

"Release me," he muttered. "Then I fuck you in the shower."

I was hard when I woke in the morning, my fantasizing of selling my body from one of the glass cubes in Amsterdam having extended into my dreams. I masturbated and then groaned and rolled over on my side, ashamed at how wanton I had become in such a short time. When I rolled over I encountered another body. I was momentarily surprised and confused.

"Mount me. Ride the cock again," Dieter murmured in a sleepy voice. Sleepy or not, he was rock hard too.

I hadn't been in Belgium for more than three weeks yet. My resolve back there after my first year in college hadn't meant much.

* * * *

My shock was total. I couldn't look at the photos, but I also couldn't take my eyes off them. All I could do was try to make my mind go blank and pretend that I was anywhere but here. But Hamilton, Hamilton Boyd, one of the embassy's senior political officers, was sitting there, across the table from me in one of the consulate's interview rooms, looking at me expectantly. Waiting for me to give a rational explanation for photos of three satyrs fucking me.

I worked my jaw, but nothing came out. I wanted to say something indignant about secret cameras and the assault on my privacy—to ask him how the photos had come into his possession in the first place—but I knew how stupid that would sound. Dieter had offered the experience to me and I had shown interest—and carried through with it. It was just a good thing—for both Dieter and me—that the photos weren't taken in my apartment. I had been pretty docile with the satyrs. I had been fully wanton with Dieter that night—even in the shower, when Dieter had mostly crouched and backed up against the tiles, holding my buttocks spread with his hands while I plastered myself to him like a spider, with my arms around his neck and fucking myself on his tool with the leverage of my feet against the tile wall.

"It's a good thing these were brought to me and not the consul general," Hamilton said. "I've always tried to be broadminded, but Sarah is about as straight laced as they come. And speaking of come . . ."

I turned my head away from the photos in embarrassment.

Sarah. He had that right. We called her Sister Sarah behind her back. She gave sour grapes a good name.

"It's not what it seems. I can explain . . ." I started to say, but I just let that peter out. It was exactly what it seemed. There was nothing to explain other than that Dieter had reopened a door for me and I had walked right through. The door led to a world and a set of desires I'd sublimated and had no idea how much I still wanted. And Dieter's world included much more than I'd ever done before—even promising more than I had done as yet—and what he had introduced me to was something that I regretted going all of these years without.

"It was just a fluke . . . just that . . ." But my voice wavered and I clamped my mouth shut when he pulled out a second set of photos. The same compromising positions; different satyrs. If he'd asked me if they had been taken on a different date, I couldn't truthfully have said no. And Dieter was shown off to the side in this set of photos, his cock out and in his hand, as he watched me being fucked.

Dieter. God, they knew about Dieter too. He wouldn't be coming to me tonight?

Shit, I thought. That's how far gone I am—sitting here with damning evidence under my nose that could put me on an airplane before dark and worrying that what Dieter gave me would be stopping.

But, still, all they'd do to me was bundle me back to the States and maybe fire my ass. There was no such thing as a dishonorable discharge in the State Department. I could just say that the life didn't suit me and go on to the next job. What could they do to Dieter? He was just a chauffeur.

I had done it with a local-hire chauffeur—had let him control and manhandle me. Some embassy officer I was.

"You realize that you could be sent back to the States and be separated from the Department," Hamilton said.

Of course I realize that, I thought. Haven't you been listening to what I've been thinking?

"If you stayed here and these fell into the wrong hands, you could be compromised. And the business of the United States could be compromised as well."

I hadn't thought about that. Good god, he was right. I hadn't thought about that. Dieter was a local, not an American staffer. He could have blackmailed me with photos like this. Would I have given him what he wanted? Yes, if I was being honest with myself—especially if he kept giving me what I wanted.

"Why, whoever held these in their hands could control what you did if you weren't sent home and separated from the foreign service." Hamilton had continued speaking through my thoughts.

Right, you've essentially said that already, I thought. And then I looked at him. He was just sitting there, looking at me, expectantly. He even was giving me a little smile. What did he . . . ? Oh, shit.

"You say no one in the embassy but you knows about these?" I asked.

"No, no one." Still he sat there looking at me expectantly.

He wanted to fuck me. He was the one who wanted to hold this over my head under the threat of being fired and sent back to the States.

"You . . . want me to let you . . . ?"

"I want you to turn this into something good for the embassy, for the United States," Hamilton said. "I want you to do certain work for my office right here in Belgium, as needed. Something that would serve the interests of the United States, something that these photos show me you wouldn't find too repugnant. Then you wouldn't have to go back to the States, you wouldn't be fired, and the consulate need know nothing at all about it."

Fuck, I thought. He's with the intelligence services. The senior political officer job. I should have known. That's often a title they give to the chief of station of the intelligence people. "If I cooperate with you, you will destroy those photos and won't turn me in?"

"You know I can't destroy the photos, Allen. But it would just be working another aspect of embassy business— more important business, I think, than issuing visas to Belgians wanting to go to the States."

I didn't say no. I didn't say yes, either. I just sat there, probably looking as miserable as I felt.

"I'm taking a little sail out of the marina in Oostende on Saturday, Allen. The consulate's closed on Saturday. I'd enjoy having your company."

I didn't say no. I still half thought that he just wanted to fuck me himself.

* * * *

Hamilton had told me to drive to Oostende separately. When I arrived and found the boat slip he'd given me the number for, he was there, on an old motor yacht from the thirties, which had a white hull and a polished teak superstructure and a large covered fantail at the stern. It was sort of like I was entering a movie set from the 1950s. It appeared that I was the last of the guests to arrive, as the yacht cast off and motored out into the English Channel as soon as I had arrived.

Besides Hamilton and a small yacht crew of silent men in white shorts and T-shirts, there was just me and a middle-aged Arab, who must have been of some importance, but that wasn't completely true. There also were two burly bodyguards who appeared to be Italian or Spanish waterfront thugs and stood on either side of the yacht at the fantail and kept scanning all of the ship traffic with their eyes and never looking back under the canvas cover where Hamilton, the Arab, and I sat, drinking scotch. They seemed more like fixtures than passengers, though.

The Arab seemed highly cultured—and rich—but he was dressed in the traditional robes of the Arab world. He was a graybeard but probably no older than his early fifties, and, although hawk-nosed, was not all that unattractive. He obviously was well-groomed and took good care of his body, and he wore gold rings, with huge gemstones in them, on multiple fingers of each hand. He spoke in refined tones— conversing with Hamilton in French, which I was only beginning to master myself, having studied it only for a short time before coming to Belgium specifically for this assignment.

I was there with Hamilton and the Arab as we steamed out into the shipping lane, but I wasn't being made any part of the conversation. I wasn't under any illusions. I figured I was there for the Arab—and maybe Hamilton too—to fuck, but they were making me feel as much like just a fixture up until I was needed as the two guards were.

The most attention I got was when Hamilton leaned over and pulled my T-shirt over my head and said something to the Arab that made him slit his eyes and lick his lips. He made me uncross and spread my legs and lean back and stretch my arms along the back of the bench I was sitting on too, which puffed my chest out.

I got the impression that whatever serious business they had to conduct—and I couldn't imagine any reason for this excursion other than that the Arab had information Hamilton wanted or engaged in services Hamilton sought, or vice versa—had mostly already transpired. Their conversation was more active as we pulled out of the harbor than later, tapering off as we reached the shipping channel. Although they were speaking too rapidly in French and in tones that were too quiet for me to fully hear, I did hear the term "al-Qaeda" mentioned occasionally, which is what led me to believe that the Arab was providing Hamilton with intelligence sensitive enough to require this venue.

As their conversation wound down, the Arab increasingly turned his attention to me. He seemed to be asking questions about me and Hamilton was answering them—in French—as he, also, looked at me. I got the distinct feeling that I was being assessed and talked of in terms of a commodity. And thus when Hamilton turned to me and said, "This gentleman would like you to retire with him into the yacht's master cabin," I can't claim that I was surprised.

"Is this what I'm along for? As part of the payoff for whatever he's told you."

"He's giving me very useful and important information, Allen. It is very valuable intelligence for the country. Surely you knew what you were being invited on this cruise for. Now, stand and strip off those shorts so that he can see what he's being offered. And smile nicely for the man. Please don't embarrass us all and queer the future usefulness of Mr. Al-Fatib by making a fuss. You are to show him a good time."

"Used like a slab of meat off a rack?"

"For the moment, here and now, yes. I know exactly what you're capable of."

I stuck my chin out at him, ready to retort that those photos with the satyrs were pretty basic, when he took the wind out of my sails and forced me to withdraw into myself.

"There are cameras in your apartment too," he said. "I've seen what you can and will do for that chauffeur."

Al-Fatib, if that was what his name really was, which I highly doubted, fucked me in the main sleeping cabin of the yacht. One of his bodyguards stood inside the cabin door, looking stalwartly away from the action on the bed, there, no doubt, only to assure that I wasn't going to assassinate his precious boss. I was completely naked, though, so if I was going to assassinate him, it would have to be with my bare hands.

I was somewhat surprised that other than the robe—which I think is called a dishdasha—the only thing the Arab was wearing were those rings and a gold chain around his neck with a large half-moon medallion. He was in good shape, the best shape that money could buy a fifty-year-old man; his cock was long, if thin, and his balls hung low.

He wanted those balls sucked as his cock lengthened. I was on my back, my feet on the deck at the foot of the bed and the Arab's body suspended over me, his knees on the bed, hugging my thighs, and his fists buried in the mattress above my head as I sucked his balls and squeezed his cock between both of my hands. When he was ready, he moved his feet down to the floor, grabbed my legs behind the knees, and raised my legs over my head, nearly flat on the mattress above my head, which rolled my pelvis up to where my asshole was pointed to the ceiling. He continued gripping my legs, holding them flat against my shoulders, as he attacked my asshole and cock and balls with his mouth.

I writhed under him, using every form of French I could think of to tell him that I wanted him inside me. I convinced myself that I was playing the role that Hamilton wanted me to, but now that I was here, in this position, I wanted to be fucked. At length, after the bodyguard helpfully supplied him with a condom, he complied, taking me in long, deep, expert, businesslike strokes. I obviously was just part of the deal for him.

He fucked me all the way back to the dock, while his bodyguard stood, there, stony faced, keeping the level of his stare at the top of the headboard.

I was still panting and moaning when Hamilton came back into the cabin, all smiles, telling me how pleased the Arab had been with me and how successful our little operation had been.

"Our" little operation, I thought. Gee thanks for giving me some of the credit.

I started to struggle to get up off the berth, but Hamilton motioned that I should stay put. And then I saw, through the cabin doorway beyond him, that the yacht's crew was lining up.

"The photos I have of you," he said. "They indicate that you have special desires. I wanted you especially for this operation, because I've borrowed the yacht and made promises to the crew. I think you will enjoy them; I know they will enjoy you. And I have to know how far you will go."

I lay back on the bed with a moan—and spread my legs. I couldn't deny what I liked, and I'd already gotten a good look at the crew members—all five of them hunks, I thought, although I was to find that there were six of them.

They were all fit and randy and, as I was later to discover on my visits to Oostende, were all expert cocksmen as they stood in line to take me in succession.

Eventually, Hamilton found out how far I would go and what Dieter had offered me was fulfilled, as one of the crewmen laid on his back and pulled me down on his cock and another one came between my legs and worked his cock in above that of the other man. It was complete. Hamilton could offer me up for double penetration if need be.

As Hamilton and I were leaving the yacht, he murmured to me, "Now, that wasn't so bad, was it?"

I didn't answer him then, but when he went on to say, "I will release you from any obligation for future operations of this nature, if you wish. Or do you wish to continue?" I hesitated only for a moment before answering, "Yes, I wish to continue."

I had made and voiced my acceptance and only had a moment of second thoughts and flash of anger when we reached the parking lot and I saw that the embassy car that had come to pick Hamilton was chauffeured by my Belgian lover, Dieter Jouret, who had seduced me and taken me to the Satyr's Grove club where the incriminating photos had been taken. Dieter was Hamilton's chauffer.

Dieter had the decency to shrug and give me an embarrassed look when I saw him standing by the embassy sedan. He wasn't so embarrassed that he failed to show up at my apartment door that night—and I wasn't so mad or embarrassed that I didn't let him into my apartment and my bed or to whisper the question in his ear in the night on whether he knew of any hunk who might join us.

Colonel's Treasure

Rob turned his head toward the open flap of the tent. He could see the tawny fringe of the Shewan subchief's buckskin jerkin at the fringe of the lamplight escaping the tent's doorway. And the two eagle's feathers sticking out to the side of the back of the native's head, up at the very top of the tent doorway. The savage must be at least six and a half feet tall, Rob thought. And he knows. How could he not know? The colonel was grunting that unmistakable sound of full rut.

Rob twitched and arched his back and stared straight up at the play of the shadows on the ceiling of the tent as the colonel nipped his belly button and stuck his tongue in it and then slurped out of the indention and ran a thick tongue down Rob's underbelly and into a fiery red thicket before tracing back up his engorged cock to the bulb. Rob twitched again as his cock was possessed by the colonel's sucking lips. He sighed and rubbed his back on the bearskin rug thrown out over the rushes that served as the colonel's mattress. There was a faint rustling at the opening flap of the tent, and Rob knew that the savage was just beyond the opening, listening and silently observing. The colonel thought no more of an Indian, even a Shewan subchief, than he did of the stray dogs of the camp, though, so it bothered him not a twit if the Indian could see them.

The shadows on the ceiling showed the hulky colonel hunched over his diminutive, lithe aide. Rob was kneeling on his knees on the colonel's beefy thighs, with his back arched behind him, his shoulder blades touching the silky fur of the robe. The colonel encased his young aide with an arm wrapped around the younger man's back. His other hand was cupping Rob's small, but firm ball sacs, and the little finger of that hand already had purchase just inside the rim of Rob's ass. The golden crest ring on that finger was rubbing roughly on Rob's rim, a familiar feel for Rob after four months of service under the second in command of Brigadier General Nicholas Herkimer, commander of American forces in the Mohawk Valley.

Colonel Seth Hampton worked his young aide's cock hard with his mouth. He'd already been sucked into arousal himself. His evening invigoration had been interrupted by the announcement that one of his spies in the English forces, the subchieftain Otetiani of the Shewan minor tribe of the Iroquois nation, had arrived and awaited his pleasure. Hampton had irritably commanded that the savage stand outside the tent until it was his pleasure to receive him—his pleasure obviously was focused elsewhere at the moment.

Hampton having had enough of his young man's cock, the young aide watched the shadows on the ceiling swirl into a new pattern, as the colonel wrapped large, callused hands around Rob's ankles and forced his legs up the length of his body. In the process, Rob was rolled up onto his shoulder blades. The colonel held Rob's legs to his body with hands pressing in under the crook of his knees, as the older man savaged the younger man's entrance with tongue and teeth and a heavy helping of saliva.

Then the colonel was up on his knees, crouching over the young man and thrusting inside him. Rob arched his back and spread his arms wide, digging his fists into the soft, grass-covered ground of the New York valley, and took what the colonel was giving him like a good soldier. And the colonel, mad and worried about the positioning of his forces and the rumors of the gathering British attack in superior force, invested all of his frustration and fury into plowing his flaming-red headed subordinate hard and fast and deep.

The colonel was grunting and groaning and voicing his pleasure in tones that could be heard all over camp, without the possibility of misinterpretation. All of the soldiers knew their colonel fucked men. But he was a damn good soldier and a brilliant strategist, and if anyone was going to conceive how to push the British out of the Mohawk Valley and back to London, it was probably going to be him. So there were few to deny him his release.

Rob had been sent from the brothels of that pagan city of Savannah precisely to be the tension reliever to the colonel that he needed. The young man had been trained to this, so there were no regrets or concern to be expended in that direction.

Rob held off on his vocalizing at first, because he knew the savage was out there, just beyond the open flap. He'd only caught a glimpse of the man, but he had frightened Rob. He was so tall and large, a man and a half. Rob had never been comfortable around the savages. He felt something primeval in them. They frightened and fascinated and aroused him all at the same time. He had known—biblically—all of the types of colonists who had washed up on the American shores. They no longer meant anything to him. No, that wasn't true. He had come to really like the colonel, to want to give him any relief possible for the responsibilities he had to bear.

It was strange to think about liking the man at this moment, when the colonel was driving his cock so hard inside Rob, making his legs ache and his back rub raw as it was jerked back and forth on the bearskin under the thrusting of the colonel's manhood. But the colonel was usually gentle with him. It was only now when the colonel was so worried about how badly the campaign and positioning was going and so worked up and frustrated that he was taking Rob like a frenzied bull.

Rob had to do what he could to help the colonel. He knew the colonel liked it when he groaned and moaned and said the colonel was spitting him and was too big for him. So that's what he did, ignoring the unsettling presence of the

Shewan warrior. And it worked. In a cry of ecstasy, the colonel shot off inside him in one, two, three lurchings and then, without extracting his cock, pulled Rob's legs down alongside his and began to kiss him on the nipples, neck, and lips. Rob wrapped his arms around the thin waist of the well-fit military officer and returned the kisses enthusiastically.

He had done his duty. Now it was time to ask for his favor.

"No, Rob, we've discussed this. I can't let you stay." The colonel had pulled back on his rump and brought the younger, smaller man with him. Hampton now was sitting on the bearskin rug, his legs stretched out in front of him. His aide was in his lap, sitting on the colonel's half flaccid cock, his legs encircling his master's thin waist, the two chests against each other, beating hearts competing, throbbing in the temporary quietude. Hampton had his lips sucking on the aide's throbbing neck vein, and Rob was staring across the light of the candle, watching the hint of the savage's persistent presence. Rob knew there would be another fucking. The colonel almost always wanted another one, and the second one would not have the fire of the first. The second one was the one that told Rob the colonel really cared for him. And this was the colonel's most vulnerable time.

"But, I don't want to leave you. I—"

"And I don't want you to go. But you're no solider, Rob. We will, almost inevitably, be in the thick of fighting within the week. Burgoyne is gathering forces up on Lake Champlain, more than 10,000 English, Canadian, and Indian forces, including the Iroquois and the Huron. They'll be streaming down here, joined by Howe's forces from the coast. They are more than we can handle. It will be a bloodbath if I cannot come up with a miracle. No, you cannot stay. You are no soldier. This is all you are good for to me. This release of my tension in the field."

Rob lowered his head onto the colonel's shoulder, and Hampton could feel the wetness of his tears.

"Nay, lad, I didn't mean it harsh like that. You are a treasure. You are my treasure. There is no way you can help me other than to leave for Albany tonight and not come back until it is safer."

"I know I can do more. I know—" Rob snuffled.

"This is enough, dearheart, this is enough." And with that, the colonel moved his encasing, heavily muscled arms down to the small of Rob's back, and Rob leaned back, as Hampton's lips and teeth went to the younger man's nipples. Rob sighed for him and felt the strong cock of his master coming back to life. Rob began to move his hips, and the colonel started to breathe heavily. Hampton turned Rob onto his side and came down with him, leaving his cock encased. They kissed and Hampton continued worrying the younger man's nipples with his fingers while he side split him in long, languid glides to mutual ejaculation.

Afterward the colonel rose, wrapped himself in a fur-lined deer-skinned robe, and sat down at his field desk, looking very official. He called the patiently waiting Shewan subchieftain, Otetiani, in. The chieftain entered the tent, all dignity and towering strength and handsome savage splendor, and stood in front of the colonel. Despite the unusual heat in the Mohawk valley in July of 1777, the Indian chieftain was wearing the same attire his tribe wore year round—side-fringed buckskin breeches with a bearskin codpiece, and a buckskin jerkin with fringed arms. His moccasins were of some sort of finely cleaned leather and he had two feathers attached to the base of whatever was holding his long black ponytail at the back of his head—two feathers to denote his somewhat exalted rank. He turned his head briefly to Rob, lying, still naked on his back on the bearskin rug, and Rob saw the Indian's eyes go wide with surprise. Rob couldn't imagine why the savage would be surprised. He had heard them fuck twice and had no doubt gotten an eyeful already as well.

Otetiani inexplicably bowed low to the young aide and said something in his own language that Rob couldn't even begin to fathom. And then he turned his full attention to the colonel.

"Is it true?" asked the colonel. "What I sent you to find out—is it true?"

"True," the Indian said, in quite good English. "Iroquois have called all of its nation—all minor tribes—to join with the Huron and serve the English in the coming fight."

"The Iroquois and the English? I'd never thought it would come to that. Damn. Isn't there anything you can do to split them? Your people hate the Huron."

"True. The Iroquois hate the Huron, and none more than my own Shewan. But the English are strong. And the Huron are strong. The Iroquois are not strong enough to resist. And the Shewan feel weak too."

"The Shewan feel weak? You are the most ferocious warriors of the Iroquois nation. How can you feel weak?"

"The signs have not been good. The Shewan wait for a sign. We need strength; the Shewan warriors need to feel the strength."

"Well, try to think of something." the colonel said. "Do whatever you can do to drive a wedge between the Indian forces. We have to try to do something to weaken St. John's forces up at Fort Oswego."

"I will try. There may be something." Otetiani sounded somewhat reassuring. Hampton knew that Otetiani was smart as a whip as well as being the bravest and studliest of the Shewan tribe. The colonel had often thought he'd like to get his cock inside him, but he knew Otetiani was too strong for him. Two determined tops did not make a promising match.

He was finished with the Indian. He dismissed him with a wave of his hand. He didn't bother to look up, so he missed the contemplative look the Indian subchief was giving Rob.

After Otetiani left, the colonel dismissed Rob as well. He didn't want to reveal how hard it was for him to let his young lover go, so he just gruffly told him to pull his breeches and jerkin on and to be on his way to Albany before the break of day.

When Rob left the colonel's tent and started moving toward his own, he heard the slight rustle of the bushes at the edge of the encampment clearing. He hoped it wasn't the sergeant sniffing around to claim his seconds. The sergeant was thicker and crueler than the colonel was.

But it wasn't the sergeant. Otetiani, the savage subchieftain, was beckoning him the edge of the light from the encampment's fires.

"You want to help your colonel?" Otetiani said to him in a hoarse whisper. "I heard you say that."

"Yes, but I don't know what I can do. If I only could get to Fort Oswego and see the English colonel, St. John, there may be some way I could help. I have heard that young men please him. Surely there's something I can do there to find information that will help our forces. The colonel's right, I'm no fighting soldier. But I have my own means of fighting."

"I could take you to St. John," Otetiani said. "I could deliver you to him as a prisoner; say you are Colonel Hampton's aide. You would have value to St. John then, wouldn't you?"

"You would do that?" Rob asked, suddenly excited about the possibilities.

"Yes. But I have orders too. You could help me with my orders. If you really, truly want to help your colonel and are truly brave. But it would not be easy, what I have to propose. Most men could not endure it."

In short order Otetiani had told Rob what he could do and Rob had agreed. It wasn't anything less than he knew what to do.

While they talked, Otetiani was fingering Rob's flaming-red hair gingerly, and when Rob agreed to the plan, Otetiani spoke.

"To do what I need to do, I need much power. I need to gather strength and power. Before I take you there, you need to give me that power."

"Yes," Rob said, although he felt his heart stop and his breath escape him. He was trembling. He'd already agreed, though, so both now and then, it didn't make any difference.

Otetiani took Rob by the arm and led him into the fringe of bushes at the edge of the encampment, past the horses staked out on a rope. The horses whinnied slightly and shifted nervously away from them as they passed. The Indian was an imposing, troubling figure. A man and a half.

Otetiani stopped in front of a smooth-barked tree of middling girth with two sturdy branches at equal heights jutting out at the side a foot above the level of Rob's head. He maneuvered Rob to where his back was against the tree. The towering Indian faced the young man with the flaming-red hair closely and pushed him gently down on his haunches with one hand while releasing his own codpiece with his other hand and letting it drop.

He was already half ready, at the very thought of what he was going to do.

The thick cock was larger than Rob had ever managed before, but he worked expertly on it with his lips and mouth as he had been trained to do at the Savannah brothel. It was mere minutes before Otetiani pulled Rob up and turned him toward the tree. Rob grabbed up for handholds on the jutting branches, while Otetiani spit on his hands and added that to the spit Rob had already lathered the huge tool with. The Indian savage lifted Rob by his hips with his hands, spreading the young man's buttocks cheeks with his strong thumbs, set Rob's hole on the bulbous head of his cock, and started working his way in.

Fearing raising an alarm in the camp, Rob stifled the scream he wanted to let loose as well as his gulps and gasps and groans as he slowly stretched inside to accommodate the digging tool. The Indian was so tall that Rob's feet were off the ground and the only leverage he had was the handholds on the tree branches.

When Otetiani had bottomed inside Rob's ass canal, he moved one hand to palm the young man's belly and the other one to cap the flaming-red hair of his head and began chanting in his native tongue. He was using the strong palm of his hand on Rob's belly to move the young man's channel up and down on his skewering member, and Rob was pulling up and releasing on the branches to try to match the rhythm.

Rob came first in a shooting against the tree trunk. Otetiani stopped his fucking and chanting long enough to bend his knees and set Rob's feet on the ground. He used the fingers of the hand he had been palming Rob's belly with to capture globs of Rob's cum, which he dabbed on his own cheeks in streaks going from ear to upper lip.

Then he palmed Rob's belly again and picked him up and resumed stroking the young man's ass up and down on his cock until he spasmed four, five times, shooting great spurts of man juice up into Rob's intestines.

The chanting stopped and the hand came off the head. But the hand remained on the belly, and Rob remained trapped against the tree trunk, while the Indian pulled a hunting knife from a sheath at his side.

Rob felt a brief stab of fear that the savage had tricked him; that he didn't intend to help the colonel's cause at all and only wanted to fuck Rob before collecting his scalp. But Otetiani just used the knife to cut a lock of Rob's flaming-red hair and tuck it into the band holding his ponytail in place.

"Is good. Is true. You are a gift from the gods. I can feel the new power. We go now." After declaring that, Otetiani just let Rob slump to the ground and readjusted his codpiece and turned to stride back to the encampment to prepare to leave.

It was several minutes before Rob was able to rise and hobble after him. He'd never been fucked like that before. Never that totally fucked before.

* * * *

The sun was going down as the ceremony in the Shewan longhouse deep in the Mohawk Valley began. It was announced with the beating of drums that required all woman and children of the tribe to leave the village clearing in the flattened hillock accessible by a secret cliffside trail and gather at the life-giving stream below to sing praises to the gods until they heard the end to the drum beats.

All was as prescribed by the chieftain, Nadie, as given on his deathbed following the previous spring's battle with the Huron. He had counseled that the Shewan were to retreat to a minor role in Iroquois affairs, subordinating themselves to the other tribes when they normally would take a lead in matters of warfare, until they had regained their strength and power, and, most important, received the blessings of the gods that they had forfeited by losing to the Huron.

As he had neared death, Nadie told his warriors to look for a sign from the gods—a being with fire coming out of his head who possessed power and would transfer power to warriors who were worthy through ritual congress. In his dying breaths, he had related in detail the requirements of the ceremony.

When assurances were given that all of the woman and children had departed the village circle, the torches were lit in the longhouse of the chieftain.

The flaming-haired Rob Winston was led, a willing participant, into one end of the longhouse. He was nude except for a tight, strong leather belt around his belly of the brightest crimson that had dyed-red feathers and strong rings of gold attached to the belt at the side of his waist, fine red-dyed moccasins, and thick, red-dyed leather bands at his wrists, also with rings of gold attached to them.

He stumbled into the tent and would have fallen if he had not been supported by two young, strong, muscular braves who were helping him to walk. These braves were costumed in the identical minimal dress Winston had, except that they both also had long, sharp hunting knives in sheaths tied to their thighs by leather straps.

Winston had spent much of the afternoon drinking ceremonial cups of a potion that largely consisted of alcohol and herbs from the forest collected for their propensity to numb and block pain. The day before he had been plied with purgatives that emptied and purified his internal systems and had his channel packed with concoctions of the numbing potions that had been withdrawn mere hours before the ceremony.

Winston and his escorts approached the center of the longhouse, where an altar had been placed and covered with a blanket made of laced-together red fox pelts.

All of the adult men of the tribe were gathered in a circle around the altar, At the outer edge of the circle were the elders and the older unselected warriors, dressed in their usual leather breeches and jerkins. The only difference in their dress on this special ceremonial day from any other day was their long, black hair. Whereas a Shewan tribesman's hair customarily was tied back in a ponytail, with a feather in the band, now every man's hair was hanging loose below his shoulders. The torches lighting the ceremony were lodged in the ground behind this outer circle of men, which included much the greater number of the men of the tribe. At the four geographic points of this circle sat a set of two drummers each, maintaining a steady, slow beat to mark the duration of the ceremony.

Inside the greater circle of older tribesmen were twelve of the youngest, most fit brave candidates of the tribe, young men who had achieved their manhood only since the defeat at the hands of the Huron in the spring, newly minted men eligible to be fully blooded warriors but not yet initiated.

And standing next to each of ten of these young warriors was an older, fully blooded, peak-condition warrior. When Winston's two escorts had led him to the altar and lifted him on top, they went to take their places next to the remaining two novitiates.

The twelve most worthy warriors, identically attired to Winston save for the sheathed knives, were the twelve selected to carry out Otetiani's plan to aid Colonel Hampton—and not only to aid the plans of Colonel Hampton as promised but also to return the Shewan to the full favor of the gods of war.

Standing at the base of the altar, facing it, standing taller than any other, legs spread wide, looking stern and magnificent, was the subchieftain Otetiani, the tribe's war leader. Attired like the twelve of the chosen, he stood with arms crossed and leather hand whips, with multiple leads, dyed crimson red, held tightly in each fist.

At a signal from Otetiani, the two warriors who had escorted Winston into the longhouse vaulted gracefully onto the altar. They raised Rob to a standing position and moved him to the center of the altar. On either side of the altar here, strong tree-trunk poles rose from the ground up to the top of the barrel-roofed longhouse, serving as part of the frame of the structure. Each of these poles had a chain wrapped around it at the height of Winston's shoulders. The warrior on each side of Winston attached the end of the chain on each side to the ring in the leather band at his wrist and pulled it taut, so that Rob's arms were stretched out fully to his sides. There were chains lower on the poles that they similarly attached to the rings at the side of his leather belt. Winston now was held in a standing position at the center of the altar with little give of movement in either direction. The two escort warriors hopped back off the altar and took up their station beside their designated novitiate.

At a signal from Otetiani, the drums changed their beat; the warriors began a chant, one that had been prescribed for this phase of the ceremony by the dying chieftain, Nadie; and clouds of incense rose from the fires set under open vents in the sections at either end of the longhouse.

Otetiani opened his arms wide.

Swish. The leather strips of the hand whips lashed out in succession. Winston raised his head in drunken, nearly numb recognition of the start of the purifying scourging. Swish. Swish. Otetiani circled the altar, scourging Rob's flesh, arms, legs, back, belly, chest, buttocks, from each side in light strokes that didn't cut deeply but that cut deeply enough to raise welts and rivulets of blood.

Winston remained stoic throughout. The ceremony had been explained in detail to him. This was all necessary to Otetiani's plan. Winston couldn't be a soldier for the colonel, but there were things he could do, perhaps things that had a greater impact than a single foot soldier could contribute. Rob was determined to do what he could. And he had been prepared well for the ordeal. He would be in great pain later, when the alcohol and drugs wore off, than he would be during the ceremony.

The ceremony of the purifying blooding was complete. Upon another signal from Otetiani, the ceremony of the congress, the actual transferring of the power from the gods through the vessel with the flaming head, began.

The two escorts vaulted back up on the altar, released the chains at Winston's side, and loosened the chains at his wrists. He was still tied to the altar poles, but each chain now had considerable give to it.

One of the warriors jumped down from the altar. The other one remained. The first to receive the power. The twelve chosen warriors, in succession, and, by prescription in different positions, and on the rhythm of the beating of the drums, consummated a congress with the flaming-haired gift of the gods. The first simply went down on his knees behind Winston's crumpled, scoured figure and pulled the young man into his lap and onto his hard cock and fucked him until the warrior's seed had been planted and the power of the war gods had been transmitted back into his body from the channel of the gift.

The fucking had somewhat revived Winston, and the second warrior lay flat on his back and made Winston hover over him, feet and hands flat on the altar cloth and slide up and down on the warrior's pole. The third made Winston stand, folded over at the waist, the warrior supporting him with arms locked around his belly, and plowing him from the rear. The next warrior pushed Winston up on his knees and took him like a dog. With Winston collapsed on his belly from this taking, the next merely straddled his hips as he lay there and rode him like a horse, stroking hard between the young man's tightly closed butt cheeks.

The sixth turned him on his back and mimicked the White missionaries. Then he was pulled back up onto his feet and made to stand facing a warrior with a long, curved cock, who raised one of Winston's legs up the line of his torso and thrust up into him in a standing position. He was taken with his wrists lashed high on one of the poles and with his legs wrapped around a warrior's waist, and the most solid, shortest of the warriors made Winston wrap his legs around his waist and his arms around his neck, and he walked up and down the center line of the altar carrying Winston like a young child and thrusting up into him from below. He was side split from both sides, and the most acrobatic of the warriors made Winston stand on his hands and held his thighs as he fucked down into his hole, the blood rushing to Winston's head and momentarily making him faint.

With each congress, the power was believed to being passed through Winston to the chosen warrior, and each warrior was smeared in the blood of the gift that had been raised by scourging. At the end of each congress, Winston sank to the ground in gathering exhaustion while the blessed and empowered warrior unsheathed his sharp knife and took two locks of hair from the flaming head.

Three of the warriors were especially blessed and, by being so were designated by the gods to be the subleaders of the raid they had been chosen to undertake. This designation came with the three ejaculations of Winston during the ceremony. The warrior rewarded with this sign of the gods' approval while they were in congress with the flaming-haired gift captured what ejaculate they could and smeared it on their cheeks as a special sign of favor.

After each warrior had received the power, he jumped off the altar and went and stood beside his designated novitiate.

When the twelfth had completed his part of the ceremony, Otetiani himself leapt up on the altar. At a signal to Winston's two original escorts, the chains at Winston's arms were pulled taut around the tree-trunk pillar once more, bringing Winston to a staggering standing position.

The drums beat louder as Otetiani bowed in front of Winston and then took the young man's cock in his mouth and just continued giving it suck until Winston had his fourth ejaculation and Otetiani had received the full force of the gods' approving nectar. Then Otetiani stood and moved behind Winston and pulled the young man's suspended body into him. He lifted Winston straight up with hands on his waist, crouched a bit to get under him and lowered Winston on his gigantic, throbbing tool for the transferring of the gods' power. As he did that, the two escorts stepped up to the side of the altar. Each took one of Winston's ankles in his hand and pulled Winston's legs back, around Otetiani's heavily muscled calves. Otetiani held Winston's torso close to his with one palm on his belly and one on his breast and took Winston in long deep glides, the rapidity and depth of the thrusts increasing with the increase in the tempo of the drums.

After Otetiani has spouted forth once, he had the escorts release Winston's ankles and then the chains on his wrists, and Otetiani gently let Winston down on the red fox pelting on his belly, without withdrawing his embedded cock. He covered Winston's body closely and gently rocked on top of him until once more aroused and then he took one last extract of power in a gentle fucking through thighs tightly encased in his own.

While Otetiani was completing the ceremony and taking his lock of the flaming hair, the short, secret segment of the ceremony was performed. Only Otetiani and the twelve chosen warriors had been told of this, concluding part, the initiation of the novitiates. As Otetiani was lowering Winston to the ground for his second taking, he signaled to the twelve, each of whom turned to the designated novitiate beside them, knocked him to ground and overpowered him.

Each blooded warrior then passed on part of the power of the war gods he had acquired by taking the novitiate's virginity by force, but, more important, lifting him up to full warrior status, and, in the end rewarding him with one of the flaming locks of hair they had taken from the gift of the gods. A privilege of this magnitude came only once in several generations. But for many drum beats, the confused, surprised, and initially angry strugglings of the prideful young men, heretofore not told that no warrior in the tribe reached full status with his virginity intact, reached a decibel level that surely could be heard down at the stream, as hard tools relentlessly dug out the last vestige of their innocence. What they were yet to find out was that they would be mastered again and again for the next three nights as part of the chosen warriors strength preparation for their mission.

The drums suddenly stopped. Loud trilling could be heard from the banks of the stream below, and the ceremony was complete.

Winston spent the next three days in a separate longhouse, recovery from the ordeal he had agreed to undertake to serve his struggling revolutionary forces, while Otetiani and his twelve chosen, now anointed and empowered warriors, prepared to go on the warpath—and the twelve newly deflowered initiates recovered from their manning into the tribe.

* * * *

"Here, I have a present for you." The senior English Indian scout, Otetiani, lifted the bundle off of the back of the pack horse like it was a peddler's sack and dropped it on the ground just inside the doorway into the log shed Colonel Reginald St. John was using as his temporary office and bedroom while the stockade and permanent buildings of Fort Oswego were under a quick reconstruction. General John Burgoyne, St. John's superior officer and the strategist for the coming British Canada arm of the Central Campaign, had ordered the Oswego fort to be fortified better before it was left on minimum garrison.

All eyes had been on Otetiani as, unimpeded, he walked the horse by the Huron chief's encampment just outside the stockade wall, through the central gates, and up to St. John's quarters. The missing sections of stockade fencing here and there didn't escape Otetiani's attention, and he permitted himself a private smile at his good fortune. The ceremony had worked; the gods of war were with them.

St. John, stripped down to his breeches and having been in the process of shaving himself, toed the bundle on the floor hard. The bundle rewarded him with a grunt of pain.

"What do we have here, then?" St. John said, the tone of disdain clear in his voice. "And why do you bother me with this?"

"I thought you would want to be the first to interrogate the aide to the American colonel, Seth Hampton."

St. John's interest was piqued by that news, and he put his razor down on the wash basin on the stool and wiped the remaining lather off his face with the cotton towel that had been hanging around his neck.

"Let's get him up, then."

Otetiani crouched down and undid the canvas sacking around his prize, revealing a much-bedraggled Rob Winston, tied roughly with rope at wrists and ankles.

"Hang him up on the hook on the center pole," St. John directed.

Otetiani did so. The hook was high enough to cause Winston to have to stretch his arms high up along the pole. He was facing the pole, his back to the two men. Otetiani untied the young man's ankles in the same movement he used to push Winston against the pole, hoping, with success, that St. John either wouldn't notice or didn't see any reason to comment on it.

"And you found him where? You just snatched him out from under Hampton's nose?"

"I found him in the forest, outside the Americans' camp. He said he was escaping, that he wanted to turn himself over to the English, that he had things he could tell your forces about the Americans' troop strengths and locations."

"And does he speak? Do you speak, young man?"

"Yes . . . Yes, I speak, M'Lord," Rob answered, although he barely whispered.

"You say you were coming over to the British to help us? And why should I believe that?"

"He mistreated me, M'Lord. He treated me cruelly. I had to leave. I hate him; I hate them all."

"And why is that I should believe that, my little friend?"

"Look at my back and my legs. All over, M'Lord. There's proof enough."

"Likely story," St. John said with a sniff.

"That part seems true, My Lord," Otetiani said. "I've seen the marks myself."

"The marks?" St. John pulled up the back of Winston's jerkin, to reveal the welts and cuts across his back.

That's when St. John's cock started to take interest. He'd heard that the American colonel, Hampton, liked his young men. He hadn't heard he liked to treat them this way. St. John, on the other hand, very much liked to treat young men this way. His urges in this direction, in fact, were almost uncontrollable.

"That will be all, Otetiani. I think you can find the mess tent. And you can tell my clerk that you are to receive the usual amount."

"Yes, My Lord," Otetiani murmured, and he backed out of the hut and left the camp directly, visiting neither the mess tent nor the colonel's clerk. He had preparations to make and plans to change. His plans could be simpler now, because of the construction under way on the fort and the missing sections of stockade fencing. As he left, he cursed the prick of an English colonel under his breath. Otetiani hadn't anticipated that he would be thanked or rewarded for bringing him this treasure from the American camps. And he hadn't been wrong.

Inside the hut, St. John's hands were trembling. He could hardly keep his hands off this one. And there was no reason why he should have to. He could use him, interrogate him, and then dispose of him.

"You say Hampton did this to you all over?" St. John asked, coming up very close to Winston's back.

"Yes. If you don't believe me, see for yourself."

He hadn't really needed the invitation. St. John shucked Rob's breeches down his legs to the ground and pulled the young man's moccasined feet out of the breeches. It was true. There were welts and cut marks on the young man's flanks and his buttocks and thighs and legs.

St. John couldn't resist. This was this colonel's weakness. He touched his fingers to the line of welting on the young man's flanks. He was breathing heavily, and his cock had gone rock hard almost instantaneously.

"M'Lord?" It was almost a whimper.

"Shut up," St. John commanded in a harsh, husky whisper. St. John ran one hand down a flank and the other up Winston's back under his jerkin, following welt lines.

"M'Lord!" Rob said more sharply.

"I said shut up. You are in no position to object. I own you now. I can decide whether you live or die." The breathing was very heavy. St. John was beyond control now. The welting was just too delicious. The young man's body just too desirable. He took his hands away from Winston's body but only so that he could unbutton his breeches with one hand and lean over and scoop soapy lather out of his shaving mug with the other.

"Not a word," he hissed as he started to rub lather into the crack between the young man's butt cheeks.

"Ohhh," Rob murmured in low tones.

St. John moved the bulb of his hard cock into Winston's crack, through the gobs of lather, and the young man went tense and moaned.

The colonel prepared to thrust past the young man's defenses, but he gulped in air in surprise when, as his bulb breached Winston's sphincter muscle, the young man's channel tightened around it and drew his cock inside the warm, moist channel. Using every trick he'd learned in the Savannah brothel, Rob set his ass channel walls rippling over the colonel's cock, pulling it deep inside him and making love to it with the muscles inside him.

"Ahhhh," St. John murmured, his fingers not being able to resist continuing to track those lash marks on the young man's body. "You are a catamite, aren't you? You're no casual lay. You were Hampton's prostitute. You have experience."

"I was his pleasure man, yes, that's right, M'Lord. But no catamite. I'm a full grown man. And I was his to release his tension, by arrangement with my master in Savannah, yes. But there was no agreement for him to treat me this foully, sir."

St. John was moaning louder than Winston was. He'd never had his cock massaged like this inside a man before, and those lovely welts on his flanks and thighs and back and belly and chest. The colonel's hands were moving everywhere, finding lovely ridges to follow everywhere.

"M'Lord, I've come to you of free will. I have information I can give you. And if it's a proper fucking you want, you only need release me. You have a bed over there. I can please you as you've never been pleased before. You couldn't be fucked better in London."

Colonel St. John was lost.

St. John laid on his back on his bed, Winston straddling him above and reversed. Winston gave St. John's cock a sucking like he'd never had before, while St. John dug at the cut lines on the proffered buttocks cheeks in rotating motion right before his eyes, smeared rivulets of blood across the luscious orbs, and rubbed fingers across loosening rim and into the channel of rippling muscles. After a tantalizing eternity of this, Winston turned and lowered his hole onto St. John's erect phallus and started the drawing in, sphincter clutch, and massaging wall treatment all over again as he rotated his hips around and around, and St. John moaned and groaned and cried out in ejaculation.

The colonel held Winston prisoner in his quarters and mostly in his bed for the next three days and nights. The young man was chained to the bed, which, fortunately for him, was still within reach of the colonel's camp desk, during the day. At various times during the day, St. John questioned the young man on the disposition and strengths of the American troops in the Mohawk Valley, and Winston told him what he thought St. John would believe and would be dismayed by if he tried to take advantage of. And at night, the colonel would bind Rob's wrists and hang them high on the center pole and lash his back and buttocks with a riding crop until the colonel's cock was rock hard and then either fuck the young man there or drag him back to the bed.

Rob was picking up some useful information during the colonel's absences to check on the stockade construction, but he hit paradise on the third day when a messenger from General Sir William Howe, commander of the eastern army of the British Central Campaign forces, both arrived with a message to be sent on to General Burgoyne and left before the colonel even knew he'd been there.

Rob identified himself as St. John's aide and said he'd give the message straight away to the colonel unopened. He'd managed all of this with his arm behind his back and not revealing that he was chained to the bedstead.

He opened the dispatch to discover that it announced a change of plans in the campaign. Philadelphia, the rebel's capitol, lay defenseless before General Howe's forces in New Jersey. Howe believed that was a larger prize than what they hoped to gain in New York with a pincher maneuver of his forces from the east and Burgoyne's forces from the north. He was willing to continue with the set plan, as it had been blessed by London, but, unless Burgoyne sent a request to this effect back to him within a week, Howe would take and occupy Philadelphia instead.

Burgoyne could be waiting for half the army to join him, not knowing it would never come, Winston realized. He rejoiced in the thought. By keeping this message from reaching Burgoyne, he, Rob Winston, could be of more service to his beloved Colonel Hampton and the colonists' cause than any soldier could.

The dispatch was quickly consigned to the fire in the hearth.

That night, after St. John had beat Rob with the riding crop, fucked him against the pole, and then dragged him back into the bed and fucked him again, like a dog, digging his fingernails into the newly opened cuts, all hell broke out in the fort.

They heard the most ungodly savage sounds from beyond the stockade walls to the west, and the sky lit up like it was day. The Huron camp was ablaze.

St. John struggled out of the bed and pulled on his breeches. He took up his long rifle propped up by the door and ran for the stockade gate.

As soon as he was gone, Otetiani climbed in the window at the back of the hut. Rob pointed to his chains in despair, but with a mighty heave, Otetiani pulled the bed frame asunder and Rob was free. Rob was naked, but Otetiani gave him no time to find his breeches and pull them on. They escaped through one of the open sections in the stockade fencing.

They reached the fringe of trees at the opposite side of the fort from the burning Huron encampment without any of the British soldiers seeing them. Eight of Otetiani's handpicked braves he'd taken on the raid were waiting for them there. A loss of four, but several fewer than Otetiani had calculated would be killed in the raid. There were ten of them, including Rob, and only nine horses. Without a moment's hesitation, Otetiani took Rob up on his horse with him and snuggled the young man into his lap. He barked orders to his braves and they all started to file quietly away from the area of the fort.

When they'd forded a river, Otetiani barked again and his braves took off in a gallop in three different directions.

None of them were with Otetiani and Rob now, though. The two rode on through the night. Rob gradually became aware that Otetiani was getting hard. And the savage's tool was free of his codpiece. That monster cock of his was rising up the small of Rob's back, and they were losing speed. The Indian warrior's palm had been on Rob's belly for many miles, helping to hold the young man steady on the horse, but now it was wrapped around Rob's cock and the young man was being stroked off has they cantered across the meadows.

Winston was trembling and becoming fully aroused. The horse was still cantering along in a rolling motion, but Otetiani raised Rob's hips, and when he brought them back down, Rob's ass channel was sinking onto that huge, thick cock. The cock was moving inside Rob's channel to the rhythm of the horse's gait. It was all too much for the young redhead. He ejaculated onto the silky mane of the horse's lower neck. Otetiani stopped the horse at that point and slid off. He pulled Rob off and laid him down on the soft ground in a field of clover on his back. He unstrapped a rolled-up blanket that had been on the horse's rump and wedged it under Rob's buttocks so that his hips were raised, his legs were spread, and his back was flat on the ground. The Indian chieftain knelt between Rob's legs; he propped a heavily muscled arm on the ground on each side of Rob's torso and his face hovered over Rob's. His hair was loose and cascaded down onto Rob's chest in long strands. Otetiani leaned down and kissed each of Rob's nipples in turn and then he looked directly into Rob's eyes.

This was no ceremony or necessary action. Otetiani wanted him. And he wanted to know if Rob would receive him with the same need. Rob reached down between them and took Otetiani's hard cock in both hands and guided it inside his channel. He closed his sphincter muscle over the base of the huge bulb when it had moved inside him and then drew the cock in slowly with his channel muscles, causing the walls to ripple over the throbbing cylinder. Otetiani's eyes opened wide and a big smile spread across his face, and then he lowered his face to Rob's and, for the first time, they kissed deeply, while Otetiani began to stroke hard and deep inside the young man.

Waves of pleasurable sensation rolled through Rob's body. He was fucked often and had more or less become numb to it, but no one had the length and thickness and strength of this man and a half. Or the staying power, as Rob learned when he was ridden and ridden and ridden while he writhed and bucked against the master fuck. Nor had any previous lover had the recovery power, when after multiple spoutings inside him, the Indian chief returned almost instantaneously to the saddle and rode him some more. The twelve fuckings of Otetiani's virile warriors hadn't left Rob this exhausted or satiated.

* * * *

The Shewan raid on the Huron chief's camp was fully accepted as an act of war by the Iroquois nation itself, and a third of Burgoyne's forces that he'd been welding together to wipe out the revolutionary forces in the Mohawk Valley evaporated into internecine warfare. The failure of half of the total forces of the campaign—General Howe's troops that now were occupying Philadelphia—to materialize at all put an end to any hopes of a knockout invasion from Canada. Weeks later Burgoyne surrendered his troops upon taking too few men into battle at the Battle of Saratoga, and the bottom had dropped out of Britain's strategy to hold on to its American colonies.

Rob Winston went on to Albany, where Colonel Hampton thought he'd been all along, and when he was fully healed and returned to Hampton's camp to take up his duties as Hampton's aide and lover once more, he was all congratulations on the miracles from heaven Hampton described to him that had made the British forces evaporate before the American forces in the Mohawk Valley.

"Yes, yes, the gods have been good to us," Rob whispered. He moaned as the colonel's tongue moved up his inner thigh and his lips closed over the young man's cock. Rob began to rotate his hips and murmured his pleasure at the fingers invading his entrance, preparing him for the second fucking of the night, the love fucking, given almost apologetically for the brutality of the earlier tension-release fucking.

Rob glanced over toward the entrance of the tent, hoping to be able to see the hint of leather fringe and feathers there. Otetiani had been here earlier in the evening, and Hampton was making him wait to give his report until after his had taken his evening pleasure with his aide.

Rob spread his legs and arched his back and wrapped his arms around his lover's shoulders, as Hampton's hard dick started its slide into Rob's hole. Rob cried out and moaned for the colonel's invasion, knowing this would please his colonel.

He looked back through the shadows to the tent opening. Yes, Otetiani was still there.

Later, after Otetiani had given his report and when a satiated Colonel Hamilton was snoring on his camp bed, Rob stole out into the night, beyond the staked horses, to the special tree to the waiting arms and the hours of riding the wave of ecstasy on the monster cock of his savage master.

Dominican Showdown

Twilight had set over the remote Puntacana resort beach on the Dominican Republic's southern coast, where the boyish, baking body of the young American tourist, Danny, had been staked out on a beach lounge bed under a palm tree all day. He watched the berry-brown Dominican beach attendant, all hulky muscle and graceful movement, tidy up the beach area for the night. This didn't take long; it wasn't an onerous task in the off season when very few occupied the small vacation bungalows dotted around at the top edges of the small semicircular, pristine white sand beach of the cove. While the beach attendant worked, he frequently let his eyes stray to the stretched out, provocatively posed, and perfectly proportioned body of the American, the last resort vacationer remaining on the beach.

Danny turned onto his belly on the lounge bed and looked up toward the nearest bungalow, where the lights had just gone on. He sighed as he felt the strong hands at the waistband of his Speedo, and the suit being slipped down over his slim legs. A warm, naked, hard-muscled body lowered on him, stretching out on top of him. He let his arms dangle over the sides of the lounge bed, his knuckles dragging in the sand on either side of it as the man above him turned Danny's head to the side with a hand on his cheek and took his mouth in a kiss. The small American, his body dwarfed by the massive muscularity of the Dominican, moaned with the feel of the cock head dragging on the small of his back. Coaxed by the touch of a hand, he spread his thighs apart. The beach attendant's cock, already half hard, dropped into the crevice between Danny's thighs, the upper side of it rubbing, rubbing, rubbing across Danny's puckering hole as the young man started to pant in response to the dry fuck.

A beefy arm laced under his waist and coaxed him up on his knees, as the Dominican's weight shifted. He no longer was lying on Danny's back. He was somewhere below Danny on the lounge bed. Danny grunted and gasped and spread his thighs further as a hand encased his engorging cock and a wet tongue went to—and into—his hole. He raised his arms above his head and grasped the top of the lounge bed. His eyes turned toward the foliage beyond the top of the bed, toward the terrace of the bungalow with the lights on inside. There was another light, the glow of a cigarette, and the silhouette in the advancing dark of a figure sitting on the terrace.

Danny tried to stifle his moans and groans as his cock was pulled through his legs and a mouth swallowed it and a tongue ran up and down the sides of the shaft. He gave a little cry as the lips closed tightly over his bulb and the tongue darted into his piss slit. A thumb was buried deep in his hole, slowly moving in and out, opening him up to the shafting that soon was to follow, seeking and finding his prostate with its pad.

"Oh, yes, yes, fuck yes. Fuck me, fuck me," Danny murmured, knees trembling and slowly rotating his hips with the attention being applied to his cock and prostate. He was trying to be quiet. The glowing cigarette was just yards away. But he involuntarily cried out as the beach attendant rose up over him, crouched over his buttocks, grasped his hips with strong hands, and slid his cock into a shimmering channel, open to him and begging for his touch.

The fuck was a long one. The beach attendant was young and virile and had great stamina—and no doubt had been thinking of this encounter since earlier in the afternoon when the two had established the twilight assignation. After doggy fucking Danny for several minutes, he turned the young

American on his back, slid in between his thighs, grabbed Danny's ankles and raised and wishboned Danny's legs. As the Dominican thrust his shaft back inside the moist, now-gaping hole, Danny arched his back and panted and moaned. Danny was fucked hard and fast to the Dominican's first ejaculation. After the beach attendant had come, he moved down the lounge bed, pulled the spent condom off his cock and dropped it to the sand at the side of the bed. He then lowered his mouth on Danny's cock and palmed Danny's pecs, worrying the young man's nipples, until Danny too had come.

The beach attendant moved back up Danny's body and they kissed, both enjoying the taste of Danny's warm cum. They lay thus closely embraced and moving their bodies against each other in a desultory fashion until Danny could feel the beach attendant going hard again. Danny was doing so as well. The Dominican went up on his knees between Danny's spread thighs and Danny narrowed his eyes in pleasure at the beautifully molded, berry-brown torso of his "for now" lover. He moaned at seeing the thickness of the man's cock, the cock that had just been inside his channel, expertly working him. The beach attendant smiled down at him, Danny watched as the Dominican slowly rolled on another condom.

Exhibiting both his strength and his control over the small, lithe-bodied Danny, the Dominican grasped Danny by the waist and raised his body in the air, over his, while he moved to stretch out his own legs toward the top of the lounge bed. Slowly he lowered Danny's body, Danny's knees going to the outer sides of the beach attendant's thighs and his face coming down to the Dominican's, where their mouths met in another long, lingering, tongue-possessing kiss.

"Perfect body, so small and perfect," the Dominican muttered as they came out of the kiss. "Such an amazing hole, first very tight and then opening right up. I didn't think it could, but it opened right up for me. You have taken many men, haven't you? That turns me on. And you are so flexible and graceful. Are you a dancer?"

"More in the line of an actor, I think you'd say," Danny answered, and then, with heavy breathing, "And yes, I have taken many men. Of those, you are one of the best. You have fucked many men too, I'll wager."

"And women too. It's part of the resort service."

"Fuck me again," Danny whimpered. "Just keep on fucking me."

Danny grasped and positioned the Dominican's cock while his own pelvis was being lowered to the Dominican's, and he lowered his channel on the shaft. Demonstrating his full acceptance, Danny leaned back and grabbed his ankles in his fists and fucked himself on the hard shaft as the Dominican laid back on the lounge bed and, smiling, arms crossed behind his neck, his muscular chest puffed out and heaving, watched Danny gyrate his body and ride the cock. After a few minutes the Dominican reached down with both hands and worked Danny's cock.

This time Danny came first.

The Dominican raised his torso up, grasped Danny's sides under his armpits, thumbs stroking Danny's nipples, and Danny arched his torso back over the upper section of the lounge bed and let his arms dangle at his sides and his head arch back, completely relaxed in his torso and his legs, every ounce of his energy and focus going to his channel and that thick, hard cock reaching up inside him. Again, the beach attendant resumed fucking Danny's channel with slow, forward and back, movements of his hips. Danny willed his channel muscles to undulate over the cock, to squeeze it and release it, squeeze it and release it. And with a jerk and deep-throated phrases of passion in Spanish, the Dominican ejaculated.

Alone, laying on his belly, panting and cooling down, listening to the waves lapping up on the beach and the breeze whispering through the palm branches, Danny raised his head and looked up at the nearby beach bungalow. The lights inside had moved to a different room. But the figure was still sitting on the terrace, the smolder of the lit end of the cigarette moving back and forth.

Danny turned and stretched like a cat on the lounge bed; raised his knees up, with his feet flat on the surface of the lounge; spread his thighs; and moaned quietly as he stroked his cock. His head was hanging over the top of the bed, and his eyes were staring toward the foliage above him, picking out and following the movement of the cigarette tip.

The cigarette arced out over the terrace of the bungalow, landing in a planter, and Danny held his breath as he discerned the movement of a darker, bulky shadow rising from the patio chair in the darkness enveloping the bungalow patio. But then he heard the closing of a door and all was silent from the terrace. Danny's hand dropped away from his cock. He sat up on the side of the lounge bed and gathered up his beach items, looking up the beach toward his own bungalow.

* * * *

Danny was already stretched out on his "claimed" lounge bed under the palm tree on the resort beach in mid morning when a couple came out of the bungalow closest to him and moved to side-by-side lounges farther along the beach but close enough that Danny could hear that they were speaking when they did so but not their specific words. He watched them over the top of his sunglasses and a paperback novel held near his face as they laid out their towels and other beach paraphernalia.

They were a couple that would arrest most anyone's attention, so it wasn't notable that Danny would be scrutinizing them closely. They were mismatched. She was somewhat of a mousey woman, probably in her early forties, who was losing the battle of weight and didn't seem to know it. She was trying to wear a bikini and not pulling the effort off very well. Dishwater blonde hair, skittish movements, facial expressions that changed moods frequently, and a whine that Danny could hear from where he sat. She wasn't bad looking, just tired looking, nervous and giving off an air of defeat. She was on the beach to swim and went to the water, up to her knees, but no farther, almost as soon as they had reached their lounge chairs.

The man, in contrast, clearly wasn't there to swim. He was bare-chested, but wearing baggy shorts, and Danny doubted he was planning on swimming with the Smith and Wesson M&P 9 mm and holster buckled at his waist. From his attitude, he was there to continuously scan the beach, his eyes stopping for a lingering moment to focus on Danny with each sweep.

He was a mismatch with the woman in nearly every way he could be. He probably was in his late twenties or early thirties, was movie star handsome, gave off an aura of confidence and capability—and all business—and quite evidently was a serious bodybuilder. Whereas his body was a temple, the woman's was a 7-Eleven convenience store.

It was very hard for Danny to see these two as a couple. He continued to watch them both as surreptitiously as he could, while the woman waded around aimlessly and rather listlessly in the surf, flinching at any sound other than the cawing birds, rustling palm leaves, and lapping waves, and the man finally settled in to a wary seated position on one of the lounges. He slowly relaxed a bit while keeping an eagle eye on the woman broken by occasional scans of the rest of the activity on the beach—of which there wasn't much—and began chain smoking cigarettes.

After a while his eyes were going to Danny almost as often as to the woman in the surf, and Danny was doing all he could in posing in his skimpy Speedo on his lounge bed to encourage the scrutiny. The man was a real hunk, and the glances Danny devoted to the gun on the man's hip sent him into flights of fancy on the other gun he was packing. The shorts were baggy and the leg holes drooped, so that Danny fancied that he almost . . . almost . . . could see far enough up the curve of the heavily muscled thighs to see the hint of a cock bulb.

Almost imperceptibly Danny turned to his side, facing the man and, as he pretended to read his paperback novel, drank in the man's bulging pecs and ripped six pack through his sunglass lenses while his free hand glided over his sweat-glistened body. It wasn't long before Danny was rewarded with seeing the man's hand drop to his crotch. He was studiously not directly looking at Danny, but Danny knew that the man was watching him as surreptitiously as Danny was watching the man.

It almost seemed like the man was poised to rise and come over to Danny's lounge bed when the woman came out of the surf, dried herself off with a towel, said something to the man, and they returned to their bungalow.

Danny rose from his lounge bed then as well and walked in a graceful half-strut across the sand toward his own cabin, being fully aware that the man had come out onto the terrace of the bungalow and was standing there, smoking a cigarette, and watching Danny walk away.

That afternoon and evening it was like the paths of the couple and Danny were continuously crossing. In the afternoon, Danny went into the small village outside the gates of the resort to view the handicraft stalls, and the couple was doing the same thing. When Danny went to the resort's beach bar for a drink afterward, the couple already was there. The two were perched on barstools, side-by-side, although leaving the impression they weren't together, she morose and he observant, not saying much of anything to each other. They certainly weren't honeymooners, as anyone watching them for any length of time could tell.

Back in the village for an early dinner, both the couple and Danny had selected the same restaurant. That wasn't something to cause anyone much concern; the village was small and the decent-looking restaurants pretty much being this one. The woman's eyes were darting everywhere while she ate, but Danny and the man mostly stole glances at each other.

Shortly after dark, Danny was back on his lounge bed, riding the cock of the beefy Dominican bartender who had been serving them drinks that afternoon. The Dominican laid on his back, stretched out on the lounge, the palms of his hands fanned out on Danny's pecs as, facing the bartender, Danny crouched on his haunches on the man's cock and leaned his torso back with his hand's gripping his ankles. He was slightly raised off the man's crotch to give the Dominican room to fuck up into his channel.

Danny was moaning and moving his hips to meet the Dominican's thrusts, but his gaze was directed toward the fringe of the beach, where a figure was sitting, in the dark, on the terrace of the couple's bungalow and smoking cigarettes.

When Danny arrived at one of the village restaurants for lunch the next day, the couple was already there. But the man leaned over and said something to the woman, after which he took money out of his wallet and they both left the restaurant even though their food was only half eaten. The Smith and Wesson was still strapped to his waist. It was there every time Danny saw the couple.

Danny's own meal was only half eaten as well when two local policemen entered the restaurant, walked up to his table, and politely but firmly requested that Danny accompany them to the local police station. There he was taken to a small interrogation room furnished with a wobbly wooden table and three chairs, one on one side of the table and two on the other. A large mirror was set in one wall, where the single chair faced. Danny was asked to sit in the single chair.

After a wait of nearly an hour sitting there all by himself, two men entered the room—an older-looking policeman and the man from the resort. They sat in the chairs opposite Danny, and the man opened a pouch he'd brought with him and had laid on the table and took Danny's passport; hotel reservation printouts for here and the Cayman Islands, where he next was booked at a beach resort; and plane tickets out of the pouch and laid them on the table.

"You've been in my bungalow," Danny said. "Those were in a locked safe."

"Yes, Mr. Wilson," the body-builder hunk with the gun on his hip said. "The local police are cooperating with me. It doesn't take much in the Dominican Republic to obtain permission to search someone's home. You have been paying a bit too much attention to me and the woman I'm with— enough to have raised questions why that was so."

"It's a small resort and off season," Danny said. "I didn't know that there were restrictions on where I could go just because you and your wife would be there too."

"She's not my wife," the man shot back. But then it seemed from the expression on his face as if he had said something he shouldn't have, and he regathered his approach. The policeman sat stoically beside him, arms crossed, saying nothing, quite possibly understanding little other than that there must be some reason for him to be cooperating with this other tourist.

Danny thought of asking the man—or the policeman—by what authority he was questioning Danny's activities, but he thought better of it and just waited for the man's next move, watching his face with a mixture of amusement and lack of worry.

"We are here for our privacy. I am, you might say, the woman's bodyguard, and I have to be very careful who shows interest in us."

"You've been in my bungalow. You've gone through my things," Danny repeated, gesturing at his documents that the man had laid out on the table. "You can hardly expect me to be more concerned for your privacy than for my own."

"Yes, sorry."

"Did you find anything that would make you suspicious that I wasn't just here on a vacation?" Danny asked.

"No, we didn't. But you have been watching the woman closely. Can you say why?"

"I wasn't watching the woman," Danny said, giving the bodyguard a level, direct stare. "I was watching you."

"Watching me?" the man said, nonplused and surprised at the comment. "Whatever for?"

"I suspect—I hope—for the same reason you have been sitting and smoking on the terrace of your bungalow the last two nights and watching me—and what I was doing."

The three sat and stared at each other for more than a minute. Only the policeman seemed not to understand what was being said—and his English probably was very limited anyway.

"Tell me that I'm wrong," Danny said. "Tell me you haven't been watching me with special interest."

Another pause of staring and then the man leaned over and said something to the policeman in Spanish. The policeman nodded, rose from the table, and left the room. The bodyguard also got up from the table, walked over to the door to the corridor, and closed and locked it from the inside. This was his one and only intentional act in that first coupling.

They fucked with the man standing with his back against the wall beside the mirror. Danny did most of the work. The man had clearly wanted to fuck Danny, but he struggled with the propriety of doing so, especially right there in the police station, until Danny seduced him with entreaties of need and with clever initiation of groping, moaning, kissing, stroking, begging, heavy breathing, and cock sucking.

Danny forced a position that the man could not resist and did not have to take responsibility for. Danny had his fists locked behind the man's neck and was draped on the front of the bodyguard, who, shorts down around his ankles but Smith and Wesson still buckled on a belt at his waist, was palming and spreading Danny's butt cheeks to give his cock maximum penetration of Danny's channel. Danny's legs were bent with his feet flat against the wall and out wide at the level of the man's waist, giving him the aspect of a crab attached to the man's pelvis. He used his feet for leverage. Taking full charge, Danny pumped his channel on the man's long and thick cock. Danny provided the Golden Ticket condom, Danny provided the opportunity, Danny provided the sensual touch, and, in the clutch, Danny provided the pumping action on the cock.

Until he was completely lost to Danny, and the irresistible need for him, the man was given no opportunity to withdraw from the brink of the abyss. What he did that night was, at least in his mind, a compensation for his lack of control and dominance earlier, letting a small, boyish-looking man dominate a macho, hulking dude like him. It became a matter of pride to reassert dominance.

That night after the resort's pool boy fucked Danny on the lounge bed under the tree and had gone, Danny rose from the lounge and walked over to the terrace of the neighboring bungalow. The bodyguard, naked, was sitting in a patio chair and smoking a cigarette. As Danny approached, he flicked his cigarette into a planter and raised and spread his arms, pulling Danny into an embrace as, facing him, the young man straddled the arms of the patio chair and lowered his channel on the man's erect, already-sheathed cock.

After Danny had ridden the cock to his own ejaculation, the man gathered him up in his arms and carried him into the bungalow, into one of the two bedrooms; laid Danny down on his back on the foot of the bed; spread the young man's thighs, slowly slid his cock into Danny's channel;

and fucked him, at great length in ever-more-rapid strokes, to his own ejaculation. As soon as the man could regain a hard staff, Danny straddled his pelvis and rode his cock again.

At length, exhausted, Danny and the man lay side by side on the bed, their hands roaming each other's bodies and Danny giving the man a hand job until with a moan and a sigh, the bodyguard drifted off into sleep. When the bodyguard's breathing had become regularized and he was quietly snoring, Danny carefully and silently rose from the bed and padded out of the bungalow, leaving the door behind him unlatched and slightly open.

He stealthily moved back to the lounge bed he had claimed for himself and lifted it and swung it away from the base of the palm tree, careful to muffle the scraping noise in the sand. Once the lounge bed was turned, he went down on his hands and knees and dug into the sand. Extracting the oilskin pouch that had been hidden under the lounge since the day Danny had arrived—two days before the couple in the nearby bungalow did—Danny carefully unwrapped the Beretta 92FS it contained, checked it over, and then screwed on the silencer that also had been hidden in the pouch.

They had been right, he thought. The best avenue of approach and the disarming of defenses had been through the sexual proclivities of the bodyguard. He already could feel the sweet taste of success. There hadn't yet been a witness protection arrangement that he hadn't been able to circumvent.

He rose and, holding the Beretta at the ready at his side, quietly and carefully stole his way back inside the bungalow.

Double-Cross Express

"I'm not quite sure what to say . . . um, Jamie, was it? We've never had a walk-in on this before. I think maybe you should be talking to—"

"You are Sam Winterberry of the special unit, aren't you?"

"Yes, but I don't know how you knew anything about such a unit or about me. Could you just sit here a minute and—"

Sam Winterberry had never in his long years with the Agency, having been through many a hairy operation, been this nonplused. He was here in Paris, because a terrorist cell was here that was about ready to go on the move, and the Agency had to know where they were going. And one of the things they knew about a couple of the terrorists in the cell made them turn to Winterberry's special operations unit, which was informally know as the Candy Store.

Winterberry had just been putting his plan into motion in Paris Station, waiting for his operative to check in, when the Marine guards down at reception had told him there was a young gentleman there who had asked for him specifically. And he wasn't even supposed to be here in Paris. The Station got a lot of walk-ins of people who wanted to talk to someone in American intelligence, most of whom were crackpots, to be sure. But they didn't often ask for a senior agency official by name who shouldn't even be there, but who was there.

"I don't think you caught my whole name," the young man said. "My full name is Jamil Jallud the Third. I'm just called Jamie for short. Do you wish to see my passport again? I did use it to get in here in the first place."

Winterberry sank back down into his chair. "Son of—?"

"Yes, Congressman Jamil Jallud the Second, of New Jersey. So, that's how I know. I know all about your unit. And, yes, my father knows about me. And I'm ready. I've been studying international relations and law. This is the perfect fit for me. I've been in the army. A communications specialist. I want in."

Not just *a* congressman from New Jersey, Winterberry thought, but the second-ranking majority member of the House Committee on Intelligence. That explained so much. How this young man knew about the unit and perhaps even how he knew about where to locate the head of the unit at any specific time and location. Congressman Jallud was one of the House's premier blabbermouths.

Winterberry took another look at the young man. If he'd seen him on the street, he wouldn't even have taken him as old enough. But he'd said he was a graduate student at Georgetown when he'd introduced himself. And Winterberry had to admit that the young man looked the part. He was well built and achingly handsome—Winterberry wouldn't have tossed him out of bed himself—with a dark complexion and curly black hair, a sultry, pouty look and bedroom eyes. Lebanese. His family was Lebanese. There was so much one could do with a Lebanese-background agent these days. Still, the unit had never taken walk-ins. Winterberry didn't like the idea of free agents; he wanted to have leverage on them. That's why he liked to trap them and suborn them to the work—and to his will. And, often, into his bed. And he'd sure like to bed this one. Bet he had a sweet hole and that he'd moan well. Winterberry felt himself going hard.

"I'm sorry, Mr. Jallud. We have never taken a volunteer."

"I'd be good at it; I know I would. Hey, Dad told me you fucked men. You wanna try me out? Take me for a test ride? I bottom like nobody's business."

"Mr. Jallud!" Winterberry's sharp response was half because taking Jamie Jallud for a test ride was exactly what he had been thinking of at the moment. "I don't . . . we don't . . . this conversation is being recorded, you know!"

"OK, then a test operation. Let me prove myself."

"What I think would be best, Mr. Jallud, is that you go back and finish at Georgetown and apply to the Agency via the normal—"

Both of the men turned their faces to the door to the corridor as it opened and a woman stuck her head into the room. "Mr. Winterberry, sorry to interrupt, but you wanted me to tell you the instant Mr. Boltov arrived. And he's in the chief's office. I'm sorry—"

"Quite all right, Erica," Winterberry stood, relieved that someone had intervened in this conversation. Winterberry didn't enjoy being pressured; he always wanted to be in control, to dominate.

"I'm sorry, Mr. Jallud. I have pressing—"

"My father knows I'm here, Mr. Winterberry. I don't think he'll be the least pleased with how this interview has gone."

"Please, Mr. Jallud. I really do have to go. But if you'll stay here, I'll be back and we'll take your information, and . . . well, just stay here a few moments, will you?" Winterberry needed some time to think this out. This had never happened to him before.

Winterberry left and went to the chief of station's office. The COS was in the south, sunning himself on the Riviera, and as the senior Agency official in the station at the moment, even if visiting, Winterberry had complete use of the station facilities.

A young, square-jawed Russian bodybuilder, who was the best of his agents that Winterberry could spring loose on the spur of the moment, was sitting, overpowering his seat, but poised like he could rise fast and strike hard, when Winterberry entered the office. Boltov was usually a power top and was employed when the subject needed to be dominated and manhandled, but he was versatile enough to roll with the punches of assignments. And he was a master of disguises, which could come in handy here, as the field of play would be really confined.

"You know what we want?" Winterberry asked as he sat down in the COS's chair.

"Yes, you want to know where the cell is moving to."

"Yes, that most of all, but there also should be a briefcase full of information they need to take with them—contacts and false documentation and such. It would tell us a lot about how these terrorist cells are being held together. This is a keystone cell. Our source says they'll take some necessary information with them—in the form of paper."

"In paper? Are you sure? Not electronic files?"

"Yes, paper," and at the thought of this, Winterberry chuckled. "We did that to them. We had someone embedded in the cell. He moved on to another cell, but while he was with the Paris group, he put into the mind of the cell leader, Samir, that we could hack into any electronic file, with or without Internet connection. I understand Samir won't trust any electronics now."

"And you don't want me to board the Orient Express before Venice?"

"No. They're taking the train from here; booked all the way to Istanbul. Chances are good that's where they'll go and then try to disperse to an unknown location from there. We need to have some idea where they'll strike next. They're taking the Orient Express as the least-watched means of travel."

"And you say there are five of them?"

"Yes, if the whole cell moves."

"But only two of them are known to be susceptible?"

"Yes. Samir, the leader, and one of the soldiers, Rashid, but that doesn't mean they all aren't, as you say, 'susceptible.' We have photos of the two who you could target. Them and one more. We don't have a name on him. Unfortunately, we don't have photos of the other two. They joined the cell after our embedded agent had left. That's one way they keep control of their information; they keep shuffling personnel around and try to keep them from getting too committed to each other. They're all Arabs, though. They shouldn't be too hard to pick out on the Orient Express European run. Give me a moment and I'll get the dossier. I left it in the other office."

Winterberry went back to the other office, to find that the young man, Jamie Jallud, had left. Winterberry was relieved, but he knew it was only for a moment, that he'd be hearing from the congressman from New Jersey before long. But Winterberry was just too busy to worry about that now. He had to scrabble around on the desk, searching for the dossier. It was not quite where he thought he'd left it, but he did finally find it and went back to his briefing of his agent.

* * * *

The first thing Serge Boltov did after he'd boarded the Orient Express in Venice and secured his cabin, tucking away all of the tools of his craft and his disguise kit so that they weren't easily found, was to walk the corridors of the train as it pulled out of the station. As soon as he'd gotten to Venice and the train had started its journey from Paris, he'd been informed which cabins the men occupied—or at least the numbers of all of the cabins occupied by Arabs. The conductor had had to be bribed for the information, and the one buying it didn't want to be too specific so that the conductor wouldn't stick his nose into the operation—and maybe ask for more, knowing how important the information was.

"And be very, very careful," his contact had said. "The agent we'd had in place with this Paris cell has been found murdered in Tripoli. We suspect he might have been compromised."

Serge ticked off the numbers of the cabins in his mind as he went down the corridor. The European Orient Express was a plush, full-night-service train, and all the passengers were accommodated in sleeper cabins with windows onto the corridor. The windows had blinds, though, most of which were pulled down. Some of them were ill fitting, however, and one could peek into the cabins at the edges of the window. Four of the seven cabins he'd been told had Arabic occupants were in the same car, and Serge assumed these were the ones he was interested in.

As Serge went down the line of cabins in this car, peeking around the edges of the blinds as surreptitiously as he was able, he heard the sounds he was attuned to in his business coming from the cabin beyond the first one assigned to Arabic occupants. One of the window blinds here was pulled away somewhat more than usual, and Serge got a clear view of the two men fucking.

A tray table was set up between the two facing heavily cushioned bench seats, and a young, lithe, sensually dark Arabic man, not one who Serge had seen in the three photos Winterberry had shown him, was on his back on the table, his legs spread. Another Arabic man, heavier, but well muscled, solid, and older, was crouched between the young man's legs and fucking him with long strokes.

The younger man was writhing beneath the other one and moaning and groaning as if the older man was well experienced and had a champion cock.

While Serge watched, the older man pulled the younger one up with his hands braced around the younger one's slim waist and turned sideways to the door and windows to the corridor. He turned the younger man on his cock to the sound of much grunting and moaning from the younger man and then sat down on one of the cushioned bench seats with the younger man sitting in his lap with his back into the older Arab's chest.

Serge could see the older Arab's face now and was able to identify him as Samir, the leader of the cell.

The younger man fucked himself on Samir's cock, using the balls of his feet on the floor of the carriage for leverage. Samir worked the young man's nipples with one hand and his nicely hard cock with the other, and the young man gave out a little cry and ejaculated in a long stream shooting out over the thick carpeting.

Serge only had time to look around and see that there were two cases on the floor by the seat across from the fucking pair, a stuffed briefcase and what looked like a computer laptop case, although Serge assumed it was just another briefcase, having been told about Samir's aversion to electronics.

Voices were approaching the other end of the corridor, so Serge moved quickly on without checking out the other cabins. He'd found the leaders' cabin and likely the sought-after briefcase, though, so the first reconnoitering outing had been a success.

There were five of them there in the dining car when Serge appeared for dinner. The seating in their area was set up variously in tables for two and four. Samir and one other Arabic-looking man were sitting at a table for four, and the terrorist Serge identified as Rashid from the photos Winterberry showed him was sitting with an unidentified Arabic man at a table for two. Across from them sat the fifth Arab, the handsome young man Samir had been fucking in his cabin earlier. Serge could see that both of the briefcases he'd seen in Samir's cabin were at Samir's feet under the dinner table.

As Serge ate, picking out a table from whence he could watch the five without being obtrusive himself, he saw the young man Samir had fucked making unmistakable signals at the Arab seated with Rashid. They were facing each other, and Rashid was facing Serge. Serge noticed Rashid watching him and decided to go to work himself. He flashed a smile at the Arab, who was slim and rather small, but well muscled, and Rashid's face lit up and he smiled back at him. Serge knew a docile bottom when he saw one and decided that Rashid was the best of the targets available to him.

Serge had come late to dinner and was served his coffee as the Arabs were finishing theirs. Samir and his dinner companion and Rashid rose and moved farther on down the car toward the next, smoking carriage, and the Arab, the young man Samir had fucked, was joined by the one who had dined with Rashid. Soon, however, they got up and passed by Serge on their way back to the sleeping cars.

Serge waited a decent interval before following this pair and ensuring that, as he surmised, they would be occupied for a while. They were in one of the four cabins identified as occupied by Arabs in the same carriage—but not the one Serge had seen Samir in.

Both were nude already, and Rashid's dinner companion was sitting on one of the bench seats and the young Arab was sitting on his cock, facing him, and fucking himself in slow, languid rises and falls.

Knowing these two would be occupied for some time, Serge walked back through the sleeping cars and the dining car and into the smoking car. There were only a couple of seats free. Fortuitously, one of them was next to Rashid and across from Samir and the other Arab.

"Do you mind?" Serge said, using his most suave voice. "There seem to be a shortage of seats in this carriage."

"By all means," Samir responded, and Serge sat down in the seat beside Rashid. Rashid was tongue-tied and seemed to be overwhelmed at his good fortune to be seated next to Serge.

As they smoked and drank Cognac, they engaged in light talk. Serge was an expert in extracting information, but he discerned immediately that Samir was an expert in deflecting meaningful talk, and Serge knew he wouldn't be able to find out what he wanted to know from Samir without a lot of effort. Perhaps from Rashid, he thought, and he turned to Rashid and gave him a smile. Rashid's automatic radiant smile back fully revealed his interest.

"These are such interesting little bottles of liquor they have on the train, don't you think?" Samir said as a parry to a roundabout questioning ploy Serge was using and had almost reached a point where it would have been impolite for Samir not to provide a useful answer.

"Yes, if truth be known," Serge, who was posing as an importer of Oriental goods, said, "I ride the Orient Express solely for their small bottles of Cognac. I steal as many as I can and take another ride on the Orient Express when I've depleted my collection."

"Well, then, you must have this one too, sir," Samir said, with a smile. "I can't use it myself. More than one glass of Cognac I can't explain away. My religion, you know. Not totally strict as I follow it, but there are boundaries."

Hopelessly turned away from his line of questioning, Serge smiled and accepted the small bottle of liquor and put it in his pocket.

In a bit, as Serge was mounting another assault on the information gap, the young man Samir had fucked returned to the smoking carriage and walked up to Samir and said, "The porter has told me the beds are turned down. Would you like me to walk you to your carriage?"

Serge saw Samir's eyes slit and could see immediately that he was smitten by the young man. The youth was, in fact, beautiful. From Samir's dossier, it wasn't at all surprising that he had managed to slip a love interest into his cell. It was ironic that suicide terrorists were told they would receive more than their share of virgins in heaven, but terrorist cell leaders made sure they got their share of them here on earth.

Excusing himself, Samir stood, as did the other Arab with him, took up the briefcases, one in each hand, and followed the young Arab, who moved with mincing step and swinging hips back toward the sleeper cars.

Serge was left alone with Rashid and took little time to turn up the heat.

A few more brief forays for information without seeming to be wanting it, and Serge was convinced that Rashid would not talk under these circumstances any quicker than Samir would.

"Do you want me to fuck you, Rashid?" Serge asked in a pleasant voice, designed to put Rashid off his stride. "I want to fuck you. I find you very arousing."

Rashid stammered, lost for words, never having been approached this directly before, certainly not by anyone he wanted this badly.

"Here, give me your hand. Feel this. This is a cock to be proud of Rashid. I can fill you as you have never been filled before. I can ride you like a stallion all night. You need a man to dominate you; to be a man like no other inside you. Shall we go to your cabin or mine?"

Rashid, on the pull-down bed in one of the four cabins in the carriage Serge had marked, was wild and needy and repeatedly sucked the seed out of Serge's cock, luxuriating in the power and size and staying power of the big Russian—first by his soft mouth and then with the talented undulating muscles of his channel walls. He loved being held down with Serge's firm grip on his wrists and spreading his legs for the Russian while Serge pounded his ass relentlessly and then being turned and brought up on all fours and taken doggy style until his knees and hands gave out and Serge rode his ass as he collapsed on his belly and just kept riding and riding and riding . . . until the exhausted Arab drifted off to snores of total satiation.

The fuck had been a five-star success, but Serge wasn't anywhere closer to knowing where the terrorist cell was going, what they planned on doing after arriving in Istanbul. Perhaps, he thought, on another night, they would progress to more pillow talk.

He pulled out of the Arab and went into the cabinet and cleaned himself off. Coming back out, he heard a door open down the corridor, and, slipping on his briefs, he opened the door and peered down the corridor.

He was almost face-to-face with the young Arab, clothed only in billowy sleeping pants that rode low on his hips. The youth was clutching Samir's bulky briefcase to his chest.

There was a moment of indecision and shock—on both of their parts—before each face took on a speculative expression, which was replaced by some mutual decision of arousal, speculation of opportunity, and intent to make the most of their situation.

"Your cabin or mine?" Serge asked.

"Mine is just here," the young Arab answered in a whisper.

"I will be just a second," Serge said, and he ducked back into Rashid's cabin and retrieved the rest of his clothes and the "just in case" satchel he'd brought along. He half feared that the young Arab would be gone when he came back out into the corridor, even though he'd been absent mere seconds. But he was still there, rooted to the spot, still clutching Samir's briefcase against his very nicely muscled chest.

Serge's cock was hardening up well. He had wanted to fuck the young Arab himself ever since he'd seen him with Samir. And it would be a little extra notch in his cap in besting these terrorists to also cock the leader's lover.

In the time it took the young Arab to stash Samir's briefcase in the narrow space left against the outer cabin wall by the prepared pull-down bed, Serge had slipped off his briefs and added those to his folded clothes and put them near the head of the bed. He'd also unzipped his satchel and placed it on top of the folded clothes, the unzipped opening facing the foot of the bed. Then he'd sat down on the side of the pull-out bed and fisted his engorging cock, wanting to be ready for the young Arab.

Serge took immediate command when the young Arab came back around the bed, and the youth seemed content to be dominated. Serge forced him down on his knees on the carpeting between his spread legs and pushed the youth's mouth onto his cock and face-fucked him, not letting him loose until he had taken Serge's ejaculate. Then Serge rose and turned the youth around between him and the bed. He reached both hands down and stripped the sleeping pants off the young Arab and took the youth by his buttocks and raised his body. The youth arched back, palming his hands on the top of the bed to take the weight of his torso and hooking his legs over Serge's shoulders and letting them dangle down the beefy Russian's back. He writhed and moaned and groaned, while Serge brought, first his cock and balls, and then, when the Arab youth had shot his load, the youth's hole in his mouth.

The Arab was begging for the fuck when Serge slowly brought his body down his chest and belly, the youth still arched back, supported on the bed with the palms of his hands, and Serge slid his throbbing cock into a recently well-used, well-prepared hole. The youth gasped and groaned at a taking that was deeper and far more of a stretch than either of the Arabs had given him.

The Russian held the Arab there to his pelvis with just one arm wrapped around the small of his back and raising and lowering the Arab's hips while he stroked in and out deep inside the young man, listening for the sighing and moaning and little encouragements of technique that assured him that he was the best lover this young man had ever had. The sweetness of the youth and of his warm and welcoming hole, his channel walls undulating over Serge's stroking cock, sent the Russian to new heights of arousal and just now, just at this time, he loved his job. The Russian played the young Arab's chest and belly and cock with his other hand, bringing the youth to another flowing, after which all of the tension and movement went out of the youth, and he just lay arched back, moaning and sighing at the working of the Russian's cock deep inside him. The Russian fucked on, fighting the rise of his own semen, not wanting the loving to end.

As Serge felt his ejaculation coming on, he reached over and into his unzipped satchel with his free hand and brought out the syringe he had stashed there "just in case."

At the point of shooting off deep inside the Arab's channel, Serge expertly pierced the youth's thigh with the needle of the syringe and pumped the drug into him.

If the Arab youth knew he'd taken a needle, he said nothing. He was burbling almost incoherently as Serge gently lowered him on the bed.

Serge put his mouth to the youth's ear and asked, "Where is the cell going? What is the mission?" but the young man was already too far gone to answer.

Dressing and retrieving Samir's briefcase, Serge quietly returned to his own cabin two cars farther away from the engine. No one stopped him, and as far as he could determine, no one saw him leave the Arab's cabin. All that came from the surrounding cabins were spent and satisfied snores.

Once in his own cabin, Serge inspected the briefcase, and as he assumed he would, found that it was padlocked. He could not risk trying to open it; he had no idea what other security devices might be attached to it, or whether forcing it open would damage the precious contents. So, he hid it as best he could and spent the remainder of the few hours before they would reach Vienna station cleaning himself in the cabinet and remaking himself into an old Zurich banker.

Discovering in the pocket of his dinner jacket the small bottle of Cognac Samir had given him in the smoking car,

Serge decided he deserved a bit of celebration for at least a partially successful night, which permitted him a bit more time to reach the primary objective, not to mention the magnificent fucking with the young Arab, and tossed the contents of the bottle down in one gulp. Then, exhausted, he slipped into a deep sleep, the sleep of the dead.

* * * *

Serge didn't awaken until over twenty-four hours later. He had missed the stop at Vienna station altogether. When he came to the train was stopped, but it wasn't in Vienna. He groggily sat up and looked out of the window. The sign for Bucharest station was staring at him from across the platform.

"Shit," he said.

And then, realizing the knocking he'd been hearing wasn't in his head, he turned and flipped aside the blinds on the window into the corridor and was staring into the red, angry face of Sam Winterberry.

"I was drugged," Serge mumbled as he let Winterberry into his cabin. "The bottle of Cognac the terrorist leader gave me." Serge was using a disguise Winterberry had seen before and Winterberry knew his cabin number, so there was no moment of Keystone Cop running about on that score.

"Well, come along and show me where their cabins are. We didn't see them dismount here in Bucharest, so they must still be in transit."

"But why?" Serge said, getting less confused by the moment. "What are you doing here? In Budapest."

"We couldn't reach you." Winterberry said. "They left one of the cell members in Paris. You should only be looking for four men. And it's not the briefcase we want, I don't think. We're sure now that our agent embedded in the Paris cell was sent to Tripoli to be assassinated there. We must assume that Samir no longer believes what he was told by that agent about electronics. Does Samir have anything that looks like a laptop case."

"God. God, yes, he does," Serge said. "But I got the briefcase. I have it right over here. Needs a key, though."

121

"Let's see it," Winterberry said, as he extracted a brace of skeleton keys from his jacket pocket.

In a jiffy the briefcase was open and all too soon they found it was stuffed with clothes.

"Where are their cabins?" Winterberry asked. "Me they don't know. And you're in disguise. We can walk right by them and check them out."

The cabins were empty. All but one.

They found the young Arab Serge had fucked and taken the briefcase from. He was lying on his bed, a "Do Not Disturb" sign on his door. The only way they knew he was alive was that he was moaning softly. He was still under the influence of drugs, though—certainly having been drugged beyond what Serge had given him. He was on his back, knees bent and legs spread. His hole looked angry red and slack and had semen dribbling out of it, and there were too many spent condoms on the floor around the bed to be readily counted. It seemed like he'd been fucked by the whole Arab nation.

His cabin was disheveled. If there had been anything here anyone wanted, they had found it.

"Oh, God," Sam Winterberry muttered when he looked down into the face of the young man.

"What?" Serge said. "He's still alive. He can tell us where they went. His comrades obviously got off in Vienna, if your people didn't see them get off here."

"This is no Arab, Serge." Winterberry said, his voice full of bitterness. "This is Jamil Jallud, an American, the son of a powerful congressman even. God, he's been playing amateur spy. And the two of you have been working each other, trying to get secrets neither one of you have. And now we have to backtrack to Vienna to try to find them."

"No. Here. Hungary, the Hungarian parliament," the figure on the bed moaned softly.

"What is that? What did you say, son? Stick with us. You'll be fine. We'll get you patched up." Winterberry was so beside himself, worried over his unit's next appropriation hearings in Congress, that he hadn't fully realized what young Jallud had muttered.

"No. No. I heard them talking as they were gangbanging me," Jallud said, his voice stronger now. "They were getting off the train in Vienna. But headed here, for Hungary. An attack on the Hungarian parliament building."

"Go out on the platform, Serge," Winterberry directed, as he sat down on the bed by the moaning Jamie Jallud. "You'll see men in suits standing out there. Identify yourself and tell him the target and then get someone back here to help this young man."

As Serge ran down the corridor, Winterberry gathered the young man up in his arms and began to rock him back and forth and tell him everything would be fine. He could not help, however, letting one hand slip down and encase the young man's cock. A very nice body indeed, he thought. He would have to have some of that.

"And, Mr. Jallud," he murmured, "welcome to the Agency's special unit."

El Presidente

"Mr. Winterberry wants to see you in the back cabin, Paulo."

Paulo Pulido unbuckled his seatbelt and gave a sigh. He was pretty sure he knew what came next. At least, though, perhaps the head of the Agency's special unit, informally known as the candy store, might shed some light on where they were going and why. At the moment they were approaching altitude after a straight-up lift off from Miami in a Challenger 604 corporate jet. And all Paulo could see out of the windows as he worked his way back to the rear compartment with its four plush seats, two on each side of the aisle, currently facing each other, were clouds and ocean.

As he entered the cabin, he saw that Sam Winterberry was alone and occupying the seat with its back to him on the right side of the cabin. From Paulo's approach, Winterberry was only seen as a head of well-groomed dark hair with graying at the temples.

"Have a seat here facing me, Paulo. I want to take a look at you. We haven't seen each other for several months."

Paulo moved past the seat Winterberry fully occupied, his bulk being more in bone and muscle mass, and turned and sat in the seat opposite. He let out a puff of air that was more a confirmation than surprise when he saw that Winterberry had his cock out of the fly of his suit trousers and was pumping it up.

"Do you know that this corporate jet flies at an average altitude of 45,000 feet and that this is approximately the level at which we're now flying?" Winterberry asked in a pleasant voice. He made no comment or gesture that indicated Paulo should be surprised that he was masturbating. And, indeed, there was no reason to expect Paulo to be surprised. Paulo was one of Winterberry's special agents, an agent employed for his sexual charms and ability to use those charms to collect intelligence. And Winterberry was his handler—in more than one sense.

"No, no, Sam, I didn't know that. Now that we're up at that altitude are you going to brief me on the operation you've called me in on?"

"In a bit, Paulo. Do you know how many miles 45,000 feet equates to?"

"No, I don't, Sam. How many?"

"Something over eight miles. Have you ever heard of the Eight Mile High Club, Paulo?"

There was a pause, and Paulo gave a sardonic low laugh. Sam was going to play it like some sort of sophisticated joke, he thought.

"Yes. It's just a term for those who have had sex on an airplane, preferably at cruising altitude."

"Very good, you got it in one." Winterberry's breathing was a bit heavy. He nearly had his cock worked up to full hard. "And are you a member of that club?"

"No."

"A more accurate answer, Paulo, would have been 'Not until now.' Strip off, completely, please, and come sit on my cock. Believe me, this is relevant to your mission. Make convincing love to me, please. Your continued employment with the Agency may depend on it."

For the next twenty minutes, Paulo fucked himself on Sam Winterberry's cock while sitting astride him, both facing him and facing away from him. Paulo was as much a slave to sex as he was to a very-well-paying job in intelligence. And Sam Winterberry was a master of fucking techniques. So, as much as Paulo felt used, it didn't take him long to be lost in what the spy master was doing to him. Paulo was about to come, having shuddered at the angles and differing paces Winterberry was using to cock him, when Winterberry raised Paulo's channel off of his cock altogether and held him suspended there, above his lap. Paulo hated this part; the part where Winterberry usually made him beg for the fuck. And he always did beg for it.

"Sam, Sam, please," Paulo murmured.

"Tell me you want it," Winterberry muttered.

"Please, Sam. You know I want it."

With a guttural laugh, Winterberry slammed Paulo down on his cock again and finished him quickly. But Winterberry wasn't finished; he fucked on, and Paulo was vindicated in knowing, from Winterberry's groans and moans, that he wanted to be finished too. Paulo did a good enough job that, in his loss in the fuck, Winterberry had raised up and set Paulo back into the facing seat and was fucking hard down into his channel with Paulo's legs waving in the air at the fountaining of Winterberry's cum into the head of the condom buried deep in the younger, lithe man.

Twenty minutes after that, they were both cleaned and clothed and sitting opposite each other in the rear cabin of the Challenger 604 once more.

"I wanted to be sure you were the right choice, Paulo. That you still could deliver in positions like this. You did well, so we can precede. You must know that I wasn't sure. I have a backup on the plane. If I hadn't been sure of you, I might have gone with Manuel."

"The assignment?" Paulo asked. He wasn't about to salivate all over Sam Winterberry about having had to prove himself worthy.

"We'll be landing at the Simon Bolivar airport in a couple of hours, Paulo. El Presidente, Eduardo Labarca, has become a bit too big for his britches and critical of U.S. society and policies. We are to bring him down a few notches."

"And so he's the target?"

"Our real target is his wife, Suzanne. Labarca is only president because of the support of his wife's brother, Jorge

Facendo, commander of the armed forces. Labarca is a figurehead, but his anti-U.S. rantings have brought attention and business away from the United States to his country, so Facendo and friends seem delighted. We want to use the emotions of Suzanne Labarca to drive enough of a wedge in this happy family for them to squabble between themselves and forget us—but we don't want to upset the apple cart completely. Labarca isn't the most unsatisfactory choice the forces of Facendo could be backing."

"I don't do women," Paulo answered.

"No, that's not the plan. We want you to do Labarca. He's spending much of his time with his mistress at the presidential retreat near the Macuto seaside resort. We have arranged for you to be his chauffeur for those trysts, and we have outfitted the limousine with pinpoint video cameras and bugs. We expect you to seduce him and give us good video and audio during the drives back and forth to his mistress."

"I don't understand. If he has a mistress, why do you need me? Just put the cameras in their love nest. And what miracle do you wish me to perform with a man who has both a wife and a mistress already?"

"Labarca has the mistress—and the wife, for that matter—because that's what's expected in society down there. We know from his earlier history that not only does he prefer men but also that, before it was inconvenient, he went wild over your type. Photographs and videos of Labarca with a mistress shown to the wife and her military power brother would get nothing more than a smile; the same photographs and videos of Labarca fucking you will be incendiary in his social circles and should set his wife to clawing—not enough to get him ousted, because she also wants the position, but enough to disrupt his yammering at the United States. That Suzanne Labarca is a real tiger."

"That's it?" Paulo asked.

"Yes, that's it. Not a nuclear bomb; just a little attitude adjustment south of the border. We can be in and out as soon as you have gotten Labarca to be in and out inside that limousine. And speaking of in and out, we are finished here and you may return to the main cabin. Oh, and will you ask for Manuel up there and send him back here, please."

Manuel was a younger version of Paulo, a Mestizo, with an engaging dusky complexion contrasted with blond-tipped hair and blue eyes and with a more hopeful, innocent look about him than Paulo could manage after his time on the job. Manuel also was a noise maker. Paulo sat in the main cabin, listening to the sounds of Manuel's reaction to the testing Sam Winterberry was giving him in the rear cabin and, like the other agents on the plane, pretending not to hear anything. The long, drawn-out moanings Manuel subsided into, though, grated on Paulo's nerves. As much of a bastard as he thought Winterberry was and as much as Paulo would like to be able to resist being taken by the spy master, he had to admit that the man gave a superior cocking, and Paulo's ass twitched in regret that the moans were coming from Manuel and not from he himself.

* * * *

The first things Paulo noticed about El Presidente, Eduardo Labarca, were his arrogance and his complete self-absorption. He was not a handsome man, but he spent a lot of time on the sculpting of his body in the gym, and he spent a considerable portion of the country's treasury on his clothing and musky scents and haircuts and manicures. He carried himself like a president of a tin horn country as well, which, pretty much, was what he was. He wore a military uniform he hadn't earned covered with gold braid and medals that he couldn't even identify.

But Paulo determined immediately that he could be manipulated if the circumstances were right.

Paulo thought the wife and brother-in-law, on the other hand, were hard as steel and cold as icebergs. They were scary. The brother-in-law, in particular, was a towering, big-boned and –muscled hulk, who looked like he not only could, but would, with great pleasure, break a man in two on whim.

Paulo didn't envy El Presidente's position when those photographs and videos were presented to the scary duo, and he hoped that he himself would be well away before then. But he didn't think that getting the photographs would be difficult. He saw that Labarca was interested in him from the first time El Presidente descended the steps of the presidential palace and entered the Bentley.

Paulo was grateful, though, that Labarca always was driven to his mistress's place in Macuto incognito and without guards. Paulo was his chauffeur for this trip purpose only, and the Bentley was not the presidential limousine.

Labarca's sexual attraction to Paulo was registered almost immediately—whenever Paulo looked in the rear-view mirror, he saw Labarca licking his lips and looking back with slitted eyes—but Paulo had to use dynamite to move to the bottom line.

Paulo had been expertly fitted out with a chauffeur's uniform that was form fitting and left little to the imagination, and Paulo always was suggestively posed on a fender when Labarca approached the car—legs spread and hands near the crotch—and spoke to him in a submissive, sultry voice. And he touched Labarca when he was handing him into the plush, commodious backseat of the car. But, beyond the looks and the slowdown while looking as he approached the Bentley, Labarca wasn't making a move.

So, Paulo created his own move. On a rural stretch of a scenic back road drive between the presidential palace and Macuto one day, one of the tires on the Bentley went. Paulo had fiddled with the tire to make sure enough air seeped out of it for it to blow at approximately the point he preferred, and the tire cooperated.

"Conveniently," neither of the men had cell phones that day. Paulo had purposely left his behind, and he'd gotten Winterberry to arrange for a planted agent in the presidential palace to let the battery run down on the cell phone kept in the president's briefcase.

"I can fix the tire, sir, or I could walk for help. That would leave you alone out here, though."

"You can fix the tire?" Labarca said.

"I can change it out, sir. But it would be dirty work. If you didn't mind, I could do it if I put my uniform to the side. Oh, and could you hold the car keys for me?"

This idea suited Labarca just fine, and when he looked down at the keys Paulo had handed him, he smiled. The tag of the chain they were on had two male symbols interlocked. Labarca knew what that meant.

Paulo stripped down to just his briefs and boots, and Labarca stood there, panting, as Paulo showed off his muscles and grace to the best advantage as he worked. He had the tire changed just as soon as he knew Labarca was hooked.

Paulo tossed the spent tire into the trunk and came around the side of the Bentley and stood there, while the two eyed each other.

"Do you really want me to put my uniform back on, sir?" Paulo asked with a smile. "Or would you prefer we do something about that bulge in your pants."

"I . . . I want to fuck you," Labarca said in a strangled voice.

"I am at your service, President," Paulo said with a sultry smile, as he slowly pulled his briefs down his legs.

They fucked in the backseat of the limousine, Paulo lapped and rising and falling on Labarca's throbbing cock—and Paulo trying not to laugh at the memory of his testing by Winterberry in the same positions. He understood now that his coupling with Winterberry in the plane really had been a test connected with the operation—the mechanics of fucking in the backseat of a car. The musky scent Labarca used signaled to Paulo correctly, and he lifted his arms, one at a time, over El Presidente's face as they fucked and Labarca went wild at sniffing and tonguing the sweat in Paulo's pits.

At Winterberry's instruction, Paulo repeated the photo-session fuckings in the Bentley three times more in the next month—and Labarca loosened up to the encounters progressively more each time. He now sat in the front seat when Paulo drove him away from the presidential palace and played with Paulo's cock and nipples while they drove. When they reached a rural spot, Labarca pulled Paulo over on his lap and fucked him there. The third time Paulo wore briefs that

131

hadn't been washed in a couple of days and that he had masturbated into, and Labarca went ape over those, putting his face into Paulo's lap as he drove and sniffing and sucking on Paulo's cock. The president kept the briefs.

Even the mistress seemed to be pleased. When Paulo picked Labarca up in Macuto now, the mistress came to the door with El Presidente and was all over him. Obviously Labarca's escapades in the Bentley translated well to his performance with the mistress.

Paulo avoided consummation—at least Labarca's—on the return trips to the palace in the capital, and by the third trip home, the dragonslaying Suzanne was also meeting Labarca at the door with a smile.

For a brief time of less than a month, everyone seemed to be getting happier and happier. But the operational plan was to lower the boom.

* * * *

Even the best of intelligence operation plans have their flaws, and it sometime seems that the simpler the plan, the bigger the snafu.

In the case of this plan, when the boom was lowered, no one bothered to tell Paulo.

"You delivered the photos and videos this morning?" said Agent A.

"Yes, at 9:00 a.m., just as you directed," Agent B answered, turning to Winterberry and addressing the answer to him.

"I said tomorrow, idiot, not today. Somebody get Paulo on his cell phone," Winterberry barked.

"He never took it back after that time he didn't want to have it," answered Agent A.

"Oh, fuck," Winterberry growled. "Somebody get our asset in the palace on the phone and have him tell Pulido to clear out of there pronto."

But before anyone could do that, Paulo had been dispatched from the garages with the Bentley to the side entrance to the palace.

When Paulo stood by the rear door and opened it at the first flurry of activity inside the side door to the palace, out stepped El Presidente's brother-in-law, Gen. Jorge Facendo. And he looked like he was about to kill something.

Paulo trembled as he held the door for the general, having no idea why there was a change in routine, fearing the worst—that the operation had been uncovered.

"Where to?" he asked, trying to keep his voice calm, when he was behind the wheel.

"Toward the coast," growled the general. "I'll give you directions as we get closer."

The general directed Paulo off the main road when they got near the coast, over a rough track where no Bentley sedan should be expected to travel, and into a grove of trees at the top of a cliff from where the thundering surf could be heard even through the closed car windows with the air conditioning going.

Paulo had a premonition that this was probably one of the general's personal killing zones, and the jig most definitely was up for him.

"Get out of the car and strip and climb into the back," the general barked, and he had a gun to back up his demand.

The general totally and cruelly fucked Paulo for more than an hour in the back of the Bentley, rocking the heavy car back and forth on its springs, exercising the Bentley in ways it never had been exercised before.

The general also exercised Paulo well and made full use of the young man's flexibility. He took him with knees under Paulo's butt as Paulo laid across the backseat, with feet scrabbling for purchase on window frames and the roof of the car, and the general's hands on Paulo's throat. And he took Paulo bent over the short-backed center section of the front seat, with Facendo's back pressed to the ceiling and his cock pistoning hard and deep inside Paulo's channel and the general's chocking arm around Paulo's neck. And he took Paulo with Paulo's knees on the floor and his chest and cheek pressed into the back of the rear seat, the general's fists grabbing Paulo's hips and his cock pounding Paulo's canal from behind. And when Paulo was exhausted, the general sat back in the seat, with Paulo facing him and lapped and the general slowly pumping Paulo up and down on his miraculously fast-rejuvenating cock by wrapping his fists around the young spy's waist and lifting him up and down on his cock and Paulo flopping around like a rag doll. And then he made Paulo suck him off.

When they were finished, Paulo had come three times and the general four, and the floor of the backseat was littered with used condoms.

"Now you will drive me back to the palace," the general said, still waving his gun. "There you will be put under guard. But tomorrow I want you to pick me up at the same time and drive me back here. We bring guards. And today was just a taste. Tomorrow I fuck you so good; you won't be able to walk for a week—if we bring you back at all. And when I'm done, I'll give you to the guards. Then we'll find out who you work for and why."

* * * *

Three intersecting elements were on Paulo Pulido's side. Sam Winterberry saw that Paulo still had usefulness to the Agency's Candy Store program, the Americans had an asset embedded in the presidential palace, and when Paulo drove him back to the presidential palace, General Facendo was immediately embroiled in an ongoing slugfest between El Presidente and his wife and then he and his sister and his brother-in-law over what the general was doing out on the road with the chauffeur in the damaging photos and he forgot to place a guard on Paulo soon enough.

Paulo was whisked away from the presidential compound, the operation marked as a glowing success—not only accomplishing its original mission but collecting incriminating videos on General Facendo as well. And the Challenger 604 corporate jet, with Paulo in the forward cabin, was lifting off from Simon Bolivar airport before the radiator of the Bentley had cooled down, let alone the libidos of the president and general he'd left behind.

Once again, the jet zoomed right up to 45,000 feet and leveled off, and Paulo was only a third finished with the flute of champagne the cute little cabin steward had handed him before one of the other agents came out of the rear cabin and walked over to Paulo's seat.

"Mr. Winterberry would like you to join him in the rear cabin," he said. He could hardly keep the smirk off his face.

Paulo rose and sighed and started toward the rear cabin, knowing that another meeting of the Eight Mile High Club was about to convene. "He probably will even tell me it's my reward for an assignment well done," Paulo thought.

Ethiopian Cabin Boy

To my surprise, when I was training for intelligence gathering, I discovered that my line of work wasn't as pristine sexually as I had tried to convince myself it was. I should already have been aware of this, as I had already gotten hints of my spy masters looking the other direction during my assignment to Bangkok when it pleased them to do so. And in my training, I learned that they could be pleased to do so if the intelligence needed was considered very important and when the options of "getting the goods" were restricted.

I was sent into the Middle East and stationed in Cyprus, which is now considered in relationship to the Middle East somewhat like Switzerland was considered to Europe in World War II—a safe haven where spies can meet on neutral ground and where it is considered ungentlemanly (although it does happen on occasion) for "wet" (meaning doing someone to death) operations to be conducted. And it wasn't long before I learned how far I might be expected to go to "get the goods" in my job. It was also where I quickly found a new answer to one of three questions that had perpetually come up in the world of "bottoms" in my Bangkok days: This question was "What was your longest?" One of the other questions, "What was your thickest?," would also be answered when I lived on Cyprus, but during a different tour a decade later. The remaining question—"What was the most satisfying?"—had already been answered years earlier in Bangkok in the form of a black Army officer (who, with his ten by two dimensions, almost answered the other two questions as well).

The "longest" question was answered in the form of an Ethiopian cabin boy on the yacht of a Saudi businessman at anchor off the Larnaka waterfront. This promenade, very European in atmosphere, enjoyed a deep, flat beach separated from a long hotel and sidewalk café front of gaily decorated umbrellas and tables by a wide boulevard. The boulevard was anchored at one end by a yacht marina and at the other by the medieval harbor castle where Richard the Lionhearted doubled back on his way to the Crusades and married his shipwrecked Berengaria.

After our encounter, the Ethiopian had me singing a couple of octaves higher than normal and walking around tenderly—although the later part might have been caused by the escapades later that night. I can't attest to how long the Ethiopian's cock was, but both my eyes and my intestines are quite sure they've never seen or felt a longer one.

When he took me, we were in a lower-deck cabin of the yacht, where you couldn't stand up straight except in the middle of the room. A double berth went in under the bulkhead. The Saudi owner of the yacht and I had just agreed on some successful business of a nefarious government nature, and the Saudi had been very attentive to me and let me know he wanted to fuck me. I had met him at a couple of embassy cocktail parties earlier and apparently had made a very favorable impression on him. I could tell by the way he looked at me that he fancied me, but I didn't make the connection at the time when I was assigned to contact him. My spy masters wanted the deal to go well, and I had been told to do whatever it took to conclude the deal—and I subsequently came to assume that my masters knew exactly what the Saudi businessman was interested in getting in return for his vital information. So, when he so directly propositioned me and connected it with his willingness to provide what I had come for, I said I would sleep with him that night on the yacht. Clearly delighted, he responded that, in appreciation, he'd send me a gift before dinner.

An Ethiopian cabin boy—not a "boy," of course, but an adult young man—had been gliding around the yacht all day as it wallowed off the colorful Larnaka waterfront, doing this and that. He was incredibly tall and thin, really out of place on a yacht with cramped head room, even if it was large. When I opened the door of my cabin to him, he was carrying a tray with a bottle of champagne and one glass on it, but I knew right away that he was my gift, because he was nude. His pecker hung down almost to his knees, it seemed—and this thighs were unusually long in themselves. I had never really thought about whether the unusual height on some African tribesmen had a relationship to dimensions elsewhere, but just then my education in that department lengthened considerably.

There was no thought of me refusing this gift from the Saudi; he hadn't given me the promised information yet, and this was no time to rock the boat—other than the rocking the Ethiopian was about to do with his performance on my body, of course.

I was still in just my Speedo, so there wasn't much undressing required. The tray also had a bottle of KY and a couple of condom packets on it, and the Ethiopian just slid off my Speedo and knelt there and sucked me hard, while pulling his own meat to erection. I fell back onto the bed, which was low to the floor, while he lathered himself and my hole up and rolled on a condom. He wishboned my legs up and out and I dug my feet into the low bulkhead that stretched out over the berth. He then knelt between my legs and just fed and fed and fed and fed that long eleven- or twelve-incher up into me.

At first he moved my hand to my ass and had me cup my fingers there so that he was pushing his cock through my cupped fingers, giving him a hand job as well as him giving me an ass fuck, when he entered me. I gasped as he reached a depth inside me I'd rarely felt before even though he had to go three inches through my fingers before entering me. But he laughed hoarsely as I panted and moaned to accommodate him. And then he brushed my hand away and I arched my back and cried out my astonishment and passion as he just dug deeper and deeper inside me. It wasn't all that painful, because his cock was pretty thin, but he had to have gotten well up into my intestines and stretched them out where they'd never been touched by an object coming from that direction before.

I looked up as he was doing this, and the Saudi was lounging in the doorway, watching me get royally fucked. The Ethiopian pumped me that way for a while and then turned me over on my belly and got that cock even farther up into me, reeling it all out and then just slamming all the way back in repeatedly until he needed to come. And he withdrew then, ripped the condom off, and shot off all over the small of my back. I was digging my fists into the bedding as best I could to hold position while he jackhammered into me. I'd already come twice by then myself, once with the help of his mouth and then with the help of his hand.

The Saudi just stood there and watched with slitted eyes, and he kept his hand busy with his own cock. His "gift" to me was even more another gift to himself. He really wanted his entertainment worth for those precious secrets he held, and the long, long Ethiopian and I gave him quite a show.

That night the Saudi and his bulky bodyguard did me in a sandwich in an all-night fuck fest in the main cabin, which was not nearly as cramped as mine was. The Saudi's equipment was nothing to write home about and he came quickly, but the bodyguard had a really thick piece and was a fast reloader and had a vigorous, long-endurance pelvis action. Lots of nice muscle. He's probably the one who was responsible for my bowed legs and shuffling walk—and big smile—the next day.

They did me in turn. Then, as a finale, the Saudi really wanted to get his cock in there with the bodyguard's, but I wasn't having any of that, needed secrets or not. The bodyguard alone was much too thick.

I never did drink the champagne, and I can only surmise that the information I collected was worth my effort—at least my masters were well pleased when I returned, and they asked me no questions about my use of trade craft in getting the goods.

Hidden Flute

It took three concerts for him to notice me. Luckily it was getting progressively warmer in Munich's spring. I had every reason to believe I'd have to attend the full season of the free outdoor concerts in the Hofgarten park before I could meet him. If I'd settled on this flutist in the fall instead, each time I had to come back would have been progressively worse.

It would have helped if I initially enjoyed flute music. I'd certainly had my fill of young men playing the flute professionally in Bavaria. I was fairly certain, though, that this was the young man for me.

He had an air of melancholy about him that I found alluring when matched with the mournful sound of his instrument, which, in his hands, was nothing like the flute music I'd heard before. I could see the attraction of him. He was probably in his mid twenties. He was small and willowy and had an angelic face. His eyes were a watery blue, his skin the glowing alabaster of the serious scholar, and he had a northern European blondness about him that was belied by jet black, curly hair on his head. It was this mystery about him that had attracted me to him in the first place—an incongruity in his appearance. This was accentuated the second concert I attended, where he managed quite well reading his music without the eyeglasses he wore for the first and third concerts.

Could it be, I wondered, that he was really a blond?

He seemed a young man hiding from something. At first I thought maybe it was from life itself he seemed so withdrawn into himself as he played his flute in concert. But then I thought it perhaps was something more earthborn, something that spoke to me in my quest. And thus I stopped attending on other orchestra performers and concentrated on this one.

He did notice me in the third concert—as I wanted him to. I sat as close to him as I could—in the seat next to the one I had occupied for the second concert. I would have sat in the very same seat if it had been available when I arrived for the concert. And I wore the same clothes for both concerts.

I watched him intently throughout the entire performance, and when he finally looked at me, with a startled look of recognition of someone there was no reason he should recognize, I smiled at him.

After the concert was over, I remained in my seat as those in the audience as well as those in the orchestra on the bandstand gathered their belongings and moved to depart.

The young man was slow to pack up his flute. I had noticed this in the first two concerts also. He moved slowly, deliberately, and I could see that he winced from time to time. He seemed to be suffering from some sort of malady that caused pain in the movement of his extremities. He was far too young to be arthritic, I thought. But I also thought that this added an attraction of vulnerability and mystery to the young man.

I wanted him. I wanted to take him in my arms and gently make love to him. But that was only a surface want. I wanted to crush and possess him—to bring passion to those eyes. He played his flute with deep passion; even I could tell that. But his face, as beautiful as it was, seemed dead even while he was playing. I wanted to bring passion to that face to match his music. And I wanted to do it by possessing his body and making him beg to have me inside him. I could see how he would have this effect on other men. I increasingly was sure he was the one I sought.

"You play beautifully."

"*Danke*," he said.

Ah, I thought. Not really Suddeutch—southern German—a northern dialect. More Nordic, as I thought.

He had thanked me, but he hadn't looked up from putting his flute away in its case. And he spoke in a soft, shy voice.

"I like it so much that I've come to all of your concerts in the park this season."

"I noticed." There was a blush on his cheeks, and he looked up at me and smiled. It wasn't making me want him any less.

"Would you . . . would you care to have a coffee with me in a café nearby?" I asked. "I would like to discuss your music further. I know of a quintet a banker has play on salon evenings that needs a good flutist. Perhaps—"

"Sorry, I have a commitment . . . a class . . . to attend. Sorry."

"Ah, you are a university student then? Studying music perhaps?"

"Yes. Yes, of course."

"Ah. I am a professor myself. But not music. My university has a very good music department, though. Perhaps—"

"I'm sorry. I'm late now. Maybe another time."

"Maybe no time, are you saying? Can you look at me, please?"

He looked up then, and I could see that I wasn't unattractive to him.

"You looked so sad," I continued. "I thought you might like to have a little company. Someone to talk to. You don't have many friends here, do you? You're not from here, are you?"

"I'm Dutch. And I do prefer staying to myself, yes. I don't mean to be rude, but—"

"I believe you would enjoy having a friend. I won't press. But I will come to all of your concerts until you decide you might like to join me for that coffee."

After the fifth concert he followed me to the Café Wein, where other musicians gathered and that specialized in playing Mozart in the background. It had threatened rain at the park as he was putting his flute away, and the elements gave him very little time to hedge when I offered him the coffee again.

"Your accent doesn't sound quite Dutch to me," I inserted into otherwise innocuous chitchat, which had included passing conversations with a couple of men I had paid to address me as "professor" and make remarks on my brilliance in musical critique.

"I've only really been to the Netherlands on holidays. I was born and raised in Central Africa. My family . . ."

But he stopped there, his voice having choked up on the word family, and he turned his head from me. He didn't do so, though, quick enough for me not to see the tearing up in his eyes.

I moved deftly into another topic—on where he had traveled in the world. I might have asked him why he'd left Africa and come to be here in southern Germany. But I increasingly thought I knew, and it might not have gone well for me to pursue that point. I was sure I knew, but I was not positive. I needed to be positive.

"Have you given any thought to the quintet I mentioned? The banker pays well, and they are quite good—I've heard them several times."

"Yes, I might be interested, thanks."

Here was the crux. "I have the information in my rooms, which aren't far from here—in fact between here and the direction of your university. You could stop in and pick the contact number up."

"Or you could bring the information to the next concert," he countered.

"Alas I'm sure they will have filled the chair by then. There is another salon night soon, and they have little time."

When we reached the apartment I had let by the week, having arrived here from Africa myself not more than a month earlier, I sat him at my small dining table with a bottle of cold beer and retreated to my bedchamber. When I reemerged, I had changed into a short cotton robe and held a slip of paper with a number that would connect to one of the men I'd hired—who would tell him "So, sorry, we have found a flutist" on the off chance the young man would have an opportunity to call. And in the other hand was a bottle of excellent Scotch whiskey. Although the young flutist looked a bit shocked—and like a deer in the headlights of an automobile—he didn't rise from the table.

I set the paper and bottle down on the table and lifted his chin with my cupped hand so that his face was staring into mine. And I took a chance and took his lips in mine.

His mouth was dead at first, but slowly, hungrily he yielded to me. I had gambled that underneath that shell he was frustrated and wanted to lie with me. The kiss confirmed this.

He was paralyzed by the situation, though. He was trembling and tearing up and seemed not to be able to stand on his own when I pulled him up from the chair. He didn't resist, but he gave nothing of himself either.

I took him in my arms and carried him into the bedchamber and laid him on my bed. I stood over him and let the cotton robe I was wearing fall to the floor. He whimpered at the sight of my nakedness, which I knew was not displeasing to a man wanting to be fucked by another man. I could see a spark in his eyes now, but his lips were murmuring "No, please not . . ."

"Shush," I whispered. "Just relax. And let me comfort you. I know there is something. Something wrong. I don't think it is that you don't want me. Let me comfort you."

I lay down beside him on the bed and took him in my embrace. He didn't fight me, but, again, he made no move of acceptance either. Only detached acquiescence. I would not be defeated, though. I hummed to him and rocked him in my arms.

"When you can speak of it. Tell me. Tell me what is a barrier to us making love. I know you want to." I had moved my hand under the waistband of his trousers and briefs and had found assurance that he wanted me. "This tells me that you want me. You have lain with another man before, haven't you?"

"Yes." It sounded bitter, almost defiant.

"And men have made love to you, haven't they?"

"No." Even harder, more bitter.

145

"You have never had a man's cock inside you?"

"I didn't say that."

"Ah, you have been taken by force then. Is that it?"

"Yes."

"In Africa?"

"Yes."

I had opened his trousers and unbuttoned his shirt by now, and I was gently fondling him with my hands—the hand of the arm I was embracing him with was stroking a nipple and the other hand was gliding along his belly and down to his cock and balls. He was relaxing a bit and was softly moaning—although I'm not sure he even realized I was already preparing him. Or that he was letting me do it.

"Perhaps if you give voice to it, let the demons out, it would be the start of healing. I am not forcing you, am I?"

"No."

"And it is giving you pleasure, isn't it? Pleasure you haven't had in some time. Pleasure you need."

He didn't answer, but I didn't give him much time or opportunity to do so. I had moved my lips to his again, and he was opening to me, letting me possess him. And then, for the first time reciprocating in the kiss, hungrily sucking on my tongue and groaning. I could feel the melting of the iceberg that had been him in the engorging of his cock in my hand.

"Tell me," I whispered when I released his lips. I had to know for sure. "Tell me of this sadness and bitterness inside you."

He lay there for several minutes, not saying anything, but his eyes held mine and his hips were beginning to roll with my slow pumping of his cock with my fist.

I was going to fuck him. I knew that. And now he knew that as well—and he was resolved to it.

"Have you heard of William Jason? Major William Jason?" the young man suddenly asked.

"Yes, I believe so. Central Africa."

"Yes, when he and his regiment mutinied and took over the government, they paid special attention to the Dutch-descendent farmers."

"You? Your family?"

"Yes." It was a whisper.

"You don't have to tell me. You can just let me make love to you and make the memory of it go away," I murmured. And indeed, he didn't have to tell me. Now I knew for sure.

But having started, he let it out as if a mighty river had burst the damning of his soul. "As they lay in wait to attack our farm, they must have heard me practicing my flute. Otherwise I would have been dead too. Who would have known that the butcher, William Jason, was a classical music lover?"

He laughed an ugly, bitter laugh, and I took his lips in mine again to keep from losing him. I had retrieved a tube of lube from my nightstand that I had left there open and I was lubricating his channel with my fingers. And he was letting me do it.

When I released his lips, though, he continued with the story. "When I was the last one, cowering in a corner, the major pushed his way through the semicircle of soldiers backing me into the wall. He is a monster of a man, you know. Gigantic in every way. He fucked me for the first time then— brutally. Not caring that I had never done it before. Then he informed me that I played the flute divinely. He used that word. 'Divinely.' It was shocking to hear from the lips of such a monster. He said he was taking me back to the palace with him, and that I would play for him. And not just the flute."

"Shush. Enough. I want to make love to you now."

"He had a special chamber—more than one—that he'd set up in the basement of the palace. Of course, as far as I knew his predecessor had had the chambers too. I was strung up every which way over the next months—and taken in every way he could think of. He laughed once, telling me that all I needed to play the flute for him were my lips and my fingers. He broke everything else in my body in his rough sex torture. You may not have noticed, but I move slowly and deliberately. I am in nearly constant pain. That is what he gave me."

"I will be gentle. Here, this will be comfortable enough, won't it?" I had moved between his thighs with my knees. His legs were bent and I placed pillows under the small of his back to raise his hips to me. I presented the bulb of my cock at his now-loosened and lubricated hole and gently pressed in. He groaned for me, but he gripped the sides of my torso as I was hovered over him. And he moved his pelvis, drawing me inside him himself.

He sucked in his breath and moaned deeply as my cock head disappeared inside him. I held there. "Am I hurting you?"

"Yes. No. Please. Oh, god. Ohhh, ohhhh, ahhhh."

I was inside him and he was opening to me as I slowly sank deeper and deeper.

"I escaped," he said in a low, breathy voice. "Those who helped me, paid for it. My freedom was their death. Yet another guilt I must bear. But I was alive. I ran and ran. And I hid. I dyed my hair, changed my appearance as much as I could. Came to Europe to forge a new life."

"Relax. Go with me. I'll love all of those memories into the back of your mind."

I began to slow pump him.

"Oh, god, oh god, ahhhh."

Later I sat there in a chair, looking at the bed, as the young man slept the sleep of the fully satisfied, exhausted by a master cocking.

I almost regretted it, but there was nothing to be done about it now.

"What? I can't! Why?" he muttered as he slowly came to. "Why am I bound?"

His wrists were handcuffed through the strong slats of my headboard and his ankles were handcuffed as well.

"I'm sorry about that," I answered in a voice that I hoped conveyed as much regret as I felt. "I'm really sorry. But the Major sent me to find you. He wants you back."

* * * *

Later, as I sat alone in my rented room and finished off the bottle of Scotch, I made the decision that I needed to find another way to earn my money. I had become too hard, too uncaring. But now I had gone too soft to be of use to the clients who sought me out. I would, of course, tell the Major that I had scoured Munich for his flutist without luck—that he must have been given bad information, or that the young man

148

had already moved on. I would tell him that I certainly was willing to follow up any other lead he might have, but that it probably wasn't worth the money he was paying.

Of all my regrets, the deepest one was not asking the young flutist where he would flee to next—so that there was always a chance I might meet, and have, him again. But if I knew the Major as well as I thought I did, it was probably best I really didn't know—in the likely event that the Major didn't believe me.

Hostage to Need

Drake looked through the picture window of the prefab and rubbed his eyes against the desert sun. Why did they have a picture window in the conference room of the administrative building at all, he wondered. Why not a cooling Alpine scene mural on a blank wall? All he could see was sand and sun and blue sky—and the plumbing equipment for natural gas extraction spreading for miles. He guessed that Wyatt in BG headquarters wanted his people not to forget what they were here for—what possessed them for eighteen-month tours in the sand at a crack.

Drake had only been here as the site manager for five months. He wasn't sure how he was going to survive the next thirteen. But then the canteen waiter, Khalil, glided by with his tray of tea and what Drake knew as cookies but that the bulk of the British work force out here called biscuits, and he thought perhaps he'd do all right on this tour.

This bleak corner of Arab desert was isolated and Drake was king here.

He leaned over to the chief of finance sitting on his right while others at the table were distracted with their tea orders. Their tea orders, Drake thought with a grimace before whispering his questions to Stan. He thought he'd go mad if they didn't start serving anything stronger at these staff meetings. At least Khalil knew to bring him coffee straightaway at the beginning of the meeting and then watch the cup to make sure it didn't go less than half full.

"Did the package arrive?" he whispered to Stanley.

"Yes, and it's in your special account. You know I could do the transfers to the Swiss bank, if—"

"I know you could, Stan, but the home office is more antsy about this than anything else. Only I'm permitted to know the account number."

"More coffee, sir?" Khalil asked as he leaned down from Drake's other side. For a moment their eyes met and there was a flash of something in Khalil's eyes. It affected Drake somewhat lower in his body.

"Thank you, Khalil. I think that will be all for now. Sami can handle the service for the rest of the meeting, I think. The meeting won't be long. You can proceed to your ancillary duties."

Khalil smiled, bowed to Drake, and backed away.

"Now, Margaret, about the production figures for the week . . . oh, yes, what is it John?"

The chief of facilities security had his hand raised. "Sorry, Drake, to break into the agenda, but we have a spot of concern in the western field, I think."

A "spot of concern," Drake thought. From his somewhat droll British chief of securities, this could mean anything from a hangnail on the secretary he was fucking to an invasion of this shaky Arab state they were operating in by its voracious neighbor.

"Yes, John, what is it?"

"Well, the thing is, that we haven't actually heard from the perimeter guards on the western fence . . . well, for twice the amount of time they are routinely assigned to check in. And we haven't been able to establish—"

"The commo equipment must have broken down," Drake interjected. If he let John ramble on like that, they could be here until nightfall. "This would be the third time this week. They sent us shit for commo equipment. Just send a patrol out to them with equipment replacements."

"We did that—an hour ago, but we haven't actually—"

152

"Just let me know when the western quadrant is back on line," Drake broke in. He had wanted this meeting to be short. There was something else he wanted to be doing. "Margaret, could we have those figures quickly, please? I have a scheduled call with London that I need to get to."

Drake was looking out over the gas extraction field, toward the west, as he walked the glass corridor connecting this building with the cross hall built against the residential trailers. The complex had been designed so every corner of it could be accessed without going out into the searing heat. He didn't see anything over to the west that should cause any alarm—maybe a dust cloud, but that wasn't anything unusual. He regretted a bit being so short with John, but the man's verbosity, combined with his stuffed British pomposity, just rubbed Drake the wrong way. He wondered if he could get the man replaced without much fuss. John had a good eight months left on his tour here. And Drake was sure he'd be a pain in the ass right up to the day he left. He didn't seem to be able to just handle these little problems on his own. He seemed to need to shove decisions on them into Drake's lap. And Drake had enough decisions he himself had to make already.

Speaking of which, he wasn't that wild about having to personally deposit the baksheesh in the Swiss bank for the hush-hush member of the ruling committee of this godforsaken backwater Arab country to cover the privilege of BG extracting gas. He much preferred having cutouts to do this and being able to enjoy deniability. It irritated him that he was expected to provide Wyatt's deniability and no one was providing any for him. Of course no one out here other than Stan and the ruling committee member knew anything about the arrangements.

Drake entered his trailer's living room and went straight to the bar and poured himself a stiff scotch on the rocks, downed it at one go, and then splashed another shot of scotch into the glass. He undid and removed his tie and then pulled the tails of his dress shirt out of his trousers, unbuttoned his shirt, and pulled it off his back. He turned to the mirror on the wall next to the bar and flexed his chest and bicep muscles and did a critical examination. He'd only been out here for five months, but the boredom of the place had already shown great dividends in the definition his body had gotten from the increased gym time. He was pleased with himself, with the look of himself.

Tossing the shirt and tie into a chair, kicking his loafers off, and clinking the ice in his scotch glass as he walked, he continued on into the bedroom.

Khalil was sitting, demurely covered in the white cotton robe the Arabs called a *thawb*, at the end of the bed. He was barefoot and was looking down at the hands folded in his lap and didn't look up when Drake entered.

Drake felt himself going hard. A man and yet still so much like a boy, Khalil was a dark beauty with brown eyes flecked with hazel, and black, curly hair. Although less than average in stature, Drake well knew that he was beautifully formed and proportioned and that his dusky skin had a luminosity about it that nearly took Drake's breath away.

Khalil had known from the beginning what his ancillary duties would be. BG knew their managers very well. And Drake had only taken the post knowing that his personal needs would be met. Drake was a valuable manager. Plus he knew where too many of the skeletons were buried in BG headquarters. He had a physical need that required constant attention, and his superiors were willing to feed that need. They had supplied Khalil fully knowing how Drake would use him. At the same time, providing him for Drake was their hold that kept Drake from taking his talents to another company that wouldn't be so understanding of his special needs.

Drake went around the side of the bed, to a nightstand. He took another swig of his scotch and then put the drink down and opened the nightstand drawer. He extracted a bottle of lubrication, a couple of packets of condoms, and the leather straps he liked to use for restraints. Then he came around to the side of the bed and placed these on the bedspread next to where Khalil was seated.

Neither men said anything. Khalil continued looking down at his hands. Drake could see that there as a slight smile on his face, though. Drake reached down and gathered up the material of the thawb on either side of Khalil's waist and pulled the garment over his head. He took his breath in again at the beauty of the young body. Khalil was naked under the thawb.

When he was naked, Khalil, still looking down, lifted his hands, the wrists held together, knowing the ritual. Drake tied the wrists together. Then he walked around to the side of the bed and took another slug of scotch. On the walk back, he unbuckled his belt, unzipped his trousers, and flared the fly out. Standing in front of Khalil, he put his hands on the back of the curly black hair of Khalil's head and pushed his now-erect cock between Khalil's lips.

Khalil gave him head for several minutes while Drake threw his head back and let the tensions of the day dissolve.

When he felt that nothing else was in his mind but sexual pleasure, Drake pulled his trousers and briefs down off his legs, sat down on the bed, and pulled Khalil's slight body over into his lap. His cock was long enough that he came up from underneath and between Khalil's thighs, pushing between the young man's balls and pressing up under his own cock.

Drake could work both cocks together, which he proceeded to do, while turning Khalil's torso sideways against his own chest and arching it back with Khalil's bound arms over his head. This position gave Drake free mouth, lips, and teeth access to Khalil's mouth, the hollow of his neck, and his pert nipples, which Drake proceeded to work along with the two cocks, until, writhing and groaning and moaning, Khalil ejaculated.

Drake had also been working Khalil's ass entrance with lubricated fingers. After Khalil had come, therefore, Drake had to lift and slightly readjust the young Arab's pelvis a bit before he could place the bulb of his now-sheathed cock at the hole and begin to work inside.

Khalil was babbling something unintelligible in Arabic as Drake turned him so that the young man's legs were split by Drake's pelvis and Khalil was arched out over the carpeted floor at the foot of the bed. Drake pulled and pushed Khalil's torso back and forth on his cock until he had ejaculated, in the first real sense of release he'd had all day.

Khalil was panting and whimpering and half sobbing, and Drake pulled him up to his chest, embraced him closely, and kissed him on the mouth and the cheeks and on his neck and shoulders while Khalil's trembling slowly decreased . . . and while Drake felt the juices in his body reboiling and himself getting hard again. These were the aspects of having sex with Khalil that pleased Drake the most—the aura he had of innocence, of being taken for the first time, each time, and for his dutiful compliance to anything Drake wanted to do with him.

Khalil's eyes betrayed a struggle of fear and arousal—and also maybe awe—all of which pleased Drake, and he moved the young Arab until he was belly down on the bed, with his short legs hanging over the end of the tall bed, not quite reaching the floor. His bound arms were raised over his head.

Crowned with a fresh condom, Drake was kneeling behind the young man's body. He was patting and kneading and kissing the plump nut-brown buttocks while he bound Khalil's ankles and calves just below his knees with leather strips. He wrapped his belt around Khalil's thighs and buckled it tight.

Khalil was pleading with him about Drake being too large for this and how he was split when Drake did this. He was close to sobbing. It was all part of the game, Drake knew, though. He had no idea how close to the truth it cut from Khalil's perspective, but it was a game they both knew—Drake liked the "feel" of taking a virgin each time. And Drake had no reason, really, to care what Khalil thought. Drake was the king in this little slice of this forsaken Arab country.

Drake stood over Khalil's hips and slowly fed his cock into the restricted channel, with Khalil crying out and begging for mercy that didn't come. When he was in and started pumping, Khalil was just reduced to sobs, groans, and moans.

At the moment Drake exploded, all hell broke out around the compound in the form of other explosions and the terrifying punches of automatic weapons fire. Drake didn't even have time to pull out of Khalil before the room was filled with Arabs in black thawbs, their heads and faces covered with black Arab headdresses known as the *keffiyeh*. Only their eyes were seen, and these were flashing with anger and triumph.

They held automatic rifles, pointed variously at the ceiling and at Drake and Khalil.

The last sensation Drake had before being hit in the head with the butt of a rifle was being pulled off of Khalil and both he and a squirming Khalil being dragged across the room by a swirl of black material and strong arms.

* * * *

Drake half awoke with a groan to the sensation of being in a pile of black-clad bodies, in the back of a truck that was driving fast across uneven terrain and jostling its occupants together. Groggily he started to rise out of the pile, but he heard something intelligible being said in Arabic over the whine of a vehicle engine and a cloth held by a hand came over his mouth and nose. A sweet-pungent smell, and he was out again.

When he next woke, he was inside an extensive tented area. The tent walls were black. He awoke to his head snapping back and forth from slaps.

He opened his eyes and groaned. He felt the hair on the top of his head being grabbed and his head lifted up. Above his face, close, was a set of those flashing eyes he recalled from his trailer, the rest of the man's head being swathed in a black keffiyeh.

Drake was bound and in a somewhat awkward position. His arms were stretched up and out and tied to the arms of an X-shaped metal beamed affair. He was sitting in something like a tractor seat, but with his butt thrust out away from the X-shaped form and his legs spread and raised and tied at the ankles to pillars in front and to each side of his body.

He still was as naked as he was when he'd been seized in his bedroom.

"Are we awake now, Mr. Manager?" the man with the face above him asked in a thick Arabic accent.

"Some mistake. There's been some mistake," Drake mumbled. His voice sounded far away and fuzzy. It didn't sound like himself. But he felt he had enough presence of mind to try to dissemble. "Just a visitor to the fields. Just a friend visiting."

"You are Drake Ellinger, and you are the general manager of the BG gas field," the man said. "You needn't play games with us. But we saw that you like to play games—that like all vultures from the West you like to fuck the Arab people."

"The others. Where?"

"That's not for you to worry about, Mr. Ellinger. Although one of your people is here. Can you see him over there . . . the young Arab man you like to fuck?"

The Arab gripping the hair on Drake's head turned his head so that he could see over in another part of the tent. A cot. And bound on the cot, Khalil. Khalil was looking at him with wide-opened, frightened eyes and, now that Drake's facilities were returning, he could hear the young man whimpering in fear and snuffling. Standing on the far side of the cot were three monster men, all muscle-bound brutes, wearing only the black keffiyeh that hid their facial features. Their arms were crossed and their cocks were huge and half hard.

"Do you value your employees, Mr. Ellinger? Like this one, for instance, that you were being so intimate with?"

"Don't . . . don't do—"

"I think you need to know how serious we are, Mr. Ellinger. We'll have a little demonstration, and then I'll ask you some questions. And if you give me the answers I want, we'll let you and your employees go."

"Who are you? What do you want? No . . . please . . . stop him. Ask me your questions. But I'm only visiting. I don't know . . . Oh, god, no."

But one of the big bruisers was already crouched between Khalil's legs, wishboning them, and working his gigantic cock inside the small channel, while Khalil screamed bloody murder. Once inside, the big bruiser began to piston hard, and Khalil's screams died out and his face flopped toward Drake and his eyes closed.

Drake watched in horror and fascination. He was almost ashamed of himself that he was watching more in

158

fascination, but such were his interests that he couldn't completely separate out his distress from his arousal at seeing the small Khalil being taken—by the second and third hulky brute after the first one was done.

When they were done, by which time Khalil was conscious again but just dully staring in Drake's direction with his tongue hanging out and panting deeply, the three unbound Khalil, one of the brutes threw his limp body over his shoulder, and they left through a flap in the tent.

Drake found that he was breathing hard. He also found that the man staring down in his face had a hand wrapped around his engorged cock, although not so tightly that Drake hadn't been stroking inside it. He was close to coming.

The Arab released the cock and slapped it, causing Drake to cry out and lose all sense of ejaculating, and stood off away from Drake.

The man was young. He wore the black keffiyeh as did all of the figures Drake had seen—there were two other burly men standing on either side of the tent flap, and wearing black thawbs as well as the keffiyeh. Each had an automatic rifle pointed in the air.

The young man, though wasn't wearing a thawb. He was stripped to the waist and was wearing billowing black cotton trousers that had some sort of flap at the groin, of material that came through his legs and triangulated out to strips that were tied at the back of his waist and held the crotch flap in place. The trousers were low risers and Drake could see the muscles and superb cut of his abs almost down to the root of his cock.

"That was just a demonstration, Mr. Manager," he said with his thick accent. "I have some simple questions for you, and if you answer them well, you all may go back to your business. If not, I can have each of your employees brought here in turn and given the attention by my men that was just given to your young friend."

"Please," Drake moaned. "I was only visiting the gas field. There's nothing I can tell you. But what is it you want to know?"

"Do you like my body, Mr. Manager?" The Arab asked. He was untying the sash of the crotch flap, which he left drop. He rotated his hips a couple of times so that Drake could see the goods—which were very good indeed. And then he dropped the trousers and stood there, undulating a bit and posing for Drake, naked but for the keffiyeh.

Drake involuntarily moaned and felt himself going hard again.

"We know what you like to do with young Arab men, Mr. Manager. Would you like to do that with me too? Just a few simple answers and perhaps you and I can enjoy ourselves before you go back to your gas field."

Drake groaned. "I was just visiting."

The young Arab came in close to Drake's body again. Once again his hand was enclosing Drake's engorging cock. "I am Farid. I find your hard body arousing. I think that I may let you fuck me after you've answered my questions and before you return to your work."

Drake moaned. His hips were moving, his hard cock stroking in Farid's loose fist.

"Three questions only." Farid's material-covered lips were close to Drake's ear. "First, we wish to know where explosives can be laid in the gas field to do the most damage."

Drake went rigid, and his eyes opened wide.

"Second, we want to know the name of the member of the Council of Ten in the capital city who is the protector of your operation."

"I can't . . . I am . . . only visiting the—"

"And third, we want to know the number of the Swiss bank account that the bribery money you have been giving this man is sent to."

Drake practically went into shock. Two of the questions he could never answer. But how in the hell did these men even know of the man in the Council of Ten and of the bank account—let alone that Drake was nearly the only man on earth—certainly the only one here in this country who would know?

"I sense you are not ready to tell me. But you will, Mr. Manager. Before long you will beg to tell me."

Without showing Drake his face, the Arab pulled the keffiyeh from his face, kissed down Drake's torso to his belly, and opened his mouth over Drake's cock. Drake moaned and set his hips in slow motion, feeling himself ready to explode.

But before he did explode, Farid pulled his mouth off, flung the keffiyeh across his face, laughed, and slapped Drake's cock again. Drake cried out and felt his cock going flaccid. But he also felt the ache in his balls. He needed to come. If only his hands were free. But they weren't.

Farid had pulled his trousers back on and already was headed toward the exit from the tent.

* * * *

"What is it that these bastards want?" the BG vice president yelled into the computer link with John Singleberry, the gas field security chief who the masked Arabs had freed to pass on their demands.

"They have all of the staff locked in the conference room," Singleberry babbled breathlessly. "They say they've set explosives to go off if anyone tries to rescue them—and explosives out at the equipment heads too."

"Steady there, John," Wyatt said. "Let's take it slow. Are all of the staffers OK?"

"I . . . I don't know, Sir Wyatt. They didn't let me into the conference room. They seemed to know who I was. I don't know how they found out. There were bodies on the grounds, but I think they were local guards. I just don't—"

"Shut up and listen to me, Singleberry," Wyatt yelled. Christ almighty, he thought. I should have replaced this man months ago. "They must have let you go for a reason. Who are you with now? Did the attackers say what they wanted?"

"I'm with a military officer. His people are making plans to storm—"

"Absolutely not, John. Put the officer on and then calm yourself and come back after I've talked with the officer. I then want you to tell me what these bastards want."

It didn't take Wyatt long to convince the military officer that the gas field could easily be turned into an inferno and that storming it shouldn't be something that should be done rashly.

When John Singleberry came back on, he was calmer. "They said they were holding the staff and the field hostage. They said they were something called the Mask of the People and were revolutionaries. They say they will release one hostage for each million dollars BG puts in an off-shore account, and for ten million more they won't fire the field. And they say that Al-Jazeera TV will have to broadcast any video they send them."

"OK. That gives us something to work with, John. They must have given you some way to contact them to agree to their terms and coordinate the releases."

"Yes. They gave me some commo equipment dialed to their frequency. And it's pretty good stuff, not the crap that—"

"Listen to me, John. Tell them we agree to their terms but must have the hostages released five at a time so that we know they'll hold up their end of the bargain. That will give the military officer there time to get a possible rescue operation planned and poised. And, John, this is important. Tell them we'll supply the names of the hostages to be released. That we have records of who has a medical problem or should be released first on humanitarian grounds. And we want Drake Ellinger released in the first set."

"Drake?"

"Yes, tell them he has a condition that requires periodic medication. That he might die if he doesn't get it."

"I didn't know that. As far as I know Drake is as healthy as a—"

"Shut up, John. Just do it. Don't think; just do as I tell you." This was at the top of Wyatt's mind. Drake held the mostly closely guarded secrets of the gas field operation—not the least the name of the host government official protecting them. They needed Drake out of that situation as soon as possible. "Now, put the officer back on, John. We have some planning to do."

* * * *

Drake was moaning and thrusting up as his bindings permitted. The Arab, Farid, wearing only his keffiyeh, was straddling Drake's lap, his channel clutching Drake's buried cock. Pumping, pumping.

The bound hostage was just about to go over the moon. His balls had ached since Farid had last teased him. If Drake wasn't permitted to ejaculate soon he was going to explode. This was Drake's condition. He had to have sex often, to evacuate his system. He had to fuck a young man.

He was coming close. Farid pulled his hips up, bringing the bulb of Drake's pulsating cock to his entrance. He had his arms around Drake, holding him close. His well-muscled chest had been rubbing Drake's, but he lifted it up now. He whispered in Drake's ear. "The three questions. If you answer those three questions now, I will bring my channel down on the cock. You will explode inside me. And you will have relief. All you have to do is to answer those three little questions."

"I don't know the answers . . . I was just visiting. I don't . . . oh shit."

Farid pulled his body off Drake's lap, slapped the cock, and pulled away toward the opening of the tent. "It's just a matter of time. And not much time," Farid said. "In many ways you are a strong man, Mr. Manager, Drake Ellinger. But in this one way you are weak. You cannot resist me in this one way. We know you well."

Drake huffed in frustration and in a dying attempt to grab at an ejaculation. He couldn't reach his cock himself. There was nothing he could do. He had tried to imagine having sex. But it hadn't worked. He needed his cock inside a young man.

And he knew he was weakening. He didn't know how Farid knew what his weakness was, but he did know. Drake knew he couldn't hold out much longer.

He didn't have time to dwell on that. The three bruisers who had taken Khalil the previous day had come into the tent and were untying him. At first he assumed that they would do the same to him that they'd done to Khalil, but he almost didn't care. If they did, maybe he'd be able to ejaculate and bring relief to his aching balls. And if so, he could hold out longer. He'd been fucked before. He wondered if Farid knew that. He might even enjoy these hulks. He wouldn't let on that he did, though. He was in a cat and mouse game with this. As long as the hulks got him off, he'd be able to endure their pounding and Farid's questions as well.

But they weren't assaulting him. They were taking him to a smaller tent. They first took him to the latrine where he'd been taken every few hours since he'd been brought here and was permitted to piss and shit and was doused with water. He'd been shocked when he'd left the bigger tent the first time. He appeared to be in a wadi of sorts out in the desert. He hadn't seen any sign of the gas extraction installation. They must be outside the parameter of the installation. And there were just a few tents. Not nearly enough to hold all of his staff members. Had he and Khalil been separated off? And where was Khalil now? Was he still alive? Had he been asked the same questions and been eliminated for convincing them he didn't know the answers?

After the latrine, Drake was taken into the smaller tent and laid on a bed, with his wrists bound over his head to the frame. Then they had left. It was almost twilight already, and, exhausted, Drake went to sleep with the fall of night.

He awoke with Farid's naked body covering his and moving on his body in a highly arousing way. They wrestled with each other, with Drake doing everything he could to get his cock inside Farid and Farid teasing him into an "almost," and then slipping away. Drake couldn't control either Farid or himself because his wrists were bound over his head.

Farid was wearing nothing, not even his keffiyeh. And his lips were everywhere, bringing Drake to an ultimate arousal and then backing off. Drake was breathing heavily and whimpering and groaning in unrealized need. Farid was hovering over Drake's body, Drake's cock head kissing Farid's entrance. But Farid just holding him there.

"The three questions," Farid hissed in his ear. "Three answers and I release your hands and descend on your cock and let you have your way with me for the rest of the night."

"One." Farid's demand cut through the silence like a pistol shot.

"Bring me a map in the morning and I'll show where the explosives could be set," Drake answered through clinched teeth. He was tired, oh so tired, of this game.

"Two."

"Ahmed Al-Sud. The ruling council member we pay off."

"And three."

"I'll write the number out for you in the morning."

"You'll recite it now. I know you have it now—memorized."

With obvious pain and reluctance, Drake recited the number. A figure hovering by, who it struck him by the person's walk as someone he should know, wrote the number down on a pad of paper and then retreated into the shadows.

Farid was going into high gear. He really did want to fuck. He started to descend his channel on Drake's cock, quickly untied Drake's wrists, and sank his face into the hollow of Drake's neck. He latched onto a fold of skin there and sucked hard. Roaring with lust, Drake threw his arms around Farid's torso and thrust up hard just as Farid thrust down with his hips. They both went wild, thrusting hard against each. Drake exploded, releasing all of his frustrated comings, and Farid collapsed on top of him. Farid moved his lips to Drake's, and they went into a deep kiss as Drake fired once, twice, three times.

They laid there panting hard for several minutes, trying to catch their breath, wanting to be melded into each other's bodies—at least Drake did; there was no telling what Farid was thinking, other than that he'd gotten what he wanted.

Drake was getting hard again. "I need to take you again," he muttered. "And I need to control. I need to take you on my terms."

"Only if I get what else I want," Farid answered.

"What else? I've given you everything."

"Not everything," Farid whispered. He moved his lips to Drake's ear and told him what else he wanted.

They held there, for a minute, still breathing heavily, Drake still getting harder. And then Drake turned Farid on his back, worked his knees between Farid's thighs, slid back inside him, and began a slow pump.

It was then that he saw it. He could see Farid's face in a beam of light entering the tent from the camp outside. Farid was looking at him and smiling. But it wasn't just Farid's face. It was Khalil's too. Brothers. They must be brothers, Drake thought. And the one writing the bank account number down. Of course. That was Khalil. Now Drake knew why and how Farid had known what he did about who Drake was, what he knew, and how he could be approached to give the information up.

But now Drake no longer cared.

* * * *

"What do you want, John?" Sir Wyatt said when he was brought to the screen. "We already sent the list for the third set of hostages to be released, and I absolutely insist this time that Drake Ellinger—"

"Switch to Al-Jazeera TV, Sir Wyatt. There's a video from the Mask of the People. They've run it once. You must see the rerun."

The technician changed the image for the BG vice president, and he suddenly found himself watching Drake Ellinger on his knees, dressed in a white thawb, and surrounded by hulking men in black thawbs and keffiyehs. Drake was condemning the West and the grasping oil companies and imploring the people of the country his gas installation was in to rise up and overthrow the Council of Ten.

A man was standing by with a sword. The clip was short and blacked out before any move was made toward Drake. There simply was a statement that there would be another announcement at the same time the next day.

Sir Wyatt was roaring curses when the communications switched back to John Singleberry. Singleberry was rattling about hoping that Drake wasn't being assassinated. That didn't faze Wyatt a bit, however. Having Drake assassinated would be one answer to the problem if he was silenced before he gave away the company secrets.

"Shut up, John. Didn't you see it?"

"See what, sir?"

"It was a tent, a fucking tent. The video was shot in a tent. There are no tents like that on the gas extraction installation. Ellinger isn't there. He isn't with the other hostages. Let me talk with the fuckin' military guy. Now!"

* * * *

Drake was standing at the side of the cot. Khalil was laying on his back in front of him, his legs strapped together and rising up Drake's chest. Khalil's arms were stretched out straight from his body and were bound with leads tied off at the head and foot of the cot frame, respectively. Khalil was arching his back and crying out the tightness of the cock in his restricted channel as Drake fucked his ass in slow, deep strokes. Drake was in ninth heaven.

Farid, standing by to replace Khalil when he was exhausted, was smiling benignly at Drake. It had been easier than he had thought to extract the information from the man and to control him ever since. As soon as they had cleaned out the Swiss bank account and dealt with the Council of Ten traitor, the Mask of the People could decide what to do with the man. But perhaps he had more secrets Farid and Khalil could extract from him. And maybe he would have other uses for Drake, if not for the Mask of the People. Farid had to admit that the man certainly could fuck.

* * * *

Sir Wyatt was sitting in front of the screen the next day as the first running of the second clip for Al-Jazeera TV came on.

It wasn't quite what he expected, although he hadn't really known what to expect. He had been confused since the morning when John Singleberry had contacted him to tell him that the rest of the hostages had been freed—or rather had been abandoned. No one had come with food for them that morning, and when they checked, they found that the conference room at the gas installation was unlocked and that the area was deserted. There were no insurgents to be found. It had been a few hours before they could make contact with the outside world, though, because the commo equipment BG headquarters had sent out to them was malfunctioning.

The insurgents and their demands for a million dollars for each hostage and ten million for the protection of the gas fields had evaporated in the night.

When the Al-Jazeera clip came up, it was a similar tableau to the one they'd seen the previous day. But this time, kneeling within the ring of black-clad insurgents was Ahmed Al-Sud, BG's man on the Council of Ten. He was babbling his sins of avarice and having been a traitor to his people and country.

After he recovered from the shock of seeing the man he was paying off kneeling and revealing all, Sir Wyatt's eyes roamed the line of men behind him. He stopped at a set of eyes swathed in a keffiyeh and his own eyes slitted. He'd recognize the eyes of Drake Ellinger anywhere. If he'd ever actually seen the young Arab man his money had paid for to keep Ellinger happy, he probably would have recognized the hazel-specked brown eyes of the man standing next to Drake as well.

This time the clip did not fade out before the swing of the sword.

Sir Wyatt roared out to no one in particular, "Someone get Interpol and the Credit Suisse on a conference call immediately."

But even as he said it, he knew it was too late. He knew the Al-Sud account had been wiped out.

The technician was nudging him, pointing out that something was on the screen for him to see again. It was John Singleberry. He was standing in what was obviously the gas installation administrative compound. Behind him, billowing flames filled the screen. Wyatt didn't have to be told that the gas field was exploding.

Hurricane

The Colombian thug Arillano Galindo was rubbing his head dry with one towel, with another one wrapped around his waist, as he stepped from the bathroom into his sea-view room at Cartagena's resort Caribe Hotel, when he was caught up short. Standing inside the closed door to the corridor was the waiter he had just been flirting with down at the hotel pool. He'd actually been assessing the young man as possibly part of the package he planned to deliver to the docks of New Orleans in two week's time—fresh ass for the male bordellos across the southern states of America. The young man was standing there, in a vest over his naked chest and short shorts—the uniform of the pool service—and holding a tray with a champagne bottle, a single glass, and a fruit plate on it. He was a Mestizo, highly valued in the trade, small of stature, almost boyish, dusky complexion but with blond-tipped hair and blue eyes. And he had the smile of a knowing flirt. Galindo probably wouldn't even have to whip him into shape if he took him to New Orleans.

"Compliments of the hotel management," the young waiter said with a smile. He moved to his right and put the tray down on the side of the dresser and then came back to the door, smiled, and said, "Anything else I can do for you, sir? Anything at all?"

Manuel was flat on his back on the carpeted floor, turning his head back and forth, crying out at the invasion, and digging his fists into the carpet pile. He was mouthing off like this was his first time, but Galindo wasn't buying that and he was feeding his ass fast and deep—and Manuel was taking him in, stretching to accommodate him without apparent trouble. Manuel's butt was raised on three pillows from the bed; one of his legs rose up Galindo's chest, and Galindo held the other one out to the side with a fist wrapped around his ankle. Galindo was on his knees between Manuel's legs and raising and lowering his body in rhythm as his cock moved in and out, in and out inside Manuel's tight hole—at an ever faster, deeper pace.

Manuel groaned and moaned and slowly pulled on his own cock, as Galindo muttered what a nice, sweet, tight ass he had, murmuring that he should see the world, that his talents should be shared—and thinking to himself that, yes, this young, boyishly handsome waiter would command top dollar in the male bordellos of New Orleans. Maybe, he was thinking, he should consider pimping some of these guys himself and letting them keep more of the take. Galindo's share of the market at this point was not-fully-willing, expendable asses. It was almost a shame to throw someone as good at bottoming as Manuel was into that short-term pool. Almost. Manuel would return top dollar anyway—almost as much as if he was a virgin.

Galindo was even more pleased a half an hour later, when he had Manuel's belly up against the wall of the shower, under a cascade of water, and the little Mestizo was able to go with a power fuck. Galindo had to be careful with the small ones, like Manuel. Galindo was built like a heavy-weight prize fighter, with the brutalized face to match, and he sometimes lost control at the height of a fuck. He could get rough, and he could crush the smaller ones under him in the heat of lust. But doing it like this was OK. Holding Manuel by his waist and raising him up and down on his cock, and Manuel making all of the sounds of full-satisfaction taking that the marks like to hear. He didn't just lay there and take it; he moved his hips and touched his taker with his hands, and murmured his love for the cock and what it was doing to him.

Afterward, as they were stretched out on the bed and Galindo was enjoying Manuel's lips with his and the little berry-brown body, lithe and boy-like, with his gliding hands, Galindo whispered to him, "Are you free for the weekend? I have a very private island. I can make it worth your while."

"Yes, I think I would like that—if, of course, your pocketbook is of the same generous size as other parts of you."

"Well, I could be very, very generous. If you can show me that you can suck cock as well as you ride it."

Manuel then showed him that he, indeed, could suck cock very, very well.

* * * *

The speedboat was skimming across the water, the beach resort coastline of Cartagena receding behind them and an islet dead ahead. The waves were choppy and white capped, and the two men were breaking off from what they had been doing to look up at the sky. Arillano Galindo was sitting in the seat behind the wheel, his bathing trunks around his ankles and Manuel sitting on his cock, his hands trapping Galindo's wrists, as the older man steered the boat, and his ass rising and falling in Galindo's lap.

"I don't like the looks of the sky," Galindo muttered. "We'll make the island, but not with much time to crank up the boat in the boathouse. If we lose the boat, we're stranded for a couple of days."

"Stranded," Manuel exclaimed. "How big is this island we're going to anyway?" Manuel wasn't at all worried about the black clouds scuttling across the sky or the sudden picking up of the breeze and drop in temperature, or the whitecaps on the waves. This had been one of the riskier aspects of all this. The timing had been very touchy, and the primary plan required the hurricane that had been building off the coast of Cuba to be making an appearance here either later today or tomorrow. It now looked like tonight was going to be the night.

"It's small. Only has one house on it," Galindo said. "I own the whole island. I'll have you all to myself." He took one hand off the wheel and pulled Manuel in close in his lap and gave him a deep kiss in the hollow of his neck.

"If your island is small, it's the only thing about you that's small," Manuel whispered, and he wiggled his butt and was rewarded with a groan from Galindo as his cock touched all sides of Manual's undulating channel walls.

And once again the international trafficker in illegal flesh, Arillano Galindo, blessed his good fortune at having added Manuel to his collection at the last moment for delivery to the New Orleans auction house. Of course Manuel didn't know yet that he was going to be sold into the underworld of male brothels. And as long as Manuel was giving him a good time, Galindo wasn't going to tell the nice little piece of ass what was what. He'd have Manuel on the ship and sailing across the Caribbean before he had any idea what was in store for him.

"There, there. Up ahead. Do you see it? Isle de Turto. And it's all mine."

"Where? Oh, that? It *is* small," Manuel said. He was doing his best acting to convey the impression that he'd never seen the island before—although he had. He knew practically every inch of the island and the house on it now.

"Shall we take a spin around it and see it from all sides?" Galindo offered. "It would only take a couple of minutes. The storm should hold off that long."

"No, I don't think so. I think I want to see your bedroom first." It was the best Manuel could think of to say on the fly. A trip to the other side of the island might have proved embarrassing to the fishing boat he knew was anchored just off the island over there. But the remark worked. Galindo revved up the engine and headed straight for the dock and boathouse.

Manuel thought the house was the perfect setup, and while Galindo was cranking the speedboat up out of the water in the boathouse, Manuel went on ahead, saying he wanted to look around the island a bit. He found the package he was looking for hidden behind a concrete vase at the edge of the stone terrace behind the house. He had its precious contents stashed away in his backpack well before Galindo came up the steps from the boathouse.

And as Manuel had requested, he was shown Galindo's bedroom first, and the wrist restraints in the headboard, and Galindo's ready cock, and the passage to paradise.

* * * *

Manuel woke in the middle of the night, encased in Galindo's arms, and in an instant he was fully awake to wariness at the sounds he was hearing—the whistling of the wind, raindrops smattering against the window shutters, and the beating of a loose shutter on a window frame. "Showtime" was the word running through his brain and he nudged Galindo—enough for the thug to wake up but not enough for him to think Manuel had purposely awakened him.

"The hurricane is here," Galindo murmured, half awake. But he became alert to the sounds of the storm quickly and sat up in bed. "It is time for me to show you the storm cellar."

The two rolled off the bed at opposite sides and reached for their clothes.

"Hurry, this way," Galindo muttered. Already the wind was howling rather than whistling.

"Just a second," Manuel answered. "I want my backpack."

They barely had made it into the store cellar under the house when the generator gave out and they heard sounds of the tin roofing giving way.

They were on a mattress on the floor, and Manuel clung to Galindo in fear of the night and the storm, and Galindo embraced him and comforted him. Manuel let his little hands roam around on Galindo's body, and they soon drifted into a slow fuck. As Galindo was at the point of ejaculation, the world caved in on him. Something hit him on the head, which stunned him, and something stabbed him in the thigh, which blacked him out.

Manuel dropped the length of wood he'd used to stun Galindo, put the syringe he'd used to put Galindo out for several hours back into his backpack, extracted a flashlight from his backpack, went to the cellar door, and let in the much bedraggled team of U.S. intelligence technical experts.

The hurricane was passing by, but it didn't give them any help in their difficult task. Still, they were miracle workers and they had trained for this. They had brought all of the supplies they needed, and the team had every move planned down to the second. The first thing they did was turn the generator back on that they'd cut off themselves.

While they worked, Manuel, with pleasure, bloodied up the Colombian flesh-peddling thug's head more than he originally had and then bandaged it with his torn undershirt.

As the team was pulling out, layering a mass of splintered timbering in their wake, the last of them, the team leader, whispered to Manuel, "You sure you know what we need? We need to know where it is and where it's going."

Manuel nodded. His thoughts had been concentrated on that for days. They were simple questions, but the answers were worth all of the effort they were putting in to get them.

By the time Galindo came too, but woozily so from his head wound—although more so from the drugs Manuel had shot into his thigh once more—the cellar had been transformed into a collapsed building trapping the two of them in a small, but manageable air pocket, with no access to an exit. The timbers were stacked precariously to leave the impression that if someone started trying to move any of them, the whole lot would come down on his head.

"Where, what?" Galindo moaned as he came closer to the surface of consciousness.

"The hurricane collapsed the house on us," Manuel said. "You got hit in the head by a falling timber. We're alive, but we're trapped. I don't think it would be a good idea to try to move any of this debris."

"Alive but trapped," Galindo muttered and drifted off again.

He woke again in an hour, as the drug Manuel had shot into him was wearing off. There was enough still in him to make him confused, however, and Manuel was prepared to keep him in that state as long as he could.

"Where? Oh, yes, trapped in the cellar," he muttered. "How long?"

"You've been out for a day—through a night," Manuel said.

"Water. Thirsty," Galindo whispered.

"We don't have any," Manuel said. He put a sob into his voice, made himself sound like he was sinking in despair. "We're trapped . . . on an uninhabited island, under a collapsed house. Can't get out. We're going to die in here."

"No. We're not," Galindo muttered. "A night you say? We can hold out. Ship. Ship will be here tomorrow."

"A ship?" Manuel asked. "What ship?"

"They know I should be here; they'll see the house collapsed and will get us out. They can't sell the cargo without me. All those people will be useless to them. I'm the only one with the contacts in New Orleans and the way to get illegals in."

"People? Cargo? What ship? Where is it coming from? Where is it going?"

Galindo started to drift off again, and Manuel patted him on the cheek, a bit hard, actually. "Please stay awake. I'm scared. What ship? I don't understand."

Galindo took Manuel in his arms and started to rock him back and forth. "Shush now, don't worry. It will be here tomorrow. Picking up cargo down the Nicaragua, Costa Rica, Panama coast. Sex flesh from all through the region. Love that in the south. Nice brown Hispanic ass—some fresh. New Orleans. Have it all set up."

"You're just trying to keep me from giving up, aren't you. We've been here so long. I'm thirsty and hungry. We're going to die here. What ship? What ship will pick us up."

"Shhh, shh, the Grego II. Wouldn't go by without finding me. Wouldn't do them any good in New Orleans."

"Oh, please get us out of here," Manuel wailed—as he jabbed Galindo's thigh with the needle again and Galindo drifted off to lala land.

Manuel extricated himself from Galindo's embrace, reached into his backpack. took out a mobile phone, and punched in a number. "It's the Grego II, coming from Panama and headed to New Orleans for a sex slave trade auction. He expects it here on Tuesday. Now get me the hell out of here."

It had all happened in an eight-hour period from hurricane damage set up, to Manuel getting the information they needed from Galindo, to breaking the staged set in the cellar of a perfectly sturdy house and bundling Galindo onto the fishing boat on the other side of the island. They called in other teams to intercept the Grego II before it left Panamanian waters, the Panamanians being much more cooperative in these matters than the Colombians were.

As Manuel climbed aboard the fishing boat, he looked up at the sky, at the black cloud scuttling away from them up toward the Nicaraguan coast. He said a little thanks to Mother Nature for cooperating. Plan B for this operation would have been much, much more complicated and risky.

Interviewing a Dictator

I rolled over to a seated position and let the balls of my feet rest on the ratty carpeting. I reached for the pack of cigarettes and lit up. I'd only started smoking in the last couple of months. Nerves. I'd stop as soon as I got back to the States. Or maybe when I changed my name and had plastic surgery so that no one recognized me anymore.

I looked around the dimly lit room, protected from the blazing sunlight beyond the French doors to the little balcony by a dirty and tattered gauze curtain. I could hear the flies buzzing and hoped that most of them were out there rather than in here. The printed wallpaper, what it represented being indistinct as faded as it was, was moldy and coming off the wall in large strips. The chamber pot on the sad-looking wooden bureau had given me pause when I first entered the room, but I was assured that there was a private bath. There was, but all of the fixtures had to be cast offs from some demolition project, which gave me new respect for the chamber pot.

Sandre Grande was possibly the worst piss hole I'd ever reported from. But I was assured that this was the best hotel in the principal town of the small tinhorn dictatorship island "kingdom" in the Caribbean. The principal claim to strategic interest of the place, the nub of what had brought me here, was that it was positioned smack dab in the center of the shipping lane across the Caribbean to the entrance of the Panama Canal.

But I was on my way back up, or so Shaun had assured me. I had gotten the assignment to interview the dictator. No one else had. No one at all had since he'd come to power. No one seemed to know exactly where he stood on anything. He was a cagey guy. One of those army sergeants who was the last man standing after the recent revolution. Did he stand with the United States as his predecessor had, or did he lean toward the Cubans and Venezuelans? No one knew—except maybe the Cubans or Venezuelans, and they weren't talking. It would be a boost for anyone who found out.

And I definitely needed a boost. I'd been riding high, with a good network. But I had been indiscreet—which was putting it mildly. I still don't know who had found out and who had told. And who had taken it to the Internet. I'd thought anyway that in today's world it didn't matter. But apparently it did. Apparently I hadn't come far enough up yet. It had worked OK for that white-haired CNN anchor, the son of whatsherface, so I didn't see why it wasn't working for me. The assignments had dried up. I was on the cusp of losing my contract.

An arm came around my waist. A hand encased my cock.

"Put the cigarette out and hand me another one of those condoms, Ted."

"Again?" I asked.

"What else is there for us to do while we wait for the summons to the dictator's presence," Shaun Madden, my cameraman, producer, and lover, all rolled into one answered. "Besides you love it."

"You treat me like a slut, Shaun."

"That's because you *are* a slut, Ted. But a very nicely put together one. You'll open your legs for any man with a big cock and a hard body. It's a talent you have. It wasn't just the congressman who did for you. You might have survived that in the press. There's some cachet in hooking up with a congressman, and the emphasis went to him. It was all those other Internet photos that followed. All those soldiers and sailors. Somebody did a real job on exposing you. A hard body and a big cock—or a succession of them. You love it."

Why yes I did, I thought. That had been my downfall. I loved it. And Shaun had a hard body and a big cock. Maybe if it hadn't been a congressman, it wouldn't have made such a big splash. But it was. But, no, I knew it was the gang bang. Only one of those had made it to the Internet. I couldn't say it was an anomaly; there had been others. But the network executive probably had been right when he'd said, "Who could concentrate on what a journalist has to say on screen after knowing—and seeing—how many randy sailors he'll just lay there and let fuck him in succession?"

And afterward it was like I was an untouchable. To all but Shaun Madden. I hadn't been an untouchable to him—he had touched me as not even the congressman had, more than any of those soldiers and sailors I became addicted to had. And he was the reason I still was holding onto the network job by a thread. He was why I had even gotten this interview. Only when he'd told the network executives he could get an interview with the elusive dictator, but only if I did the interview, had the wheels on printing up my termination letter ground to a halt. It would be a temporary halt if I didn't bring this interview off.

He'd said he'd help me on the way up. He was helping me get it back up right now.

"There's a hard-bodied soldier out in the hall," Shaun whispered as he nuzzled his face into the crease where my thigh met my underbelly. "You saw him—one of the men they've had guarding us since we entered the country. Don't tell me you didn't look him over good and set your mind to thinking. He gave you a good look too. If I told you to get up and go get him and let him fuck you right here while I watched, you'd do it for me, wouldn't you?"

I hesitated, but only for a moment. "Yes," I answered in a quiet voice.

"Well?"

I started to get up from the bed, but he grabbed my wrist and set me back down. "Told you so," he said. "Now, put that cigarette out and get me a rubber."

I sighed and stubbed out my cigarette. I reached over to the nightstand and picked up a condom packet. As I split the foil, he sat up beside me. He had a beautiful, muscular body—and a cock to die for. He'd had no trouble picking me up after I'd been knocked down when the rumors about the congressmen and me became photographs on the Internet. I'd started with him even before the photos with the soldiers and sailors were posted by whoever it was who had it in for me.

While I extracted the condom from the packet, he rolled the used one off his cock—his nice plump cock—and tossed it in the wastebasket. The maid tomorrow—if there was to be a hotel maid tomorrow, or even a tomorrow in this humid hell hole—would get a thrill. There now were three used condoms in the basket.

"You do it," he said, as he continued to hold me to his side, his hand working my cock.

I rolled the Golden Ticket condom on his cock, engorged again. He was three years younger than I was, fit and virile. Not long out of the Marines. As lovers went, I was very lucky to have him—if he didn't kill me trying to keep up with him.

"Knees on the bed," he said. "You're gonna fuck yourself for a while." I stood up from the bed and moved to in front of him, facing away from him. Then I came back on the bed on the fronts of my calves, my legs bent, on the outside of his muscular thighs. Reaching under my buttocks, while he continued to stroke my cock, I positioned the bulb of his thick cock and slowly descended on the shaft.

"Do it," he commanded, grabbing my waist with his big hands.

I rose and fell on the cock, using the leverage of my bent legs. He was humming and I was moaning. He was thick, and always just got thicker as my channel stretched to accommodate him. But he was right. I loved it. My channel muscles began to ripple over the cock as only a young, virile, hung man like Shaun could make them do. He was moaning too now, enjoying the feel of that.

"God, you're good," he whispered. "This. This is what all those soldiers and sailors sniffed around you to get. What the congressman risked it all to have."

I was jacking myself as I rose and fell on the cock. I felt his hot breath between my shoulder blades and the nipping of his teeth on my skin. I ejaculated, shooting out over the worn carpet, already smeared with so many stains that more wouldn't be noticed.

"Grab your ankles," he commanded.

I unfolded my legs, being careful not to lose his penetration of my ass, leaned forward and down, grabbed my ankles, and went up on my feet. He came up on his feet behind me and started pounding my ass hard, deep, and fast. He spent some time at it—long enough that I came again before he did.

Yes, he was just the lover I needed to make being in this room in this backwater of a tinhorn dictatorship—if he didn't kill me in the process—bearable.

* * * *

The fast and jolting drive across the town from the fleabag hotel to the presidential "palace" was a harrowing one. We had been pushed into the back of an ancient army truck with a tarp over the bed just the same as if we were being carted off to prison. The presidential "palace" was a ramshackle wooden, bullet hole-pockmarked building badly in need of paint that, visually, at least, appeared to lean a bit to the right—something Shaun no doubt would work into the editing of his introduction to the filmed interview to suggest the dictator's political leanings unless the man proved to be a lefty.

The venue of the interview couldn't have been any more weird, and the content couldn't have been more fascinating and revealing. It was content that would light up the networks—not just mine—when and if we could get the footage back to the States. The "if" was to become the kicker.

The venue was a large, dark room, containing not just the sitting area in which the interview was to be filmed but also a massive four-poster, canopied bed, which Shaun would have to almost hang from the ceiling to avoid getting into the frame.

The dictator was no less a weird part of the venue. I had expected him to meet me in a khaki army uniform dripping with braid and medals, but he was in a dressing gown—and one that indicated that there wasn't much in the way of clothes underneath it.

I'd like to have been able to say that he wasn't a fat slob, but he came too close to that to deny it. He was tall and heavy. It was deceiving, though, as much of what looked like fat centered on a beer belly. Much of the rest of the bulk actually was muscle. He'd been a drill sergeant. That he'd worked his body hard was evident. That he enjoyed food and drink was equally evident. That he used drugs was suspected. His eyelids drooped almost as heavily as his jet-black mustache did. He was a dark man, with black hair—on more than his head. He spoke English, but not well. There was no evidence that he was educated. The only hints of his vanity were the thick rings worn on four of his fingers, and, as revealed later, the thick gold chain with the medallion pendant he wore around his neck.

Four bruisers, in army fatigues, were spaced around the room, during the interview. Two were at the door, as if Shaun and I planned to escape in the middle of the interview, and one each was stationed near Shaun and me. The dictator was paranoid and not taking any chances.

Shaun was calm as a cucumber. I wasn't, but I was doing all I could not to show that on the film. I quickly lost touch with my nervousness, though, because almost as soon as the interview started, the dictator was ranting on about the imperialist United States and of what he claimed were secret military pacts he had not only with Cuba and Venezuela but also with Russia and a few Mideast terrorist groups that I was flabbergasted to find he even could pronounce the names of let alone consort with.

He made no bones about being dismissive of his own people, who he planned to break on the wheel of padding the fortunes of the president and laid out specific plans on disrupting the passage of shipping to and from the Panama Canal, unless the United States became very generous with its foreign aid program.

As delighted as I was to hear all of this—with the man coming up with a news blockbuster every thirty seconds—and to know that Shaun was getting it all on film, I increasingly couldn't understand why he was telling us all of this.

That is until I made the mistake of asking him that specific question.

"Why, because I am enjoying talking about it and because you are never going to put any of that on your television. What you're filming is going to be for my private viewing pleasure"

"I'm not going the televise it? Why not?"

"Because you aren't leaving the country. Why did you think I specified that Ted Thompson be the one—the only one—who I'd give this interview to? Especially after the publicity you have gotten recently."

"I don't know," I said, flustered, and motioning to Shaun that maybe it was time to turn the camera off.

"Precisely because of the publicity you have gotten recently. I've watched you on TV for a couple of years. You are a sexy little thing. I wasn't at all surprised when you were caught being fucked by a congressman from the behemoth to the north. And all those military men you took—very impressive. I've wanted to fuck you myself. Now I will."

With that, he stood up from his chair, dropped his robe to reveal that, in fact, he had no clothes on underneath the robe, and signaled to the four soldiers in the room. Two went for Shaun, pinning his arms behind him in the straight chair he was sitting in, taking his camera from him, and producing rope to tie him to the chair.

The other two were at me, dragging me over to the bed, pulling my clothes off me, and pulling restraints down from the canopy at the foot of the bed and down from the headboard. While they trussed me up, naked, with my arms stretched over my head, wrists tied together, and my legs raised, spread, and tied to the restraints dropped at the foot of the bed from the canopy, the dictator walked over to a sideboard and popped some pills. Since his cock filled right up into a huge erection extending out from under his pot belly, I had no question what the pills were for.

I writhed for what seemed to be a half hour or more as the dictator crouched between my thighs and fucked me. No one said anything in the room. All that could be heard were his grunts of pleasure and my whimpers and involuntary moans as, when he set up a steady rhythm, I couldn't help but go with it and to move my pelvis to the fuck and to shoot off when the hand he was stroking my cock with proved to be very proficient.

As far as I could determine only two soldiers remained in the room during this taking. Both were standing by the chair Shaun was bound to, one on each side of him. One solider had his cock out, forcing Shaun to service it with his mouth, while the other played with Shaun's camera. At some point the two traded positions. Shaun was gagging on the cocks, but doing as he was told.

When the dictator had creamed my channel in three strong spurts, he grunted and pulled out of me.

"Time for a break," he said, and he and the two soldiers left the room.

After a few minutes of being alone in the room with Shaun, both of us bound, he said, in a hoarse voice. "It'll be OK, Ted. We'll get out of this."

"I don't see how," I mumbled. Shaun, ever the optimistic one. But what other choice was there at the moment? I had brought this on myself—I and whatever bastard had exposed the congressman and me.

"Just don't make him mad," Shaun said. "Take it. No, more than that. Make him think you enjoy it. Make him want to have you again."

The dictator and the two soldiers came back in the room. The soldiers released my ankles while the dictator popped pills and his cock popped up again in response. But they didn't release my wrists. They returned to their station next to Shaun's chair, and one of them picked up the camera and played with it again, while the dictator came up on the bed on his knees and pushed me up onto the center of the bed.

He stuffed a pillow under the small of my back; grabbed my ankles and spread and bent my legs, placing my feet flat on the surface of the bed; and slid his knees under my buttocks.

Remembering what Shaun had advised, while the dictator was entering with his cock, I arched my back and cried out, "Yes! Oh, god, yes! You're so big. Fuck me, fuck me hard. Ram it up me. Give me your cum."

And, god, yes, the enhanced cock *was* huge—thicker, longer than the first time. I panted and gasped in taking it inside me. He was fat and ugly, but the cock on him . . . Closing my eyes and relaxing my channel, I could enjoy it. I needed to stretch more, so that when he started to pump, there would be room for friction. I willed myself to open to him. He was throbbing inside me, the pills still working to thicken him.

Startled, but clearly pleased, the dictator began to piston me hard and deep. I was opening enough by panting and relaxing. It was working; the friction was there. Skin. No condom. He was barebacking me again. My channel muscles started rippling over the plunging cock. Something I did for the young, hung, hard-bodied soldiers and sailors. And for Shaun. Never for the congressman. But I was doing it for this ugly and fat man. Because the cock was unnaturally huge and arousing.

His hands ran up my chest and he thumbed my nipples for a few minutes before returning his hands to my waist. Again there was a flash of surprise as I wrapped my legs around his back and stroked his buttocks with my heels in rhythm to the fuck. I managed to raise my torso enough to take the medallion dangling from his neck into my mouth and suck it while giving him a lustful look with my eyes. He stroked hard and faster. He was huge inside me.

Shaun had told me to pretend I loved it. I wasn't pretending.

His face came down to mine, and I closed my eyes to the ugliness of him and opened my mouth to his as he was ejaculating again inside me.

He collapsed on me for a brief moment and then started to rise.

"No, please. Stay inside me," I whimpered. "I need you again. Stay inside me until you are hard again and then fuck me again; fuck me hard." I did need him inside me still. But huge inside me.

He seemed willing, but his pills weren't cooperating anymore, and I was coming back to my senses. At length, with a grunt, he pulled himself off me.

"No, no," I cried out. "Don't leave me. Don't take it out. I want you again." *Now* I was acting. Flaccid, there was nothing of him that I wanted.

He sat next to me for a few minutes, looking at me with eyes that seemed almost affectionate now, and ran his hands over my torso and thighs. He grabbed my cock and stroked it, and I did everything I could to give him an ejaculation, eventually succeeding, while whimpering, "Fuck me again. Please, please."

"Later, my sweet young man," he said as he stood from the bed. "You have taken all I have for now. But later."

Clearly he was pleased with my response to his assault—and how I had played on his vanity. But also, clearly, we weren't any closer to being released and sent back to the States in one piece with the interview film under Shaun's arm than we were before Shaun told me to win the dictator over.

"Take them to the citadel," he said, with a sniff, as he pulled his robe back on. "Bring the one on the bed back to me after I have had my supper. Bring him back in good condition. Tell the men there that they can have the other one. Leave the camera with the secretary in my office downstairs."

I was released and given my trousers—and only my trousers—to wear, by one of the soldiers, while the other soldier was untying Shaun. We were shoved through the door to the corridor and out of the presence of the dictator and hustled down to the street, where the same old army truck that had brought us to the presidential palace was waiting to take us away.

The soldiers at the truck, though, weren't the same ones who had brought us across town. And, as we were hustled into the back of the truck, where there were four soldiers—none of them ones I'd seen earlier in the day—strung along the benches, one of the soldiers who brought us down from the

186

dictator's bedroom winked at Shaun and handed his camera back to him.

"Got good footage?" Shaun asked him in Spanish.

"Really good," the soldier answered.

As his face disappeared from the back of the truck, I whispered, "What?" to Shaun.

"Shush," Shaun said. "The two soldiers were assets of ours. I told you I'd get you out of this." He handed the camera off to one of the other soldiers in the back of the truck—all of them with rifles gripped in their hands and pointed at the tarp overhead—and pushed me back between two soldiers and onto the bench. The soldier he handed the camera to merely nodded and put the camera in a padded case as if it were the crown jewels, which, it was dawning on me, it probably was.

"Assets?" I asked. "Who are you, Shaun? Are you CIA?"

"Don't ask," he said. "Better you not ask. Just be glad we're getting out of here. These are our men. There's an airstrip. You'll be in Key West in another hour or two."

"You set this up, didn't you? You and the CIA. You used me to get this footage of the dictator not only revealing his politics but also laying me." I didn't go to the lengths of asking him what part he had had in putting those photographs of me being gangbanged on the Internet. Somehow I knew the answer to that already.

Shaun laughed. "The footage of the interview will be bombshell great in Washington. The footage the soldiers took when the dictator was fucking you will be great to show here in the country. These people aren't going to like the idea of knuckling under to a faggot."

"A faggot? Shaun, you've used me. You're using the network."

But Shaun wasn't listening to me. He was crouched in front of me, unzipping my trousers, pulling them down my legs, unzipping and releasing himself, pushing his thighs between mine. Grabbing our dicks in his fist and pumping them together, telling what he was going to do right there and then to me, while I moaned and could only think of him doing it. The soldiers sitting close beside me were looking straight

187

ahead, stony eyed—at least at first. Not a source of help or comfort. As Shaun fucked me, I saw that they had released their own cocks and were stroking them and watching Shaun's cock appearing and disappearing in my hole.

He was shushing me, thinking that fucking me like this would calm me down and take my mind off the big picture. I can't say he was wrong.

"God, I nearly creamed myself as I watched him fuck you," Shaun growled, keeping my attention on his words while he worked his cock inside me. "I wanted to break out of my bonds—not that they really had me tied so I couldn't if I had to—you are such a luscious piece. As much as you want it, your saving grace is that you have an incredible body, that you're an incredible fuck. Didn't really have to be told to play up to him, did you? Those pills really did for him. Cock that big, you were in heaven, weren't you? You were never in danger. You must understand that. The two soldiers were local assets of ours. They could have stopped it at any time. But when I saw what those pills did to his cock, I knew you'd want it."

I didn't answer him. I had my legs hooked on his hips, my arms around his neck, and my forehead plastered to his, moaning and whimpering to him the same words I had to the dictator as Shaun pumped my ass. "Yes, yes, fuck me. Yes, yes, like that. Oh, fuck, oh shit."

He knew me too well. He knew how to control me, and he knew that I would do this for him again if he wanted me to. I knew he was doing this just to bend me to his will. And I knew he would be successful. I didn't fight him. I moved my pelvis with him, determined to fully enjoy what I couldn't fight.

He also knew that I would lay under any of the four hunky soldiers in the back of the truck—all U.S. Marines, I was sure—if he told me to and they wanted me.

"Shaun," I murmured.

"I told you already. All you need is a hard body and a big cock. Tell me I'm wrong."

I couldn't.

"You want to stay with me, you have to do what I want. What will it be? You want me to spin you off at the network and try to rise again on your own and not stick with me, say it now. You want me, you have to show me you'll do whatever I want."

I lay back against the bench, relaxing to him, giving in to him completely, as he came deep inside me.

"OK, guys, who else wants a piece of him? He'll love it. You've rescued him and he'll want to express his appreciation. Look at this hole," he said, turning my body so they all could see how open I was. I clung to him, burying my face in the hollow of his neck, embarrassed because what he was saying aroused me. "Who else wants to take a dip? I know each of you guys—what each wants."

Curse me, I wanted to hear one of them say yes. They all were hunks.

Two of them did say yes, right then, fucking me on the floor of the bouncing truck as it raced toward the air strip. All four had magnificent bodies. I was resigned to what I liked. When Shaun told me what he wanted—what they wanted, I lay on my back on sacks of grain on the floor of the truck, spread and raised my legs, and held out my arms for each of the hard-bodied young Marines, both big cocked, both vigorous and fast shooters in the excitement of what we were doing and where we were doing it. As I set my hips in motion at the first pump of their cocks, Shaun and the other soldiers watched, grinned, licked their lips, and stroked their cocks.

As the second, one, a big, black stud, slid into me, his heavily muscled arm lifting my waist, my torso arching back to the floor of the vehicle, my mouth opened to a silent scream at the thickness and length of him. My hands went to his hard buttocks, holding him close to me as he pumped deep. Shaun leaned over, kissed me on the lips as I looked up at him, eyes glazed, already swimming in cum, and whispered, "Trust me. I know what you want. I'll always take care of you if you do what I tell you to do. I can give you this and so much more. You will be a great asset for us."

The truck paused at the air strip long enough to accommodate the other two soldiers, plus the truck's two drivers, all admitting that they wanted it too. They took me in quick succession, the next entering me right after the one before him had shot off and withdrawn, as Shaun told them to hurry, anxious for the plane to lift off. This seemed silly a short time later, as the Marines continued to trade off on me as we were flying to Key West. My own little gang bang, moaning for each throbbing monster cock. Shaun stood over me, filming it all. I knew the film would be one more thing held over me to keep me compliant to the wishes of Shaun's masters. I didn't care. No more denying what I wanted, what I'd do to get it. Shaun had swept every ounce of my guilt and resolve away. I loved every thrust of the hard-bodied, big-cocked Marines Shaun and whoever he worked for—although, of course I knew who that was—had selected just for me. Of course I'd do whatever he—and they—wanted me to do. Just as long as they took care of me. Young, hung, hard-bodied soldiers and sailors—and, of course, my very own handler, Shaun.

I felt very lucky, very, very lucky—and not just because I was being saved from the dictator.

Labyrinth

"I will not buy boys," Xanthos said with a dismissive wave of his hand, although the gleam in his eyes suggested otherwise. "They are unreliable and too inexperienced, and they break the crockery while playing their childish games."

"These are no boys, excellency," the slave master simpered. "These are all past their playing stage and have been trained in service, in special service to a nobleman such as you. Besides, I was told—"

"You did tell me, Xanthos, that you liked your servants lithe and blond and graceful and small enough not to overturn the furniture," General Lykaios said with a smile. "Come, select one of these and be done with it. You have done us a great honor by breaking with Morini and coming to us. We can surely take Morini with your help. Accept our gift of your own serving man; you must be tired of calling upon Senator Lykaios's servants after he has done with them."

Within, Lykaios was less patient. "Get on with it, you treasonous sea slug," he was thinking, and he was not fooled for a second that it was a kitchen servant they were shopping for here.

"Well, I don't know," Xanthos replied as he reached over for his wine cup. As soon as he set it down, Senator Ixsandr's own serving man stepped forward to refill his cup.

Xanthos bounded off his couch. "Well perhaps if I saw them in the light, and without those loincloths. Come, bring them out on the terrace."

Xanthos pranced out onto the terrace, and the slave master fell in step behind him, tugging on the chains of the three small blond men struggling along behind him and hissing at them to strip down while they were moving to the terrace.

"How can we be sure he'll pick the right one?" Ixsandr whispered to the general as he watched Xanthos clucking and prodding the bodies of the young men out on the terrace, spending as long as he thought the slave master would tolerate in narrowing his choice to one—in the process getting some pleasure out of all three.

"They are all the right one," Lykaios muttered back, and then he laughed. "Our best-trained spies. Whoever he picks will keep us apprised of his activities here in Brixia. It was indeed a small victory when he deserted from the Morini and came over to us—he was one of their best military minds, despite his stupidity in other matters. But I don't trust a traitor."

"And look at the fool out there," Lykaios continued, changing the subject. "Who does he think he's fooling? He's not picking out a servant. He's picking out someone for his bed. But that's fine. We want him besotted with whoever he selects. He will be more ours with a Brixian catamite than otherwise. Ah, there you are, dear brother Xanthos, back with us again. Boy, refill the flagon of wine for our hero brother. Have you selected? Yes you have, and a very good choice it is too. Nyke, is it not?"

Xanthos' selection was standing in the center of the room now, demur, his hands at his sides and his face looking shyly at the floor. He was small, as they knew Xanthos really liked, and with blond curls falling down into his face. His body was lithe, that of a graceful dancer, and he was perfectly muscled for the role—not anything either overdone or underdeveloped. He had the cock and balls of a boy, which was particularly in demand this season. His lips were full and sensual and his eyes hazel and sultry, as Lykaios knew without the young man having to raise his head. Of the three, he gave the greatest impression of being innocent and virginal—although Lykaios knew full well this was just a trained pose. He knew this because Lykaios was a master of diplomacy through the art of subterfuge and spying and also because he had very intense and personal experience that belied any claim Nyke might make to being either innocent or, the god's laugh, virginal.

And Lykaios was supremely pleased that Xanthos had chosen Nyke, because Nyke was his best sweetmeat spy. If Nyke could not get the armies of Brixia inside the walls of Morini, no one was likely to.

Ixsandr turned to a nearly trembling Xanthos, who was barely able to contain his excitement at the gift of a blond beauty in service to his every need. And Xanthos was aching to have his needs serviced at this point. Ixsandr easily discerned just how aroused Xanthos was. Togas were not built for modesty.

"I regret we cannot indulge ourselves in small talk and wine when your coming to us opens so many possibilities for moving at last against Morini, Xanthos," Ixsandr said in his most magisterial voice. "I must be off to the Senate to arrange the resources General Lykaios and you will, I'm sure, make brilliant use of. And there is much preparation for General Lykaios to complete before you will be needed in counsel. Perhaps you would like to take your new servant back to your apartments and show him how he can best serve you." Ixsandr could hardly keep a straight face at the hidden meanings in his last sentence. He and Lykaios, the functional dictators of Brixia, wanted Xanthos under their complete power as soon as possible.

"Well, I suppose that might be something I could take a few minutes from more important matters to do," Xanthos said dubiously. But he was already shuffling toward the passageway to his quarters and herding the shy Nyke before him, his hand on the servant's naked buttocks.

"Silly dolt," Lykaios muttered under his breath as he smiled his happy farewells at Xanthos's departure—happy principally at the departure. Then he turned to Ixsandr and said, "I wonder how much flimflamming I need do in war counsel before managing to convince that ass that it's his idea that he is going to return to the court of Morini."

When Ixsandr had all of his plans in order and his minions in tow, he moved down the corridor toward his scheduled meeting of the Senate. As he passed the door into Xanthos's apartments, he saw that Nyke was already at work. Xanthos was lying on his back in the mountain of pillows, and Nyke was astride his pelvis riding his cock like a ship upon the Ionian sea the day after a tempest. From the sounds Xanthos was making, he was quite content with the service his man was providing him.

* * * *

"I will not do it; they cannot expect it; what were they thinking?"

Nyke raised his head up from the task at hand and asked, "What, noble sire? What do they expect of you and who is they?" Nyke knew damn well what this was all about. His assignment was to make Xanthos fall for the plan.

Xanthos was laying on his couch just beyond the line of sunshine flowing in from the terrace of his apartment. Nyke knelt between his thighs at the end of the chaise, Xanthos's legs raised and resting on Nyke's shoulders, and Nyke was working Xanthos's cock in his mouth. Sucking on the bulb and flicking the piss slit with his tongue and then taking the whole shaft in with one long slide, listening for the sigh from his master, and then slowly pulling his mouth back. Down again and listening for the sigh. Feeling Xanthos's body go tense and his hips start to jerk, grabbing Nyke's golden curls in his hands and emitting little chirps of pleasure. Nyke taking him down to the root and applying pressure to the root with his teeth while gently squeezing Xanthos's balls in his hand. And then swallowing the spurted semen as quickly as he was able, trying not to gag or to spoil the moment in any other way for his master. Then sitting up and looking down into eyes glazed with the satisfied remembrance.

Eyes that quickly cleared and set into an expression of the spoiled pout.

"Wine, Nyke. Must I tell you whenever my glass nears empty? And it's long past time for my massage. The games this morning were grueling."

"Grueling for your adversaries," Nyke voiced in honeycombed praise as he scrambled off the couch and trotted off for the wine pitcher and the oil, sponge, and marble phallus. That was one thing Xanthos was an expert in, though, Nyke had to admit. Prissy and self-possessed as he was, Xanthos was master at the games, and, Nyke assumed, therefore also a champion on the field of battle. Nyke had watched in the stadium and had slowly and involuntarily taken on Xanthos as his champion. His muscled body was beautiful to Nyke as he watched Xanthos win one throw after the other, and when they had returned to the coolness of the senator's villa in the heat of the day, Nyke hadn't minded at all sponging water over Xanthos's body in the bath as Xanthos sat back in the water and lapped Nyke and raised his hole up and down on a strong, firm cock. That was another thing Xanthos was. Young and virile and quick to recover and ever ready for the fuck.

His strength was also his weakness, though. Xanthos became ever more controllable as Nyke spun a web of lust and want around him.

"You did not tell me what was troubling you," Nyke whispered in Xanthos' ear as he had him laid belly down on the couch and was massaging his neck muscles. Nyke had his own agenda to work to.

"The fools want me to return to Morini and be their spy inside the court—to undermine the Morini from within. Do they have any idea what that would take, what the dangers are?"

"They must, master," Nyke spoke in a soothing voice. "They have devised this as their best stratagem, laying it all, the future of Brixia, on your shoulders. They must trust you very much and must see the great talent that is within you."

"Humph," was Xanthos's reply, and then, in a huskier voice, "Yes, that is good, deeper there. Oh yes, and there too."

Nyke had moved his oiled fists down to the small of Xanthos' thin waist and then down to roll and knead his meaty buttocks. Nyke pulled the cheeks apart as he was working them and bent down and blew on Xanthos's hole, which puckered right up, the action earning a sigh from Xanthos. And then Xanthos was grunting and slowly churning his hips as Nyke's tongue went to the opening.

"Enough," Xanthos growled huskily, and then he turned onto his back, saluting Nyke at three-quarters' staff. "The marble phallus," he murmured.

Nyke oiled up the marble phallus as Xanthos watched with slitted eyes and licked his lips, and then Xanthos, his legs bent, hips rolled up, and a hand encasing Nyke's cock, moaned, as Nyke moved the bulb of the oiled phallus around the rim of Xanthos' opening, slowly worked it inside his channel, and rubbed the smooth tip on Xanthos' prostate. Xanthos was slowly working Nyke's small, thin cock and his pert little balls while Nyke worked both Xanthos' hole with the phallus and his staff with an oiled fist—at first—and then with his mouth, until Xanthos had ejaculated once more and Nyke had swallowed his essence again.

While Nyke was massaging Xanthos' legs and chest then, he endeavored to complete his essential assignment.

"Who but you could bring off such a feat, master? Isn't it, upon reflection, a brilliant plan? And aren't you the perfect man to bring it off? Your story and name will be sung down through the ages."

"I suppose you are right," Xanthos said in a faraway voice, already composing his own song to his glory. "But you have had enough rest, you lazy slave. Here, I want you."

As Xanthos sat up, picked the small servant up from the floor with hands encasing his waist, and seated him on the couch in front of him and facing him, Nyke worked in the last, burning question he'd been told to have answered. Xanthos was here, but no one in Brixia could tell the senator and general how he had gotten here, how he had gotten out of Morini unnoticed—which may just be the key for getting the army of Brixia inside Morini.

"But it may all be just dream, you cannot return to Morini. It is too heavily guarded. You cannot get back in. Oh, sire!"

196

Xanthos had pushed Nyke onto his back below him and barked, "Spread your legs and grab your ankles," and Nyke was groaning at the invasion of his hole by oiled, thick fingers.

"That is no problem for such as I," Xanthos boasted, as he straddled the couch with his legs and grabbed Nyke's hips with his hands. "I will just go back in the way I came out. And speaking of getting in—"

"Oh, sire, oh, SIRE, OHHHH!" Nyke cried out as Xanthos pulled the youthful torso of the blond servant toward him along the now-slippery couch surface, and his long, thick cock slowly disappeared into a tight ass channel.

Later in the night, when Xanthos was finished cocking Nyke again, they were laid, stretched out on the sleeping divan, bringing their breath back to calm.

"But, what about me, my lord?" Nyke whispered in a small voice. "I don't know how I would live—"

"Hush, hush, my sweet one," Xanthos murmured as he brushed the sex-wet blond curls out of Nyke's face and embraced him closely. "This cock has not had its fill of you either. I will take you with me."

Nyke cooed and snuggled closer into Xanthos' embrace. This part of the mission accomplished.

* * * *

"Master, why are you leading me this way?" Nyke asked in a whisper. "Morini is on the west slope of Mount Fotia. You are leading us to the east."

The night was dark and they had placed sacking on the hooves of the horses and were moving as silently as possible. It was a moonless night, and the only illumination other than the stars was the glow from atop Mount Fotia, which had been smoldering and sending up clouds of ash and noxious fumes since before Nyke was birthed.

"Yes," Xanthos answered with a low laugh. "And why is it that your searchers from Brixia have never found our secret entrance into our city? It's because you look on the wrong side of the mountain."

Hours later, standing on a shelf of rocks outside the yawning entrance to a cavern on the east slope of Mount Fotia, Nyke held back in fear when Xanthos would have plunged right into the mouth of the cavern.

"This is the Labyrinth of the Underworld, isn't it?" Nyke muttered in awe. "I've never been here, but I have heard of it. Our foretellers came here for signs until they all died of mysterious illnesses. I've heard that to enter here now is to die."

"Yes, it is, and it indeed is a home of the dead," Xanthos answered. "But if you follow me, very close behind me, we will soon be inside Morini. You must trust me, Nyke."

"Yes, yes, I must," Nyke answered. And indeed he had to. His mission was to get inside Morini and return to serve as guide or not return at all.

They walked into the dark, and Xanthos lit a torch. Nyke saw that it was a maze of many choices, many decisions to be made. There were far too many passages leading off from the entrance cavern for him to have any idea which to follow. And it was not in total darkness here, any more than it had been on the trail around the base of the mountain from Brixia. There was a soft glow down some of the passageways and trails of vapors wafting out of the entrances to these shafts as well as others.

Xanthos was doing something strange with the torch. He was not holding it high; he was holding its tip close to the ground and was training his own gaze there as well.

Nyke instinctively moved to his left, assuming that passage they sought was the one farthest away from the ones with the glowing interiors. But as he moved to the entrance, Xanthos grabbed his arm and pulled him back.

"Not that one, little one." He skipped a rock into the dark of the entrance to that passage, and Nyke's stomach turned over as he heard the hollow sound of the rock tumbling down into a hole.

"As I said, stay close to me," Xanthos said. "And watch along the base of the rock walls."

Nyke looked down and then he saw them—painted symbols, small and noticeable only if you were watching closer.

But they were there, and by following them through the many winding passages and across crystal-columned caverns, at last they came out into the rear room of a small, unoccupied house in the mountainside wall of Morini at the start of a busy and noisy market day.

Nyke was completely surprised as they led their horses through the bustling streets of the city state toward the consul's villa. He had been led to believe that the three-year-long siege of the town by the forces of Brixia had reduced it to a starving cesspool, but, as much as the smell of the place—indeed of any healthy city state in the world—was that of a dung heap, the town looked prosperous and the inhabitants appeared to be perfectly pleased with their living conditions. And they seemed pleased with Xanthos too, which was the most shocking to Nyke. He was not seized upon as a deserting traitor but was hailed by the more prosperous-looking citizens, who no doubt knew him, and was given way to with bows and admiring looks by all others, who seemed to know of him.

But then the truth dawned on Nyke. Xanthos was held in such esteem in Morini that the citizens had not been told he had deserted lest this imperil the false sense of security they had all taken upon themselves.

"We shall see what we shall see when we get to the consul's villa, though," Nyke thought.

And when they did, Nyke was not all that surprised that as soon as they strode into the reception hall, four hefty guards formed up beside Xanthos, with one of them prodding Nyke off to the side as inconsequential. A tall, straight-limbed and imposingly toggaed man of many years appeared in the doorway opposite to the entrance to the villa.

"Hail, Consul Aeneas," Xanthos boomed out in a voice dripping with affection and totally absent of fear. Nyke admired his courage at this moment.

"So, you return to us, do you, General Xanthos? Enjoy your little excursion, did you? Perhaps you will join me within for a little meeting of the minds."

The consul turned and disappeared from the doorway, and Xanthos followed him, hemmed in closely by four burly, straight-legged, empty-expressioned military guards.

This was what Nyke knew would be one of the trickiest times for him. The plan had never been for Xanthos to regain his place in Morini and serve the interests of Brixia. The functional leaders of Brixia, the senator Ixsandr and general Lykaios never had any use for Xanthos. All that they wanted from him was to show Nyke how to get into and out of Morini. And all Nyke wanted to do at this point was to get safely out of the villa and back to the Labyrinth of the Underworld while he still had the route of the maze in his mind.

"I wouldn't wait around here, if I were you—not unless you want to share the punishment that is being meted out to our traitorous Xanthos." Nyke turned and found he was looking up into the eyes of a handsome, well-built man with auburn hair and laughing hazel eyes, dressed as a servant, older, taller, and more solid than Nyke was and obviously very comfortable in his environment.

"If you come with me and would like to have food in your mouth and a place to sleep in the lap of luxury, I'll perhaps make a position for you here," the young man said. "My name is Cirillo, and I serve the consul Aeneas. But unless you want to be here to explain yourself when the guards reappear, you'd best come with me."

Nyke blindly followed Cirillo into a passageway that led beside a garden atrium and into the bowels of the villa, which was some sort of labyrinth of a century of haphazard expansion. They stopped and then walked more gingerly at the sound of lashing and a man crying out. Cirillo paused at the corner of a doorway and motioned Nyke to peek inside.

Xanthos, naked, was on his knees at the foot of a couch, with his lower belly on the edge of a low divan's surface and his torso stretched up to where his arms v'd out above his hanging head and were bound to posts at either side of the couch. The consul, also naked, and superbly fit for his many years, was crouched over Xanthos' hips and fucking him while half-heartedly lashing at Xanthos' back and buttocks with a many-thonged whip.

After only a glimpse of this, Cirillo took Nyke's hand and led him quickly back into the back labyrinth of the villa, where the furnishings became coarser and the rooms smaller and with less access to the sun. When they reached a small room off a side corridor, with a single narrow couch in it, Cirillo pushed Nyke down in a seated position on the couch and turned to him.

"I serve Aeneas in every way. Am I to surmise that you have served Xanthos in the same way?"

"Yes," Nyke said. It was no shame and he saw no reason to deny it.

"And are you pleased with Xanthos?"

"What do you mean?"

"I don't mean politically. Hades may have the lot of them for their politics. I serve no man but myself. And if I could leave this hell hole of a city pretending that life is just as it should be as it quietly starves and creeps to its enslavement, I would do so."

"You would go over to Brixia?" Nyke said, trying to fill the tone of his voice with disbelief and censure.

"In a moment's time, yes. They are the ones who live free on the plains as we grovel here inside our trapping walls. But that's not what I meant. I meant does Xanthos have a cock as good as this one?" Cirillo pulled his tunic over his head and stood there in the nude. His body was beautiful, but neither his body nor his cock were any more beautiful than Xanthos' were. Nyke saw no reason to disappoint or alienate this young man who had rescued him from a quite possibly very sticky situation at the entrance to the villa. And, besides, the young man was very nice and Nyke did need a place to hide until he could return to the labyrinth. And, Nyke did like to be fucked; otherwise he would not be in Ixsandr's special service.

"No, you are beautiful and manly, and superbly manned," Nyke answered.

Cirillo seemed pleased. "I told you back at the entrance that perhaps I could give you a place here. The perhaps is if you will serve me as well as you have served Xanthos. I know you are no simple wine holder. I know a catamite when I see one. Do you service well?"

"As well as you may wish, sire," Nyke said, as he reached out for the cock Cirillo had been stroking. As Nyke opened his mouth to Cirillo's cock, he was thinking, "My good fortune that you take me for a mere catamite and not for a spy."

When Cirillo lifted Nyke's tunic over his head and pushed his back down onto the couch, Nyke spread and lifted his legs and rolled up his hips, and then gasped and cried out and moaned as Cirillo thrust inside him and made him feel that, indeed, the cock of the consul's man was longer, thicker, and more vigorous than that of Xanthos.

Not fully trusting him, Cirillo kept Nyke bound and imprisoned in his room for several days, appearing occasionally and fucking the beautiful small blond with the curly golden hair until, after purposely letting Nyke go for two days without sex, Nyke begged him for the fuck. Then, deeming Nyke completely within his control, Cirillo released him and let him work in the kitchens during the day and come back to his bed in the evening.

For Nyke's part, he played Cirillo's game, always looking for the opportunity to leave, but being totally lost in the maze of the villa. He would not have been impatient about the time it was taking except that the longer this game went on, the less sure he was that he could renegotiate the Labyrinth of the Underworld.

Cirillo solved that problem for him.

One night while they were languidly fucking, Nyke asked, as innocently as he could, "Were you speaking truthfully that first day when you said you had no allegiance to Morini."

"Truthfully," Cirillo answered, and then he let loose with a long litany of all of the ills that Morini had done to him and those he had lost.

"Would that I could leave, I would take you with me," Nyke whispered, worried lest the walls have ears. "But I have no idea how to leave."

"I do," Cirillo answered. "There is a way through the Labyrinth of the Underworld. I know it well."

* * * *

Weeks later, Cirillo was standing on the terrace of the Senator Ixsandr's villa in Brixia, waving to the vanguard of the army of Brixia as it was departing the city for the eastern side of Mount Fotia. At the head of the army was General Lykaios, and beside him rode the servant Nyke, put in the front of the column as guide through the Labyrinth of the Underworld.

Cirillo waited until dark, giving Brixia's army time to enter the maw of the labyrinth. Then he stole along the corridor of the senator's villa, meeting no one to challenge him, as Ixsandr had assured him would be the case. Cirillo had spent considerable effort cultivating the senator since he and Nyke had escaped from Morini. Cirillo had become Ixsandr's favorite, which was why Cirillo had not accompanied the forces of General Lykaios as auxiliary guide—there had been quite a row over that between the senator and the general, but the senator simply would not part with his new lover.

As Cirillo massaged Ixsandr's back, his mind wandered to the image of the forces of Morini entering the maw of the labyrinth and following the signs at the base of the wall, the signs that Morini's consul, Aeneas, had caused to be reset after he and Nyke had passed through, the reset signs that would pull the Morinis ever deeper, ever more confusingly into the heart of the volcano and the welcoming arms of its noxious fumes.

Ixsandr raised his hips, which was a sign for Cirillo to pull his cock through and stroke it as his lips went to Ixsandr's hole, opening it up for the last cocking. Once Ixsandr was moaning and begging for the thrust, Cirillo reached under the couch and then crawled over Ixsandr and mounted his hips and thrust inside him. Ixsandr yelped and cried out and clawed at the sides of the couch as Cirillo's cock thrust inside his channel and, with each of those thrusts, Cirillo's dagger thrust into Ixsandr's back.

Across the plain, on the western slope of the glowing Mount Fotia, the Brixia consul, Aeneas, had just finished fucking and whipping his lover, Xanthos, the two now exhausted after a coupling that brought out the depths of passion in both of them. Aeneas unbound Xanthos, and they stretched out on the sleeping couch in each other's arms, as Aeneas kissed the welts on his lover's torso.

"There has been no alarm from the street," Xanthos murmured. "That is a good sign. None of them have made it through the labyrinth and to the wall. We have men in force there just in case, but there seems nothing for them to do. Cirillo has done well. He sent word that he would take care of Senator Ixsandr personally. Brixia decapitated in one blow. We can open the gates of the city again."

"Yes, but it is a big price for Cirillo to pay," the consul murmured. "I did so enjoy Cirillo. And he was the best of my special spies."

"No, master," Xanthos answered. "Cirillo should be safe if he's kept his wits about him and the gods are favorable. I told him to steal out of Brixia in the confusion and to remain in the wilderness at a town called Theron for a week. By then we will have remarked the passage through labyrinth. We have it marked by cuttings as well as the painted symbols, so we can easily restore the route. Cirillo will be back in your arms soon and with many an interesting secret to tell us about Brixia."

As the two cooed and kissed and ran their hands over each other's bodies in anticipation of the return of Aeneas's man strength and desire to be moving deep inside Xanthos, a figure felt safe at last to move from the shadows near at hand into the deeper shadows of the chamber and beyond. As he silently glided out of the chamber, the consul's night steward, Dymas, kept going over the phrase in his mind so that he would not forget it, "Cirillo in the village of Theron." He would go directly to his messenger who would then contact the men of Cenopolis who lingered outside of the city to the north of Mount Fotia. The time was ripe for his city. Not only was Brixia crippled by the loss of its army and of its functional rulers, but Morini also was ripe for the picking in its false sense of security. And the spy Cirillo was the key. There was so much he could tell the men of Cenopolis with a bit of persuading. Not only the secrets of Brixia but the way into Morini as well.

Murmansk Delights

I was sitting at the bar of the Meridien Hotel in the Russian seaport of Murmansk, one seat away from Lev and with Mariana, a blowsy blonde, sitting on the other side of me, chatting up a businessman from Moscow. I liked sitting next to Mariana at the bar. It got a thought into men's minds, and, if Mariana and others of her gender weren't who they were looking for but Mariana put into their minds what they were looking for, their eyes could slide off onto me. And maybe stick.

I was in my working clothes. Tight black stretch pants, molded in the buttocks and showing a little basket in the front and a billowy, long-sleeved, black-satin shirt, open almost down to the navel and showing off a simple gold chain suspending a unique gold charm—two male sex symbols intertwined. Not all that tasteful but nothing too subtle. Subtlety didn't get understood much on the Murmansk docks.

I was turned toward the room, elbows in back of me, resting on the bar, legs slightly spread with my butt barely perched on the stool, when he appeared at the door to the bar. He took the full room in a sweeping glance, passed over me, and then brought his eyes immediately back to me. After dwelling on me for a few seconds, his eyes broke away and continued the sweep of the room. But they came back to me.

He looked like all I ever wanted. In fact, he was exactly what I wanted. Oleg Isakov, captain of the Kresta-II-class Russian guided missile cruiser stationed at the nearby Severomorsk naval base. I was here because his ship was in port on the first night after a three-month at-sea hush-hush dispersal, and we had been building a nice file on Oleg, a very personal file.

He stood there, solid and sparkly in his navy blue, well-pressed summer uniform, dripping in medals. He'd taken his hat off his head and held it under his arm. His steel-gray hair, lighter gray at the temples, had been trimmed, as had his close-cropped beard and mustache. He looked robust and tanned from months on the bridge. I hoped those had been lonely months.

Our eyes met. He smiled and I smiled back. I turned around toward the bar top and he was at my side, between me and Lev. His hat and gloves and a Meridien Hotel room key on a big brass tag with a room number engraved in large characters on it went down on the bar top.

"May I buy you a drink?" he asked. His voice was smooth, cultured. It sounded a little breathy though. It sounded like he was ready.

"If you wish," I answered coolly, and I looked over to Lev, who nodded that he had seen the room number on the key and who then pushed away from the bar and was gone even while Isakov was mounting his stool. I began the countdown of how much longer I'd need to keep Isakov in the bar.

Isakov indeed had been lonely those three months, and he tried to make up for all of that time between my legs on the bed of his hotel room.

En route to the room, I whispered to him, "I hope you are forceful. I love it rough. I love being taken like it's the first time and not of my choice."

This aroused him to the point that I didn't think we'd even make it to the room.

Inside the door, he turned on me and embraced me and started to pull at my clothes. I arched back at him, asking in a tense voice what he was doing, and tried, unsuccessfully, to avoid his mouth in searching for mine. He laughed and then kissed me hard again. I bit his lip and he slapped me hard across the mouth, and I took his mouth in mine, sending him aflame.

He had me trapped under him on the bed, naked, his pelvis pressed against mine between my spread thighs, his fists holding my wrists out from my body. He was a big man, barrel chested with a heavy matting of salt-and-pepper hair, and thick waisted, although all of it was muscle, and meaty thighs thicker than my waist. There was no question who controlled, nor did I want there to be.

I writhed under him and moaned and begged him not to do it, as he crouched over me, forcing my thighs wider apart with his monster cock rising out of a thatch of thick salt-and-pepper hair thumping on my lower belly.

He dragged that up my belly and sternum and forced it between my lips and made me give suck as I gagged and grunted a bit more than I really had to.

As he dragged it back down my chest and belly, hard as steel now, I begged him to be gentle, having given up on forestalling what would happen. And then I screamed out and arched my back and tensed my body against him as he thrust inside me hard and long and deep.

I cried out that he was killing me, splitting me apart, and he laughed and thrust again and again, harder, deeper, aroused to new heights by this game we were playing.

Eventually I gave up my seed to him, up his heaving belly, and subsided into whimperings and moans and lay there, docile, as he ejaculated and fell on top of me. When his breathing had become calm, I felt him rising inside me again, and he started to fuck me a second time. And this time I gave him a ride he wouldn't forget, clawing at his back, taking his nipples between my teeth and meeting the thrusts of his pelvis with counterthrusts of my hips. I wanted his last memory of us together here to be something he savored—if possible something he obsessed over and wanted again.

And when we finished, he showered and then came out of the bathroom in full erection, showing that he did want it again, but he also said he wanted a drink. I told him to dress and go on down to the bar and I'd shower and join him in the bar for a drink and then we'd come back to the room.

He asked me how much he'd have to pay for more sex, and I told him we'd discuss that later.

When I heard the elevator door shut on Isakov, I opened the door to Lev, who went around the room taking down the miniature video cameras in the corner of the room and stutter-shot still camera, all of which had been trained on the bed, and the bugs from the side of the mattress. While he did this, I went back into the bathroom and took my shower. When I was finished dressing, Lev was gone.

I met Lev and my handler at the door before entering the bar. Lev handed over a packet of photographs taken from the still camera. I entered the bar and went over to Isakov, who was sitting on a stool, and suggested that we move to a booth in the back corner. We went to one with a U-shaped bench around the table, and as I pushed Isakov around the bench from one side, my handler was moving in on the other side of him.

"Excuse me, Who—?"

"Allow me to introduce myself, Captain Isakov," my handler said. "My name is Sam Winterberry, and I'm an American. I'm an exporter, and I think you have something I would like to export."

Isakov was speechless, even after Winterberry fanned out the photos of him fucking a young man in his hotel room and assured him that the video and audio versions would make it clearly seem he was raping me. Chances were good that I also would look to be underage in those photographs. The naval captain didn't do much more than look hangdog and give little irking sounds as Winterberry explained what Isakov could do for the Americans and continue to lead the life he was leading—even lead some of that with me, if he liked.

"How would that be, Captain Isakov? Would you like to go upstairs again with our friend Pietr here—knowing that you will be cooperating with us anyway?"

After a long pause, Isakov gave a shamed and quiet, "Yes."

"Well, not tonight, Captain. But come back next week with a few answers to this set of questions, and we'll see what we shall see."

Winterberry was still going over questions on a sheet of paper with the guided missile cruiser captain when I stood and walked out of the Meridien Hotel. Motioning Lev, who was sitting in the lobby with his cameras, to follow me, I strode toward the Murmansk waterfront.

It was a cool night and I wasn't dressed for walking in it, so I hoofed my way as quickly as I could to the wharfside Alyosha Nights bar, where Russian commercial sailors from the docks of Murmansk mingled with the naval sailors from the nearby Severomorsk naval base to seek out each other and, if lucky, something a little softer and less connected with the monotonous sea. If they wanted to fuck each other, they could just stay in their ships. I had to grit my teeth, though. It was too rawly cold for me to be on the streets only in what I was wearing. This was as warm as Murmansk, sitting high on the Kola Peninsula on the Barents Sea, just below the Arctic circle, was going to get, despite being Russia's only northern port with an unfrozen exit into the world's sea lanes throughout the year. It was just this sort of accessibility to the sea that had made Severomorsk Russia's leading submarine base. And this, principally was why I was here. But I would only come here in the summer, no matter what Sam Winterberry, head of the Agency's special unit, informally known as the candy store, said.

I knew immediately where I wanted to sit when I entered Alyosha Nights, even though all eyes turned on me when I was at the door and each man in the crowded bar would have been grateful to get the nod.

But near the back of the smoky main room two sailor sat at a table and seemed to be pretty much into their cups. They were talking animatedly to each other and were almost oblivious to my appearance. Almost. I could see that they still were interested in what I had to sell.

I walked back to the area they were in. There were two tables that were possible. One with two hulking longshoremen, who looked mean as rot, but who were salivating at the sight of me, and another with a lone commercial sailor who was good-looking but slender and looked a little hesitant. I sat down with the lone sailor and told him that he could buy me a drink. When he got over the shock that I had singled him out in the bar, he motioned for the barkeep. He obviously had no intention of leaving me alone at the table for any length of time, which showed that he wasn't any dummy.

I sat with my back almost touching the table where the two sailors were sitting, and I almost didn't have to do anything else that night but sit there and listen and remember to get enough intelligence on the Russian submarine fleet to make the night's outing profitable even if we hadn't hooked a naval captain already.

It was eureka time for me. Both were submariners but were from different subs. One was a chief petty officer on an Akula-class hunter/killer sub and the other was a senior sailor on a Yankee-class guided missile sub. Although the specs of these were pretty well known, the Russians had completely redone their use and float patterns for the submarine navy since the cold war period, and even the most mundane daily schedules and routines were of value to us. The two submariners, half drunk—which wasn't a nonfunctional stage by any means for a Russian sailor—were comparing notes on life and maneuvers of their individual subs.

I had almost decided to pack in the night, because the sailor I now was with had worked up the courage to blow in my ear and feel my basket and start making some suggestions, when I felt the hand of one of the sub sailors at the other table start on the small of my back and move to my butt. I turned and gave him the "yes, I really would prefer to be at your table" smile.

In short order the two sailors, Nikolai and Vladimir, had been successful in a standoff against the young, slender sailor, which I could not have counted on if I'd chosen the table with the two bulky longshoremen, and the two submariners were preceding to work on getting me drunk enough to take them both. I pretended a low capacity, but not so low that I hadn't gotten their name and rank and submarine assignment and the next time they planned to be in port—and that they'd be happy to see me then.

As we were dickering on a price and I was making sure they realized I wasn't so anxious that I'd go cheaply, Nikolai asked me if I had a day job.

"Yes, I am a cleaner at the Taybola base," I answered.

This impressed them greatly and Vladimir whistled and said, "That's an ICBM base. You have to have top clearances to get anywhere near that base. You must really have connections."

"Yes I do . . . of course," I said, and I smiled at him.

"And speaking of connecting . . ." Nikolai said with a low growl while he palmed what he very much wanted to be connecting with.

They fucked me doggy style in a dark, backroom of the bar, although I managed to get them over near a window with a street light outside, where I was belly down on the top of an old table as they took me in succession.

Before that, I'd stripped for them while they pulled off their white pullover shirts, and I told them how beautiful they were standing there in their white trousers with fully developed, finely sculpted chests. And I meant it too. They were young and virile, the cream of Russian manliness, and I enjoyed my encounter with them.

I told them to stand in a V where I was kneeling and I fished two fine cocks out of their buttoned-fly trousers and sucked them together until they couldn't take it anymore and bent me over the old table and pumped me.

The cock sucking turned out not to be the only thing they wanted to do together. They wanted to fuck me together at one time, and I could tell that our little sex scene had turned them on toward each other as much as to me. I quoted an impossibly high price, and when it looked like they were working up to accepting that, I demurred and told them not this time—that maybe the next time they both were in port together we could make a party of it and we could include that.

When I left them, with Vladimir sitting with his butt on the edge of the table and his torso arched back, supported on his stiff arms and grunting and groaning with Nikolai crouched between his spread legs and fucking him hard and deep, I met Lev in the shadows of the room and we departed by a back door, with Lev off to deliver the photographs he'd been taking of my encounter with Nikolai and Vladimir to Sam Winterberry and me back to my room to transcribe as much of the information I had picked up from the two sailors that I could remember. And I had a very good memory.

It had been a satisfactory night. One big fish bagged and two small fish—but with very useful information of their own—playing on the hook, ready to be reeled in when and as needed.

Early the next afternoon I was one of several in a crew of cleaners who rolled up in a battered old bus to the first perimeter fence gate to the Taybola intercontinental missile base in a remote area nearly 100 miles south of Murmansk. At each gate, the documents of all of us were scrutinized, and I trust that I was the only one who noticed the cleaner supervisor sweating and glancing in my direction with a worried look each time we rolled up to a gate and were challenged.

At the third gate, I was taken over to the side by the guard leader and I thought the cleaner supervisor was going to go into catatonia. He calmed down, however, when the Russian soldier told me that Lieutenant Titisov had special duties for me that day and that I should follow him. The cleaner supervisor looked at me with slitted eyes, no doubt sure of what special duties a lieutenant would have for me. But he was only half right, and he'd been paid well not to think about it at all.

Once ushered into Titisov's corner office in an old barracks building that should have been torn down after World War II, but wasn't, I walked over to the desk and stood in front of it. Titisov, a fit, square-jawed soldier in his mid thirties, locked the door behind him and just stood there, looking at me.

"Do you have something for me?" I asked.

"Yes, I most certainly do," he said. And then he laughed. "But I'll give you what your handlers wanted from me before I give you what you deserve and get what I want from you."

The information he had to pass was on three sheets of paper, which, when rolled, fit easily into the false handle of the mop I was carrying along with a bucket. Those three sheets of paper replaced two more sheets of new questions from my handlers, which I laid on his desk top.

And then Titisov walked over to his chair, behind a battered wooden desk, slipped the sheets of paper I had put on the desk in a folder and slid the folder under several others. Then he rolled his chair back a bit and stood in front of it and unbuttoned the fly of his brown worsted trousers and fished out his cock. I came around the desk, and he sat down in his chair and spread his legs as I hooked my elbows over his thighs and brought my mouth down on his cock.

While I gave him a blow job that brought him near to climax, I shucked off my clothes and he unbuttoned his tunic and ran his hands across his nipples.

When he was more than ready, I rose and straddled his lap and slowly descended my channel on his cock, making noises of appreciation and surrender to the power of him. He was moaning and groaning too. I didn't descend all of the way but left space for him to pump up into me with hip action, as I buried his face in my chest and then pushed him back and savaged his mouth with mine and moved my sucking and gnashing teeth down onto his nipples until he started to cry out, only to have his mouth taken in mine again as he ejaculated.

There were tears in his eyes when he was done and I looked into his face.

"What is it, Fedor?" I murmured.

"When will it end?" he whispered.

"You want me to stop coming?" I asked.

"No, no. I'd love to see you elsewhere. I'm besotted with you. I mean where does all this duplicity, this disloyalty end?"

"It goes hand in hand, Fedor," I said. "It was sealed when you asked me up to your room in the Meridien Hotel. It was sealed for both of us. If you want me, and if you want your life to remain unexposed, we keep on like this, people like you and me. If it hadn't been you, it would have been someone else. If it hadn't been me, it would have been someone else. We are all pawns. We can only play our part."

"I suppose . . . but you and I."

"Do you feel I hold back when we fuck, Fedor?" I asked. "Do you not feel that this at least, is real and honest?"

It was a line I sometimes had to use when the first blush of lust melted off a relationship such as this.

"Do you not feel it when I kiss you here . . . and here . . . and here. And touch you here."

He was breathing heavily, and I felt him rise again inside me. We fucked more slowly then, more intensely, and at the height of his passion, he rose from the chair, laid my back on his desk, and fucked me like there would be no tomorrow. And who knows, from day to day, whether there will be a tomorrow.

Afterward I told him what else I wanted. "Send me to a barracks today to clean the latrine."

"You don't have to do that. I can send you over to the colonel's office. Maybe you'd want—"

"An enlisted men's barracks is exactly what I want," I cut in. "And one where the men are off shift, in the barracks, with little to do."

I started it in the latrine. The first two guys who came in to take a piss while I was mopping the floor got the universal signals I had been taught. I blew them both and while I was doing the second, the first was out in the barracks telling his bored comrades out there what the deal was. By the time I came out of the latrine, they were lined up by a bunk, money in hand. I leaned over the side of a bunk and rested on elbows on the mattress, the first in line doggy fucking me from behind and the next on the other side of the bunk working up his dick in my mouth. Each time a new dick approached my mouth, money was slapped down on the top of the bunk next to me.

I could tell that some were more into it and more experienced than others. There were two or three shy ones, ones who seemed to be looking for more than a quick poke on a boring day, and I hoped one of these would be my newest recruit.

The soldier stopped me outside the barracks as I was leaving and introduced himself as Aleksei. He was a young guy, no older than I was. In good shape, but the "just from the farm" type. He apologized for what had gone on in the barracks, even though it was clear that I had initiated and controlled it all, and, shyly, he asked if I ever went to any of the bars in the local town where we might maybe meet and share a beer someday.

I told him no, that I came all the way from Murmansk. I asked him what he did at the ICBM site, just to be sure, and was gratified to learn that he worked maintenance on the missiles. He would know a hell of a lot about the SS-18 Satan and SS-19 Stiletto missiles we knew to be at this site. And so I told him I'd love to see him again, under better—and more private—circumstances and indeed was just melting to see him. And we made a date.

From the bar in Murmansk I took him back to the small apartment I rented for only one month—just one room and a bath, really, with a counter for cooking—and I undressed him and covered him with kisses and sat on the bed and clutched his buttocks to me in the palms of my hand while he stood between my spread thighs and I gave him a soft and slow blow job.

He came quickly and was in love before he'd squirted his last youthful, virile seed down my throat.

Then he made love to me—just like we were new-found lovers and this was the beginning of a life together. He had no idea what life this was beginning.

Aleksei laid me on my belly on the bed and, using lube, he gave me a sensuous full-body massage that had me panting for his loving attention and his freshness and his lovely body and for his innocence. While working my buttocks, he ran his hand under my balls and brought my cock through and stroked it as his other hand worked my butt cheeks and thighs.

My sighs for him were as real as it gets, as were my moans and the slow movements my hips began to make as he took my cock in his mouth and then sucked on my balls and then moved his lips to my hole and opened me up with his tongue.

When we fucked, it was like riding a camel across the sand dunes. He was astride my ass, his cock buried inside me and both he and I were rolling our hips as I moaned and he groaned and he got bigger and bigger and sank deeper and deeper and deeper and throbbed more rhythmically, both of us rolling across the sand dunes toward an oasis of fountaining bliss.

Sam Winterberry and Lev entered the room while I was taking my shower, and Lev had already extracted the cameras and shown Aleksei the replay of behavior that, in Russia, would go far worse with him in the top-secret clearance missile corps than a mere reprimand or change of assignment.

Aleksei looked like a crushed flower, and I couldn't stand being there. I left the apartment and went down to the small park across the street from the building's entrance and stayed there until Lev brought Aleksei down to the street. They walked off in different directions, Lev far more jauntily than Aleksei.

I caught up with Aleksei in the next two blocks. He didn't want to say anything, didn't even want to look at me. But I pulled him into an alley, pushed him up against the wall, and assured him that, although this was a web we all were caught in, my sex with him had been real. That he should know that at least. That what I'd felt and given to him was all real. Crying, he pulled me farther into the alley, behind some trash bins and pushed me up against the wall and covered my face and neck—and then, when he'd opened my shirt, my chest and nipples—with his kisses. I unbuckled his belt and mine and unbuttoned the fly on his brown worsted trousers and unzipped mine and pushed both pairs of trousers down to the ground while he was devouring my mouth and nipples. We stood there rocking back and forth against each other, as I fisted our cocks together and stroked. Aleksei sank to his knees and devoured my cock, while I moaned and scrabbled at the coarse bricks in the wall behind me.

I gave him what he wanted, and then, when he stood up, I climbed his legs and hips with my legs and helped him gain purchase with his cock at my entrance and, as he slid into me, met his thrusts with mine to exhaustion.

"I'm so sorry, I'm so sorry, Aleksei," I muttered like a mantra.

"It's all worth it, all worth it, if I can have you along with the rest," he murmured.

"Yes, yes," I answered, knowing all along that I probably would never see him again.

When I returned to my apartment, Sam Winterberry was sitting on the bed. He looked up at me and said, "You were waiting for him downstairs, weren't you?"

"Yes," I answered. I had no secrets from Winterberry.

"Yes, you were," he said, satisfied that I hadn't lied to him. "I saw you follow him from the window."

"You let him fuck you again, didn't you?"

"Yes."

"You know you can't afford to take any of this personally."

"Yes."

"Well, go wash the stink of him off you now."

"Yes." After I showered, I came back out with a towel around my waist. Winterberry was still there, sitting on the bed, but he was naked now—and in full erection.

This was the part of the job I didn't care all that much for.

"Drop the towel."

When I did, he took a deep breath as he always did and smiled.

"Come lie here on your back on the bed and open your legs to me," he said.

"Yes." I answered out of habit.

~

217

About the Author

Habu is one of the pen names of a former supersonic spy jet pilot, intelligence agent, male model, movie actor, and diplomat. A wild youth in South East Asia was spent enjoying whatever sexual opportunities came his way, and much of his gay male writing is about recalling incidents from those days and inventing ones he'd perhaps have liked to experience. He now leads a very quiet and ordinary happily married family life.

An American, he is a published mainstream novelist and short story writer under another name and in another dimension of his life. He has written or cowritten (with Sabb) approaching 1,000 published short stories and over 100 published erotica e-books, primarily of gay fiction but also memoir, straight fiction and ménage fiction. His hand and creative writing can be seen in stories and books by habu, sr71plt, Dirk Hessian, Shabbu, and Stephen Kessel—among unrevealed others that might surprise readers. The fictionalized GM memoir *Flying High, Diving Deep* is loosely based on his life experiences. He can be found at the adults only gay male site www.BarbarianSpy.com, which he shares with Sabb and Dirk Hessian.

Our authors always like to receive feedback, and appreciate it when readers post reviews at distributors and other sites.

BarbarianSpy

FOR LITERARY HEAT

Not all books listed below may currently be on release.
* indicates the book is available in paperback and e-book.

BOOKS BY DIRK HESSIAN

Xtreme Erotica

The King's Men
Shores of Tripoli
Prophecy of Noto
Pretender's Fate

General Erotica/Romance

Fire Down the Valley*
Constantinople*
The Beautiful Way*
Blue and Gray
Colonel's Treasure
Beginning of Time
Labyrinth

BOOKS BY HABU

Gay Erotica

Memoir Faction

Flying High, Diving Deep*

Xtreme Erotica

Apyko: The Greek Pimp
Visits of the Schlange
Second Coming: Emile La Cour Unleashed
Vortex: Sacrificed by Curiosity*
Dark Angel Sounding *(in e-book & included in Sounding:Ultimate Control Paperback)**
Sounding: Ultimate Control *(Print Only)**
Sounding Five *(in e-book & included in Sounding:Ultimate Control paperback)*

General Erotica

Romance

Snowy, Snowy Nights (Christmas Romance)

Four Coins
Lower Than the Heart
Brambleton
Gotta Keep Trying
Finding Amnad
Platres Conclave
Other Novels/Novellas
Cruising Gigolo
Prepared in Cape Verdi
Gilded Cage
House on Park
Anything for Ambition
Dance of the Ravishers
Hard Knocks U*
My Neighbor's Spa*
Man's Man: Tales of a High Priced Gay Hooker*
Trip Money
Clint Folsom Mysteries Compendium Volume 1*
Death to Blonds - Stolen Judgment (Clint Folsom Mystery)
Clint Folsom Mysteries Compendium Volume 2*
The Indian Doctor
Sailorboy
Home to Fire Island
Choke Hold
Gay Erotica Anthologies
Spy Tails 001*
Spy Tails 002*
Doubled*
Doubled Again*
Tails in the Tropics*
Tails in the Med*
Tails in the West*
Rough Riders*
Grab Bag 1*
Grab Bag 2*
Grab Bag 3*
Grab Bag 4*
Grab Bag 5*
Beyond the Beaded Curtain*

Habu's Christmas Balls
The Sporting Life*
Fetish Galore!*
Literary Gay Erotica
Cairo Surrender*
The Handyman*
Homeward Bound
Journey to Mirage*
Menage Erotica
Cruising Gigolo
13 Ways for Halloween
Luther*
The Indian Prince
Literary GLBT Fiction
Summer of Denial
BOOKS BY SHABBU
Finding Jason
Dirty Pool
Operation Black Jade
Cigars!*
Angel in the Barn
Gayly Complicated*
Despoiling David
The Tree of Idleness*
I Met a Man
The Interview
Rough Road to Happiness
BOOKS BY SABB
Hiring in Hollywood
The Legend of Holleystone Grange
Surprise Encounters
She is He
Wrong Man
Loyal to his King
Barbarian Tales - Book One - Traveler's Tales*
Barbarian Tales - Book Two - Journeys Begin*
Barbarian Tales - Book Three - The Inheritance*
Barbarian Tales - Book Four - Road to Persepolis*